Francesca Scanacapra was bo
mother and Italian father, and her e
Bologna, the city whose rich history
the Bologna Chronicles series of no
has been somewhat nomadic with periods spent living in Italy, England, France, Senegal and Spain. In 2021 she returned to her native country and back to her earliest roots to pursue her writing career full time. She now resides permanently in rural Lombardy in the house built by her great-grandfather which was the inspiration for her Paradiso Novels.

Also by Francesca Scanacapra

PARADISO
RETURN TO PARADISO

THE LOST BOY OF BOLOGNA

Book 1 of the Bologna Chronicle

Francesca Scanacapra

SILVERTAIL BOOKS • *London*

First published in Great Britain by Silvertail Books in 2022
www.silvertailbooks.com

A catalogue record of this book is available from the British Library

978-1-913727-18-5

For my mother, Victoria Scanacapra.
For my children, Jake and Nellie Lowe.
And for all mothers and children
separated by geography and circumstance.

PART I

RINALDO AND EVELINA

CHAPTER 1

Bologna, Italy, 1929

The Foundlings' Wheel at the orphanage of San Girolamo was more commonly known as 'the Bastards' Wheel'. It was a wooden turntable set into the outer wall, like a small, one-way revolving door, where mothers in desperate circumstances could leave their babies anonymously.

Mimi looked at the hatch which concealed it and ran her hands over her swollen belly. She could imagine nothing worse than giving up her precious baby to the Bastards' Wheel – but nor could she imagine raising a child alone. Mimi had been trying to trace her baby's father since her arrival in Bologna and now there was such a short time left for a miracle to happen.

She had searched in all the places she might hope to find him, but Bologna was a big, unfamiliar city and her hunt had proved fruitless. She tried placing several personal advertisements in the local newspaper, hoping that he would see them, but she had received no response. And so Mimi had found herself here, at the Bastards' Wheel, alone and with all hope lost.

A little further along from the orphanage was the Clinica Santa Monica, which housed both a normal maternity ward and one for unmarried mothers. A sign at the main entrance requested that all Child Welfare Service patients should use the side door.

Although the function of the Child Welfare Service was to assist unmarried mothers through birth and the first weeks of their baby's life, it had also at its discretion the power to remove infants from their mothers. If Mimi was perceived as being unfit, or too young, or not having the means to support her baby, the Child Welfare Service had the right to take the infant away. Mimi reasoned that a girl in her circumstances might just as well put her baby straight into the Bastards' Wheel.

On learning of Mimi's condition, her step-mother had made provisions to send her to an institution for unwed mothers and had signed papers stating that Mimi's baby would be placed for adoption. Mimi had begged her not to, but her step-mother had made it clear that the wayward girl had no choice in the matter; that her shameful condition was to be kept secret and that after the baby's birth it was never to be spoken of again. There was to be no evidence of her disgrace. Mimi implored her father to do something to change her step-mother's mind, but Mimi's father was not permitted to disagree with his wife.

Determined that she would keep her baby, Mimi had gathered together enough money to cover the cost of a one-way train ticket to Bologna and a few days' living expenses. Although she was not worldly-wise, Mimi was a resourceful girl. On the day of her departure she took her late mother's emerald earrings and raided the sideboard for saleable items of value – two brass candelabras, a silver jug and a set of ivory-handled spoons. She left the family home before daybreak knowing that she would never see her father and step-mother again.

Once in Bologna Mimi had rented a cheap room in the former Jewish quarter. She had been prepared for an interrogation concerning her circumstances, but the landlord hadn't even asked her name. He had simply taken a month's rent in advance and told her not to put rubbish down the communal lavatory. He hadn't noticed her swelling belly, carefully hidden under the folds of her clothes.

The sale of the items from the sideboard raised only enough to pay for the first month's rent. Mimi could have sold the emerald earrings, but she was reluctant to part with the only thing which connected her to her late mother unless her circumstances became truly desperate.

She found a job peeling vegetables and washing dishes in a workmen's canteen, but the pay was pitiful. It was only thanks to the fact that Mimi could steal mouthfuls of food as it was being prepared and eat leftovers from the workmen's plates that she didn't go too hungry. But one day, less than a month before she was due to have her baby, the canteen proprietor caught her eating half a cold boiled egg in the back-kitchen.

'Don't think I don't know what you've been doing!' he shouted angrily. 'I know you've been stuffing yourself all day long with food from my kitchen! You came here a few months ago a skinny little thing, and ever since you've been growing fatter and fatter. I won't have a thief working for me. Get out!'

Mimi left without argument, slipping an apple and the butt-end of a salami into the pocket of her apron, just as her baby kicked in her belly.

Despite having benefited from a good education, Mimi felt poorly prepared for life. Nothing she had learned at school was of any practical use. What purpose did it serve to know her Latin declensions, or the history of the kingdoms of Italy, or any of the mathematical theorems she had memorised? She was a bright girl with many talents, but none of them seemed relevant.

Mimi had no experience of babies. She had never even held one. Nevertheless, she made what preparations she thought might be necessary and lined a vegetable crate with clean towels to use as a crib, then spent almost three days' wages on the softest wool she could find. The little yellow blanket she crocheted wasn't perfect, but it was crafted with love.

She had a basic idea of what giving birth might entail, having talked her way into the university library and gleaned what information she could from a book on midwifery. The book warned that childbirth was painful and that it was messy. Mimi found this to be something of an understatement. When her contractions began, she thought she might be torn in two, yet somehow she managed the delivery alone and without attracting attention. Even when during the final throes of her labour, the landlord had come rapping on her door demanding payment of her rent arrears, she had managed to stifle her cries by biting down on a blanket.

But the moment Mimi saw her baby boy she knew that there was something wrong. She had been prepared for blood, and there was plenty of that, but her baby was covered in a sticky white substance, like the rind of a soft cheese. Once she had cut the cord and tied the end off with a piece of clean ribbon, just as the midwifery book had instructed, she washed him carefully in a bowl of warm water, but what she discovered under the waxy coating was worse. Her baby boy was yellow. Every part of him was yellow, even the whites of his eyes. There had been no mention of such coloration in the midwifery book.

Mimi dropped to her knees and thanked God that she and her baby had survived the birth, and survived it without major injury. She prayed that her son's peculiar colour was normal, or at least temporary. He pulled a face when her tears landed on his cheek.

Yet despite its strange yellowness, there wasn't a blemish on her baby's skin. Mimi examined him meticulously, counting his perfect miniature fingers and ten tiny toes. His eyes were brown, like his father's, and he had his father's curly hair too, but just a little tuft, like a corkscrew, right in the middle of his forehead. He was the most beautiful and wondrous thing that Mimi had ever seen.

Although she had prepared a vegetable crate crib, Mimi didn't want to put her baby down, even for a second. She needed to feel every inch of his skin against hers. He was so warm and so lovely and he smelled so good. He made a funny little noise when she tickled him with her fingertips and his hands reached out to touch her face.

A combination of euphoria and exhaustion overwhelmed Mimi. The weight of responsibility for the little being in her arms felt like the greatest honour that could ever be bestowed upon her. In that moment she felt altered beyond recognition, knowing that whatever happened in her child's life, there would be nobody more important to him than her. She had grown him in her belly, given him life and that was something that nobody else could ever do. Mimi tried not to think about not having any money, or the stigma of being an unmarried mother. She would find a way to bring up her son with love and dignity, even if she never found his father.

She stood at the window with her little darling boy cradled in her arms, rocking him and gently murmuring all the loving thoughts in her head. He seemed soothed by the sound of her voice, and when she sang to him, he curled his fingers around her thumb and gripped tightly. His gaze never broke from hers.

As Mimi stood looking down at the street below and the passing traffic of people and bicycles, she tried desperately to ignore the reality of her situation and to hold onto the feeling in her heart that her love would be enough to raise her child, although in her head she knew that it could never be.

Mimi decided that her baby boy should be named after a great man – perhaps Giacomo after Giacomo Puccini, or Antonio, after Antonio Vivaldi, or perhaps even Michelangelo. After some consideration she decided upon Leonardo in honour of Leonardo Da Vinci as he was not only an outstanding artist, but also a man of brilliant ingenuity.

Mimi had been concerned that a baby's crying would disturb the neighbours, or alert the landlord and draw unwanted attention, but little Leonardo seemed content just to lie in her arms and nuzzle her neck. He had cried only once, just after she had delivered him – although surely, she thought, he must be hungry. She inspected her breasts, supposing that milk would come before too long, yet nothing seemed to be happening.

But as the hours passed, Mimi's breasts swelled to the size of oranges and began leaking something which looked nothing like milk and smelled sour. It tasted even worse than it looked and she was reticent to feed her baby something so foul. Nevertheless, she knew that she must try to feed him, so she cupped little Leonardo's head in her hand and drew him close to her breast, murmuring soft words of encouragement, but he wouldn't suckle. Mimi didn't know whether she was doing it correctly. When she parted his lips gently with her fingertip, he sucked feebly on her finger, but there was no such reaction when she offered him her breast.

As the day progressed Mimi's breasts grew to the size of grapefruits and became so hard and sore that even the movement of her baby's breath made her wince. She felt some relief when the sour discharge gave way to something which looked more like milk. It was watery, but sweetish. Still, despite numerous attempts and much encouragement, little Leonardo refused to suckle.

Mimi fretted, knowing that he wouldn't survive if he wouldn't feed, so she gave herself an ultimatum. If by the following morning there was no improvement, she would take him to the Clinica Santa Monica.

She didn't want to. She was filled with the fear that the Child Welfare Service would take him from her and never give him back. The thought of Leonardo being taken and given to somebody else, or being raised in an orphanage when he wasn't really an orphan, terrified Mimi. Nobody could ever love Leonardo as much as she did.

She held her little golden boy close, kissing his soft skin and stroking her cheek against his. She wanted to give him all the love she could in the time she had, because she knew that the possibility of him being taken from her was very real.

But by the next morning little Leonardo was still yellow and clearly very unwell. He could barely open his eyes and he wouldn't even suck on her fingers. He just lay limply in her arms. Mimi knew she had no choice. She had to get him to the hospital for medical treatment, and quickly.

Still she hesitated. Perhaps she should make up a story about being married, although she doubted whether such a deception would be believed. Proof might be demanded. Suddenly she had an idea.

With little Leonardo cradled in her arms she hurried to the room upstairs, which was rented by a single man. Mimi didn't know his name, or anything about him. They had only ever exchanged a brief greeting when they had crossed on the stairs, but perhaps he could be convinced to go with her to the hospital and pretend to be her husband. She was willing to pay him for his trouble with her late mother's emerald earrings.

Mimi rapped on his door, but there was no answer. She knew that the man worked nights and was usually home by 8 a.m. It was already past 8.30. Mimi feared that she couldn't wait much longer. She paced the landing outside his room for ten minutes, but there was no sign of him

Suddenly Leonardo gasped, coughed, and his little body stiffened and shook, then went limp. Mimi rushed back down the stairs clutching him tightly to her chest, but by the time they reached her room he had slipped out of consciousness and had turned from yellow to a bluish colour. Mimi tried frantically to revive him, rubbing his little body and his little arms and legs, but Leonardo remained totally inert.

'Wake up! Wake up! Wake up!' she cried with a scream so desperate that her throat was scraped raw.

There was no reaction. Leonardo was utterly unresponsive.

Mimi was overcome by such an explosion of distress that everything around her fell away. Anguish crushed the breath from her. Her mouth couldn't speak. Her ears couldn't hear. Her eyes were rendered blind. She could feel nothing but the vibration of her body. The building might have collapsed on top of her and she wouldn't have known.

When at last the room came back into focus Mimi found that she was on the floor on her hands and knees. Little Leonardo's limp body lay in front of her.

Why had she waited? What had she done?

She was a murderer, and she had committed the most unforgivable of all murders – and to make it worse still, little Leonardo had not been baptised so Mimi had condemned him to a state of eternal limbo. Her tiny baby, who was innocent of any wrongdoing, would not be allowed into heaven in his unbaptised state.

Mimi begged God to be compassionate and to grant her baby clemency. God could punish her as much as He wanted and however He saw fit, but please, He should find it within His merciful goodness to let little Leonardo into heaven.

She held him, kissing his little clammy cheeks and trying to decide what she should do. She knew in her heart that she should alert somebody, admit what she had done and face the consequences, yet part of her hesitated once more. Nobody knew her in Bologna. Nobody knew that she had been pregnant and therefore nobody knew of little Leonardo's existence. She could leave quietly and disappear and nobody, except God, need ever know.

Mimi kissed little Leonardo one last time, told him that she loved him and always would, and that she was so, so sorry. She wrapped him carefully in his yellow blanket and placed him in the crate, then tore the margin from a newspaper and wrote – *Leonardo: 20th March 1929 – 21st March 1929. Forever in Mamma's heart.*

Somebody would find him and they would know what to do. Mimi hoped that they would find him quickly.

She stoked the stove, because she couldn't bear the thought of little Leonardo's body being left to go cold in a cold room, and slipped away just a few minutes later, placing one of her mother's emerald earrings in the crate to cover the burial costs.

*

When Rinaldo Rossi returned from his job at the brush factory that morning with fresh bread and milk for his breakfast he had quite a spring in his step, the reason being that he had also treated himself to a whole smoked Scamorza cheese the size of his fist, and he was very much looking forward to eating it. Its smoky aroma was making his stomach rumble.

He climbed up to the first floor and noticed that the door to the girl's room was wedged open with a chair. He would have thought little of it, but as he passed he heard a strange squeaking noise coming from inside and stopped. The noise continued.

'*S'gnurina?*' he said, tapping on the door, but he wasn't sure whether the girl spoke Bolognese dialect, so he tried in Italian: 'Signorina? Signorina, is everything all right?'

There was no answer, but the squeaking increased to a feeble wailing. Rinaldo Rossi poked his nose tentatively over the threshold, but clearly the girl was not there. The bed was stripped and the room was bare. The only thing which looked out of place was a crate on the floor.

Rinaldo Rossi stood looking down at the small, yellow infant in the crate, whose crying had now grown so urgent that he felt compelled to pick it up. He was not alarmed by the baby's colour as two of his sisters had been born jaundiced but had turned a normal colour eventually.

'There, there, little one,' he cooed. 'Where's your Mamma gone?'

There was a strip of newspaper draped over the baby. As he couldn't read, Rinaldo Rossi paid no attention to the fact that Leonardo's name was written on it. He was halfway through sucking a boiled sweet, which he spat out, wrapped in the scrap of newspaper and put in his pocket. He would finish it later, after he had eaten his bread and cheese.

It was then that he spotted the emerald earring. It was a beautiful thing, with a single stone set into a gold drop. He held it up to the light for a moment to see the emerald sparkle, then placed it in his pocket with the half-sucked sweet.

Rinaldo Rossi stood bouncing the infant gently in his arms hoping it would sleep, but the child's crying became more distressed. He paced the room with the baby resting on his shoulder and began to sing a lullaby which his own mother had sung to him, but the infant would not quieten. Still there was no sign of the girl.

He knew that a crying baby was usually the sign of a hungry baby, so he sat on the bed with the infant on his knee and slowly began to feed him milk from a spoon. The baby was quite suddenly animated and lapped at the milk like a cat.

Rinaldo Rossi's stomach rumbled loudly. With the baby tucked into the crook of his arm he reached across to his parcel of food and tore off a piece of bread, then fumbled, one-handed, with his package of Scamorza cheese. When he looked from the Scamorza to the jaundiced infant he thought how funny it was that the baby bore such a remarkable resemblance to the ball of cheese, both in form and colour.

'You're like a little Scamorza,' he chuckled.

It took an hour to feed the baby almost a quarter of a bottle of milk.

'*Dio bono*, you've got an appetite, little Scamorza!' exclaimed

Rinaldo Rossi, at which point the baby belched, screwed up his little yellow face and let out a long, reverberating fart.

'Shall we have a nap, little Scamorza? Maybe by the time we wake up your Mamma will have come back.'

He lay on the mattress with the infant and before long they were both asleep. Rinaldo Rossi was woken by the landlord some time later.

'What are you doing in here?' the man bellowed, lunging forwards, ready to drag Rinaldo Rossi from the bed. Then he saw the baby. 'And what the devil are you doing with a baby?'

Rinaldo Rossi did his best to explain, but he was not very good at expressing himself clearly, particularly not in Italian, and particularly if he felt under pressure. He knew that people often misunderstood him, which made him anxious, and that made his confusion worse.

'The girl's gone,' said the landlord. 'Left me a note this morning. Should have given me a month's notice and paid rent until then, but she's gone.'

'She forgot her baby.'

The landlord grunted. 'Forgot it?' he scoffed. 'The little trollop knew perfectly well what she was doing. If I'd known she was about to drop a kid I would never have let her have the room.'

A policeman was summoned, which made Rinaldo Rossi very afraid. Although he had never been in trouble with the law, in the past he had attracted the attention of various policemen by virtue of the fact that his anxiety could easily be mistaken for guilt. Finding himself interrogated, Rinaldo Rossi panicked.

'What can you tell me about the child's mother?'

'I – I only saw her when we passed on the stairs, Officer. But I can't say I got a good look at her. It's dark on the stairs, Officer. There's no lights on the stairs.'

'Do you know her name?'

Not knowing the answer and not wishing to anger the policeman, Rinaldo Rossi blurted out the first name he could think of, his own mother's name.

'Giuseppina.'

The policeman noted it down.

'Do you know the child's name?' he continued, to which Rinaldo Rossi answered, 'Scamorza.'

'Scamorza? Like the cheese?'

Rinaldo Rossi nodded.

'And the Christian name?'

Rinaldo Rossi was so relieved that he had given not only one but two satisfactory answers, that he hadn't properly understood the third question and assumed that the policeman was asking him his own name.

'Christian name? It's Rinaldo, Officer,' said Rinaldo Rossi.

The policeman wrote it down. Thus on the twenty-first of March 1929 the baby was registered as Rinaldo Scamorza, son of Giuseppina Scamorza.

'This was in the box with the baby,' said Rinaldo Rossi, taking the emerald earring from his pocket.

'Where's the other one?'

'I don't know, Officer. I only found this one.'

'Only one earring? And what was it doing in your pocket?'

'I put it there to be safe.'

'Empty your pockets!'

Rinaldo Rossi laid out a handkerchief, a length of string and half a boiled sweet wrapped in a sticky strip of newspaper.

'I'll give you one more chance to tell me what you've done with the other earring,' warned the policeman.

It was then that a woman turned up from the Child Welfare Service. She took a look at the yellow baby and shook her head. He was the fourth abandoned child she'd been sent to retrieve that week.

'I don't know whether this one will survive,' she said wearily. 'We'll do our best.'

'Will you take him to the Clinica Santa Monica?' asked the policeman. 'I could get one of my colleagues to run you in.'

'No, no,' replied the woman. 'This child has a far more pressing commitment. Look at the state of him! He needs to be baptised before anything else.'

The woman made off with the baby and headed for the nearest church. Within the hour the infant had been christened Rinaldo Scamorza.

The policeman left too, taking Rinaldo Rossi with him. Having been unable to produce the second earring, the unfortunate man was arrested for its theft. He spent two days in a cell but was released without charge when the space was needed for another offender.

Rinaldo Rossi lost his job at the brush factory for having been absent without leave. Unable to pay his rent, he also lost his lodgings.

The policeman, being an honest and upstanding fellow, took the single emerald earring to the orphanage of San Girolamo so that it could be returned to the child at an appropriate time.

CHAPTER 2

Little Rinaldo Scamorza knew about the emerald earring. He also knew where it was kept. The orphanage of San Girolamo had a box in which identification tokens left by mothers were stored in the event that a mother should wish to reclaim her child. One of the nicer orphanage ladies would let him have a look if he'd been good.

It was a dismal collection of keepsakes – bits of ribbon, buttons, barely literate notes, even half a chicken bone. Rinaldo's earring stood out, for it was the only thing of any value. The boy would hold it up to the light to see the emerald sparkle.

Rinaldo invented a thousand reasons why he had ended up at the orphanage. He was certain that his mother had not really abandoned him, but simply mislaid him. He was convinced that she was looking for him and therefore it was only a matter of time until he was found. He would know immediately who she was because she would be wearing the other emerald earring. He checked the ears of every lady he met, but to no avail.

Still, he held on to the belief that one day he would be reunited with his mother. Sometimes, when he knew that there was nobody to overhear him, he would practise saying her name in different ways and in different tones of voice – *Mamma, I'm hungry. Mamma, I've hurt myself. Mamma, I'm happy. Mamma, I'm sad. Mamma, I love you.* Often he would just repeat the word by itself, like an exercise, so that his mouth wouldn't forget how to make the right shapes. *Mam-ma. Mam-ma. Mamma. Mamma.*

Being a healthy and manageable child, there was no shortage

of would-be parents willing to adopt him, but each time the circumstance arose, Rinaldo would scream and kick and beat the floor with his fists. Sometimes he would bite. Rinaldo was determined that he would only leave with his real mother. He couldn't risk leaving with anybody else. What if they wouldn't give him back to her when she came to claim him?

The Child Welfare Service couldn't understand why a child as agreeable as Rinaldo would turn into such a monster whenever anyone showed interest in adopting him. They concluded that there was probably something wrong with his head. He had, after all, suffered from convulsions during the first few days of his life. Still, despite the orphanage's best efforts, no adoption could be secured, therefore there was no option but to try to have him fostered.

Aged five, little Rinaldo Scamorza found himself under the care of Ada Stracci, although 'care' was not the most appropriate description of the service provided by his new foster mother. Rinaldo hadn't wanted to leave the orphanage, but he'd had no choice in the matter. Some people had come to collect him in a car. He'd had his wrists and ankles bound with twine to stop the usual tantrums, and his mouth gagged with a bandage to avoid the risk of biting.

Ada Stracci took in as many orphans as she could squeeze into her house. The Child Welfare Service provided her with an income for the maintenance of each child, almost all of which she spent on herself. She usually only took girls, but had taken Rinaldo on account of the fact that a boy could be useful. And as he was small, he would be cheap to feed.

The Child Welfare Service considered Ada Stracci to be an excellent foster mother as she kept a very clean house and ensured her charges' regular church attendance. None of the children were ever asked whether life in the Stracci house was happy, or fair. Playing was prohibited. Instead, Ada Stracci filled the children's days with chores. There were always floors to scrub, windows to clean, laundry to wash and iron. She even took in laundry from other people in the neighbourhood, which was a lucrative side-line. It would have been stupid not to make the most of all the free labour she had at her disposal.

On the rare occasions that the welfare inspectors called, Ada Stracci would change, transforming herself into an attentive and benevolent foster mother, showering her charges with a false, exaggerated affection. One time she had even sat Rinaldo on her knee, playfully pinching his cheeks and ruffling his curls whilst the inspectors drank coffee and ate pastries in her kitchen. When Rinaldo had made an attempt to wriggle free, she had grasped him so tightly that he had felt her fingernails dig in between his ribs, and whilst maintaining an expression of tender motherly affection, she had hissed in his ear: 'Stay where you are, you little bastard, or you'll be spending the next week locked in the cellar.'

Once the inspectors had finished their refreshments and left, Rinaldo lifted his shirt to reveal purple half-moon bruises on his flank left by Ada Stracci's fingernails. But as far as the welfare inspectors were concerned, the verdict was the same as always. Ada Stracci was an exemplary foster mother. The house was spotless. The children's church attendance was consistent. There was nothing untoward to report.

Most children were obedient. The insubordinate ones were brought into line with a beating. Being a woman of unparalleled laziness, Ada Stracci couldn't be bothered to beat the children herself. She left that task to her gentleman friend, Gigio Lingua, a stoat-faced little fellow with a cartoonish moustache to disguise his bad teeth. He simmered with the aggression of a man conscious of his small size and was always causing fights, although he rarely stuck around long enough to join in.

Ada Stracci was a shrewd businesswoman. Once girls reached

the age of fourteen or fifteen she sold them to a man who procured girls for brothels. The pretty ones she sold even sooner. If the Child Welfare Service made any inquiries concerning the girls' whereabouts, Ada Stracci would tell them that she had found work for them, which was not untrue. No further questions would be asked.

But there was one girl, Evelina Brunelli, to whom Ada Stracci gave special treatment. At the time of Rinaldo's arrival, Evelina was nine years old.

During his first night at his new foster home Rinaldo had wanted to cry, but he had learned at the orphanage that being seen or heard crying was an admission of weakness, so he lay immobile in his unfamiliar bed holding his breath. Evelina heard him sniff and squeak and knew that something was wrong, so she slipped into bed beside him and put her arms around him.

'Don't cry,' she said softly. 'I'll look after you.'

Rinaldo explained his predicament, but Evelina assured him that the orphanage kept a list of all children's names and where they were living. If his mother went looking for him at the orphanage, which was the most obvious place for her to search for him, the ladies from San Girolamo would simply find him on the list and direct her to Ada Stracci's house.

'Until your Mamma comes for you, I'll be your big sister,' said Evelina, stroking Rinaldo's hair to soothe him. 'I'm glad you're here. I've always wanted a little brother.'

Rinaldo hated nicknames. From as far back as he could remember, other children – and even sometimes adults – had made up silly names for him, all related to cheese. None of them were clever and none of them were funny. Evelina never teased him about having the same name as a cheese. She called him 'Aldino', and he liked it very much.

Evelina had not been fostered through the orphanage. Her

mother, who was known in certain circles as 'La Bella Brunelli', had worked in the same brothel as Ada Stracci, although this element of her past was one that Ada Stracci was careful to keep from the child welfare authorities.

Following Evelina's birth, her mother had tried to earn a living as a wet-nurse, but the pay was not enough to feed herself, and if she was not fed she couldn't make milk, even for Evelina. She had no option but to supplement her wet-nursing income, and for that she had no choice but to put her body back on sale again.

As Evelina grew she learned to be still and perfectly quiet when her mother draped the blanket over her cot. Sometimes if the blanket was not quite pulled down far enough she could see men without their trousers on. She didn't like it when the men came into the room and her Mamma's voice went soft, but her Mamma had explained that if the men didn't come to see her, there would be no food and no money to put in their special savings pot.

The pot was shaped like a strawberry and Evelina's mother would put a lira into it whenever she could. It was their fund for their move to Milano Marittima, a pretty little seaside town where her Mamma said Evelina would be able to play in the sand and swim in the sea and eat ice cream every day – but it would take a long time to save enough money to move there.

La Bella Brunelli was cautious and always checked her clients for sores, so she couldn't think who had given her syphilis. She didn't know that it could be passed to the babies she wet-nursed. By the time the police and sanitation inspectors came for her, she had infected five babies.

Evelina's mother died when her little daughter was four. It was unclear whether she had entrusted Evelina to Ada Stracci, or whether Ada Stracci had taken the child without her mother's consent.

A legend had grown around Evelina's mother, fed in great part by Ada Stracci, who said that La Bella Brunelli had been a creature of singular beauty, renowned for her thick raven hair, green eyes and alabaster skin – not to mention the full, perfectly-proportioned form of her body. Ada Stracci claimed that men had travelled from all over Italy and sold their valuables for the privilege of a night spent with La Bella Brunelli.

If indeed any of this was true, Evelina's mother had had nothing to show for it. She died in the state syphilis hospital, leaving just the threadbare dress and green shawl in which she had arrived. The savings, along with the strawberry-shaped pot, had disappeared.

To Ada Stracci, Evelina was valuable capital. She fed her adequately and prohibited her from doing chores that might damage her hands. Evelina knew her intended fate and was untroubled by it, for Ada Stracci had explained that hers was to be a future far brighter than any other girl's. Evelina believed her wholeheartedly.

'What will you be when you're grown up, Aldino?' asked Evelina.

'I don't know,' the boy replied.

'Ada says I am going to be a very beautiful woman,' announced Evelina with absolute confidence. 'My Mamma was the most beautiful woman in the whole of Italy and I shall be just like her. I shall be given fine clothes and be taken to dine in fine restaurants. But even when I'm a grown-up lady, I'll still be your sister. I'll share my food with you and when they give me money I'll give some of it to you. And when I have a fine house you can come and live there too.'

Rinaldo hoped it was true, but he did not share Evelina's faith in Ada Stracci.

'I shall ask for my house to be in Milano Marittima,' she added.

'Where's that?'

'It's a little town by the sea. It's where my Mamma was from. People go there for their holidays. It has shops that sell things made of sea shells, and ice creams, and parks full of pine trees. And there are even boats there that you can pedal, like bicycles. I think I shall ask for one of those boats too. Wouldn't it be fun to ride on the sea like that?'

Evelina's recollection of her mother was always loving. Rinaldo liked to listen and he wished that he too had some memory of his mother. He hoped that she had loved him at some point, even if it was briefly.

'I'll miss you when your Mamma comes for you, Aldino,' said Evelina sadly.

'I won't go with her unless she takes you too,' replied Rinaldo.

Evelina grinned and hugged him. Although Rinaldo meant what he had said, he was beginning to question whether his mother really was looking for him. Maybe she had given up, or lost interest. Perhaps he would never have a mother, but somehow that thought didn't feel too bad because Evelina was there to stick up for him. If Ada Stracci was cross, as she often was, Evelina would step in and defuse the situation. If ever he was sad, Evelina always found a way to make him feel better. She made sure that his curly hair was brushed and that his fingernails were cut. He didn't even mind when she scolded him a little. Rinaldo loved Evelina very much.

*

Ada Stracci's quarters were in the attic of her house, an area into which no child was allowed. The door had locks and bolts on both sides. Even her man-friend Gigio Lingua was only allowed in by invitation, and would be sent home once Ada Stracci had finished with him.

There was much speculation amongst the children as to what treasure Ada Stracci hid in her room. Stories abounded about trunks filled with gold and sacks of silver, boxes of diamonds and rubies.

One day, curiosity got the better of Rinaldo. He knew that trying to tamper with the locks or the bolts would not only require tools, but would also alert Ada Stracci. Stealing the keys was impossible as she kept them on a chain around her neck. However, there was a small skylight in the roof at the top of the attic stairs. Rinaldo stood on the landing contemplating it and wondering whether it would be possible to squeeze through it, make his way across the roof and slip into Ada Stracci's room through the dormer window. The window was always open when the weather was fair. Rinaldo could see it from the yard.

There were several problems. Firstly, getting up to the skylight itself would be a challenge. Even if he stood on a chair Rinaldo was far too small to reach it. A ladder would be ideal, but he didn't have a ladder and even if he did, being seen carrying one up to the attic would arouse suspicion. This thought occupied the boy's mind for months. He would often sneak upstairs to stare thoughtfully up at the skylight.

One day a delivery of crockery arrived packed in a wooden chest. It was a flowery porcelain set which Ada Stracci had bought with the profits from the sale of a girl called Bianca. After it was emptied, the chest was left on the landing and used to store blankets. The moment Rinaldo saw it he knew that it was just right.

The opportune moment came one Friday when Ada Stracci was at the market. Rinaldo ran out into the yard to check that her window was open, then dashed back up to the top of the house, placed the chest under the skylight and balanced a chair on top. It was a perfect height.

Getting through the skylight was a bit of a squeeze, even for a skinny six-year-old boy, but he managed and found himself on the roof of the building. Thinking it best not to look down, he shimmied his way across the tiles then swung in through Ada Stracci's window.

The room was jammed with things. Every surface was covered in ornaments and china figurines. There was a collection of porcelain dolls, the new crockery from the sale of Bianca and a display case filled with gaudy coloured glassware; but there were no trunks filled with treasure, nor boxes of jewels. Despite the temptation to take something, Rinaldo left Ada Stracci's trinkets untouched. He had satisfied his curiosity and that was enough.

Evelina gasped when he told her where he'd been.

'You'll be in so much trouble if Ada finds out!'

'She won't find out unless one of us tells her.'

'You know I won't, Aldino.'

'Then she's not going to find out.'

Evelina said that they must never talk about it again in the house in case one of the other children overheard. She knew that Ada Stracci would have Rinaldo punished for it. The girl had witnessed him getting more than one whipping with a belt, which had turned his back purple.

*

Rinaldo realised that his permanent unwell feeling was due to hunger, but he knew that requesting more food from Ada Stracci would be tantamount to requesting a beating. The other children ate their food in rapid, ravenous mouthfuls, but Rinaldo found that eating in such a way only made him hungrier. It was better to eat slowly, taking small bites and chewing for a long time to trick his body into thinking it was a satisfying meal, but it was only a temporary solution. Within an hour of finishing his food, he would be hungry again.

Competition amongst the children was fierce at the table. Each one protected their plate, defending their food and prepared to stab their fork into any hand which strayed too close. Every mouthful, every morsel, every breadcrumb and every smear of sauce was guarded like the most precious thing in the world.

Evelina would share her supper with Rinaldo by passing things secretly under the table. She would always tap his foot with hers to warn that something was on the way, but the other children soon realised what was going on and didn't like it. They didn't like the fact that Evelina was better fed than they were, and they didn't like the fact that she only shared with Rinaldo. They threatened to tell, so Rinaldo asked Evelina to stop. Instead of passing him morsels under the table, she would wrap things in her handkerchief and give them to him later. Still, it was not enough to satisfy the appetite of a growing boy.

Rinaldo became entirely obsessed with food. He would stand outside the pastry shop with his nose pressed against the window, gazing at the cakes. There were tarts glistening with glazed fruit, pyramids of almond and hazelnut cones, meringues oozing *zabaglione* and rich chocolate custard. His craving was all-consuming. Sometimes it was all too much. It was as though Rinaldo was being devoured by the cakes.

He had tasted one once. A kind lady had given him a cream-filled choux bun when he had helped to carry her shopping, and it had been the most delicious thing that the small boy had ever tasted.

Then one day, as he was walking down a side street not far from Ada Stracci's, Rinaldo had stopped dead in his tracks, struck by the hot, sweet fragrance of a freshly-baked something. Whatever it was, it came from the sill of a ground-floor window, but Rinaldo was too short to see exactly what it was. He stood for a while, filling his nostrils with the aroma, until the ravenous wrenching of his stomach became intolerable.

Snatching up a bucket on which to stand, he found himself at eye-level with a *crostata* – a huge baked tart, topped with a thick layer of apricot jam and latticed with strips of sweet, crumbly pastry. It sat on the windowsill still in its baking tray, steaming as it cooled. The sight and smell of it made the boy's knees tremble so much that he almost fell off the bucket.

Unable to control himself, he reached out to take it, but the dish in which it sat was too hot to hold. Rinaldo pulled down his sleeves over his hands and grabbed the dish. It was not only very hot, but also very heavy. As he jumped down, the bucket toppled over with a loud clatter, taking Rinaldo and the *crostata* with it, but he managed to land on his feet, the *crostata* held aloft.

The noise alerted the woman in the kitchen, who leaned out of the window. To his dismay, Rinaldo realised that he knew her. She was the nice lady who had given him the choux bun for carrying her shopping.

'Stop! Thief!' she cried.

Rinaldo made off as fast as his toothpick legs could carry him. Almost immediately a man came out of the tobacco shop and gave chase. Rinaldo ran, still holding on to the *crostata*, but the heat from the dish was radiating through his sleeves and his hands were burning. The man from the tobacco shop was closing in. Rinaldo slipped down a side alley. He would have run faster, but he was slowed by the weight of the *crostata*.

'Oi! I know who you are! You're one of Ada Stracci's urchins!' yelled the man.

Realising that he had not only been rumbled, but also identified, terrified Rinaldo. He continued to run, but when he turned to look behind him, he tripped and the dish slipped from his grasp.

The beautiful *crostata* flew through the air before hitting a wall and sliding in a slow, sticky, jammy way to the ground. Rinaldo ducked into an open cellar and sat blowing on his burned hands. He could hear the angry tobacconist outside, cursing him. Eventually the kind lady came to retrieve her baking tray. Rinaldo remained hidden in the cellar until long after they had gone.

The mess of the *crostata* had been scraped from the wall, leaving only a smear of jam. Rinaldo pressed his finger into it and rubbed it on his tongue to taste it. It made his longing worse.

Although he had not satisfied his hunger, Rinaldo had learned two lessons that day. The first: if he was to steal, he would have to be clever about it. The second: he would never steal from someone unless they deserved it.

*

There was a private school in Via Saragozza. The boys who attended it wore smart black smocks with white collars and a turquoise bow. The school crest was embroidered in gold on the breast pocket. These boys fascinated Rinaldo. They weren't like the boys from the ordinary schools whose smocks, if they had them, were a rag-tag of faded, mismatched things made from old shirts and anything else which came to hand.

Rinaldo imagined that if his mother had not been forced to leave him, he would have been one of those smartly-smocked boys. A mother rich enough to leave an emerald earring would surely have been rich enough to pay for school fees and a smock.

The students from the private school never ventured into the streets around Ada Stracci's, but following the incident with the *crostata*, Rinaldo was also avoiding the area, preferring to take his walks further afield.

One day he was sitting on a wall not far from the school minding his own business when the thwack of a stone hitting the back of his neck knocked him off it. It took him a few moments to understand what had happened. It was the laughter of two private-school boys which made him realise that the stone had come from them. They didn't run off when Rinaldo saw them. They just kept laughing. The second stone hit Rinaldo on the forehead.

Once the stars had cleared from his vision, Rinaldo got to his feet, retrieved the stones and threw them back, but his giddiness made him miss and the boys sauntered off, calling him a poor boy and an idiot. Rinaldo decided that it would not be the end of the matter.

He spent several days observing the boys from a vantage point behind some dustbins opposite the school. The boys, obviously brothers, one older than Rinaldo and one of approximately the same age, would come out at four o'clock and make their way along Via Saragozza. They would stop for sweets almost every day. Rinaldo noted that the man in the confectionery shop was very nice to them, often giving them a little something extra. This annoyed Rinaldo. He had never been given anything by a shopkeeper. More often than not, he was kicked out of shops for looking shifty.

The boys' home was a grand mansion on the Viale. On their arrival home they would be greeted by a maid, who, having set a table for them on the veranda, would immediately set about serving them cake, or bread and honey and peach juice, despite the fact that they had just eaten sweets. Rinaldo gazed into their garden from behind the railings as the boys ate some of what the maid had served them and fed the rest to a little fat sausage dog.

Several things played on Rinaldo's mind. Revenge for the stone-throwing was one of them, but above all, it was the way the boys were treated by the shopkeepers. He wondered whether if he too was dressed smartly, he would be given the same treatment.

Finding himself once again outside the mansion on the Viale, an opportunity arose. The boys had finished their afternoon snack – or rather, they had started it and the sausage dog had finished it – and had gone inside. Shortly after, the maid brought out their smocks to beat the chalk-dust from them, then left them to air on the washing line.

At lightning speed, Rinaldo darted into the garden and took the smaller smock. He rolled it under his arm and was about to make his escape, but then he spotted a little fresh dog turd on the grass. He picked it up with a leaf. It was soft and still warm. Rinaldo placed it in the pocket of the remaining smock, then gave it few firm squeezes to make sure it was well-rubbed into the fabric.

'That's for the stones,' he said quietly and slipped out of the garden.

Rinaldo hid the smock under his bed. He would take it out and look at it whenever the dormitory was empty. It was a beautiful thing crafted from the blackest, finest quality fabric. The collar was so white that it gleamed. As for the bow, it was made out of something which was so soft and so shiny that Rinaldo never tired of running his fingers over it. Evelina said that it was silk, which was the most expensive material in the whole world.

He longed to wear it, but there was a problem. Although he had a smock, and one which fitted surprisingly well, he only had old boots. One had come unstitched where his toes had broken through and both soles had holes. The problem plagued him. He had been back to the mansion on the Viale numerous times in the hope that the maid would put the boys' shoes outside to air, but luck had not been on his side.

Nevertheless, the urge to wear the smock nagged at him like an unreachable itch. Unable to stand it any longer, Rinaldo decided he would risk it. He smuggled the smock out of Ada Stracci's and changed into it in the cellar where he had hidden from the tobacconist.

He felt so good in the smock, like a better version of himself.

He paraded around the cellar practising talking like the private-school boys, dropping his heavy Bolognese dialect and enunciating the words in his best Italian. Pronouncing the letter 's' was tricky. It was best done through his front teeth with his chin in the air.

He crept out of the cellar with some trepidation, thinking it best not to venture too near the school, so instead made his way down Via Sant'Isaia. It was not long before he realised that people were looking at him differently, respectfully even, although a few did cast questioning glances at his broken boots. Emboldened by their reactions, Rinaldo strode with confidence, practising his private-school boy voice in his head, until a lady in a fur stole stopped him.

'Whatever's happened to your shoes, dear boy?' she asked.

Rinaldo stood dumbstruck for a moment and considered making a run for it, then blurted out, 'A poor boy took them.'

'Oh, how awful!' exclaimed the lady. 'You have to mind the horrid little hooligans around here. Is that why you're not at school, dear?'

'Yes,' replied Rinaldo solemnly, remembering to pronounce his 's' properly.

'What's happened to your spare pair?'

Rinaldo stood up a little straighter, his confidence boosted by the fact that dressed in the smock he looked rich enough to own spare shoes.

'They're being mended,' he said.

He thought that would be the end of their encounter, but the lady took his hand and accompanied him to the cobbler's shop.

'This young man has come to collect his shoes,' she announced in a commanding tone, which made the cobbler put down his hammer immediately. 'I sincerely hope that they're ready. The poor child has had his other shoes stolen by an urchin and he's unable to go to school until he is properly shod.'

The cobbler squinted at Rinaldo, although he didn't seem to pay much attention to Rinaldo's face, only to his smock and to the fact that he was holding the hand of an elegant lady in a fur stole.

'What's the name?' he asked, spitting out the tacks from between his lips. 'Zappatelli?'

'Yes,' replied Rinaldo, trying to keep his voice steady.

The cobbler cast his gaze along the numerous pairs of shoes lined up on the shelves behind his bench and without further question handed over a pair of newly re-heeled shoes. Just as Rinaldo was reaching out tentatively to take them, prepared to snatch them and run off with them if necessary, the lady raised her hand to stop him. Rinaldo's heart leaped into his mouth.

'No, no,' said the lady. 'These shoes are not ready to be worn. They haven't been polished.'

The cobbler took them back with a slight roll of his eyes, turned and pulled a lever on a machine which comprised a series of angled brushes. It came to life with a high-pitched whirring sound and he set about buffing the shoes. By the time he had finished and handed them back, Rinaldo could see his own reflection in the toes so clearly that he could look up his own nostrils.

'I'll put them on the account,' said the cobbler and Rinaldo left the shop in Zappatelli's shiny shoes thinking that it had all been remarkably easy.

From then on, and with significant self-assurance, Rinaldo adopted his new persona of wealthy private-school boy, although he was careful not to be seen in the vicinity of Ada Stracci's, nor anywhere near the school when he was dressed in his smock. He also avoided the cobbler's.

As he had suspected, being well-dressed made people treat him very differently. Shopkeepers would let him have things and demand no payment when he said, 'Thank you. Please put it on my mother's account.'

On the rare occasions when he was asked for a name, he would reply, 'Zappatelli.'

'You're such a lovely, polite young man,' said the lady who ran Rinaldo's favourite confectioners. 'You're a credit to your parents.'

'Thank you very much, Signora,' replied Rinaldo in his most charming voice and with his best-pronounced 's'. 'I'll be sure to tell them.'

Despite the temptation to raise the stakes, the memory of the *crostata* episode and the lessons he had learned from it remained at the forefront of Rinaldo's mind. He was never greedy. He never placed large or expensive items on account. He would limit himself to a daily allowance of one cake – two if they were small. Occasionally he would treat himself to chocolate, or an ice cream. Most of the time he took half his bounty home for Evelina. Evelina was the only person he told because she was the only person in the world he trusted.

Being better fed caused a significant growth spurt which meant that within six months of appropriating the private school smock and shoes, he outgrew them.

Rinaldo had been a victim of his own success.

CHAPTER 3

As the Stracci house was such a miserable place, Rinaldo and Evelina would go out whenever they could. Ada Stracci didn't care, as long as their chores were done. At least if they were out, her charges didn't get under her feet, or make the house untidy.

During the late spring and early summer, once a fortnight on a Saturday afternoon, there was a free Burattini puppet show in Piazza Maggiore. A platform which was half-stage and half-tent would be set up in the piazza and great numbers of people would come to watch the performance. It was so popular that many a hopeful spectator would end up sitting on the steps of the Church of San Petronio, even though it was much too far from the stage to see or hear what was going on.

Rinaldo and Evelina would weave their way through the crowds in the hope of catching a glimpse of the puppets with their brightly-painted faces, big noses and silly hats. If they were lucky enough to get really close they could even hear what they were saying. The Burattini puppets all spoke in Bolognese dialect; sometimes they even used some rude words. Rinaldo and Evelina would laugh so hard that their cheeks and their bellies would ache.

Rinaldo's favourite puppet was Fagiolino. Fagiolino was poor, and he was nearly always hungry, but he never let anyone get the better of him – and those who tried to cross him received a vigorous beating with a stick. His best friend, and often also his partner in crime, was Sganapino.

There was only one girl puppet, Fagiolino's wife, Isabella, but nobody called her that, particularly not Fagiolino. Instead she was known as 'Brisabella', which was a play on words in

Bolognese dialect that translated to 'not beautiful'. Evelina was disappointed that the only girl character was ugly, so when she and Rinaldo re-enacted the shows they'd seen and Rinaldo played Fagiolino, Evelina invented her own girl version of Sganapino, whom she called 'Sganapina'. They even made up their own rhyme:

Aldino-Fagiolino, Evelina-Sganapina,
Aldino-Fagiolino, Evelina-Sganapina,
Aldino Fagiolino ...

They would chase each other around, talking in nasal, sing-song voices, just like the Burattini puppets, but they never beat each other with sticks. At worst they would tickle one another, and because Evelina was bigger, it was usually Rinaldo who succumbed to the tickling attacks. He didn't mind too much, because Evelina always knew when to stop. But most of all, whether they were being Aldino-Fagiolino and Evelina-Sganapina, or simply Rinaldo and Evelina, they made big plans of how one day they would be rich.

How they would make their fortunes was always a subject of lengthy and animated discussion between them. Evelina was confident that she was going to be very beautiful one day, so she would have lots of money. But Rinaldo understood that as he was a boy, he couldn't count on his looks and he'd have to rely on his muscles and his wits instead.

When there was nothing in particular to see in town, the two friends would go exploring, but Rinaldo knew that wherever their wandering took them they would end up in at least one church. Evelina loved churches and couldn't pass one without wanting to go in. Rinaldo didn't share her religious fervour, but he never complained about visiting churches. He could occupy himself for hours looking at the painted ceilings and the frescoes on the walls. It was a glimpse into a rich world, where things that to Rinaldo seemingly had no function but to be beautiful, could be admired. He loved the carved wood, the silver candlesticks and the religious ornaments all covered in gold.

Evelina's favourite church was San Paolo Maggiore because it contained a life-sized statue of a pretty Madonna who she said looked like her mother. The Madonna was clothed in a blue shawl, as all Madonnas were, but in the sombre light of the church it looked quite green. Evelina said that her Mamma had owned a shawl just like it.

'What happened to your Mamma's shawl?' asked Rinaldo.

'I don't know,' replied Evelina sadly. 'I don't know what happened to any of her things. She had a pot which looked like a big strawberry with money in it, but Ada said that was stolen by thieves. Mamma had a special picture of the Virgin Mary too. It was very precious because it was blessed by a priest who had blood coming out of his hands like Jesus did when they crucified Him.'

'Ugh!' grimaced Rinaldo. 'That's disgusting.'

'It's not disgusting at all! It was a miracle.'

Rinaldo wasn't convinced. 'I thought miracles were supposed to be good,' he said. 'Like when Jesus gave all those people bread and fish. Or when He made the water turn into wine. But He could have done better miracles though, couldn't He? If I'd been Jesus I'd have turned the bread into *tortellini* and the fish into pork chops. And I wouldn't have turned water into wine. I'd have—'

'Shh, Aldino!' hushed Evelina. 'You shouldn't disrespect things that Jesus did, and especially not in a church. God can hear everything.'

Rinaldo fell silent immediately, but his stomach rumbled loudly. The thought of *tortellini* and pork chops had entered his mind and would not leave.

‘I hope I see a miracle one day, like the girl in Lourdes,’ sighed Evelina. ‘I wouldn’t be at all frightened if the Virgin Mary came to me and spoke to me.’

Rinaldo looked up at the statue. It was so realistic that it wasn’t difficult to imagine it coming to life. Evelina seemed to read his mind.

‘I think all the statues come to life at night when the church is closed,’ she said.

Rinaldo shuddered and tried not to imagine it. He turned his thoughts back to *tortellini* and pork chops instead.

No church visit would be complete without the lighting of at least one candle. As they never had money to put in the offerings box they would put in whatever they could find in the street – buttons, bottle tops, discarded tram tickets and anything else small enough to fit through the coin slot. Evelina said that it didn’t matter what they put in, because it was all they had.

‘In the Bible there’s a story where a very rich man made a big offering to the temple,’ she explained.

‘How much?’

‘I don’t remember exactly. At least a million lire. But he had plenty of money left. His house was full of money and gold and precious things. Then there was a very poor widow. All the money she had in the whole world was two lire, and when she went to the temple she made an offering too. She gave Jesus her two lire.’ Evelina’s expression turned very serious. ‘So, Aldino, who gave Jesus more money – the rich man, or the widow?’

‘The rich man, obviously,’ replied Rinaldo.

Evelina shook her head with great conviction. ‘No, Aldino. It was the widow because she gave Jesus everything.’

The story didn’t sit well with Rinaldo, and not just because of the maths. He thought that Jesus should have given the widow her money back and given her the rich man’s million lire too. He didn’t care whether God, or Jesus or the Virgin Mary heard his thought because taking all of the widow's money just wasn't right.

'Why do we light candles for dead people?' he asked.

'Because they can see the flame from heaven,' replied Evelina, snapping a candle in half. 'And then they know we're thinking about them. I'll light one half for my Mamma and you can light the other half for your Mamma.'

'My Mamma isn't dead. I don't think so, anyway.'

'You can light candles for people who are alive too. You have to say a prayer for them and the candle helps God notice the prayer.'

Rinaldo knelt beside Evelina, screwed his eyes up tightly and prayed hard that his mother would find him. It was the only thing he ever prayed for, apart from food.

'We should light one for our Papás too,' said Evelina.

'I haven't got a Papá.'

'Everybody has a Papá somewhere.'

'Who's your Papá then?'

'My Papá is a prince from a country a long way away, but he had to go back to his kingdom to fight a battle against an evil prince who wanted his lands. He couldn't take Mamma and me with him because it was too dangerous.'

'Did your Papá win the battle?'

'Of course he did! He was very brave and very strong and very good at battles. He had a sword made of a metal that was even more precious than gold. And he had the most beautiful white horse. The biggest horse anyone had ever seen!'

It was then that Evelina's expression changed. She sighed and said sadly, 'But the evil prince who lost the battle and didn't get my father's lands wanted revenge so he sent a letter to Mamma to say that my father was dead – and then Mamma died of a broken heart.'

'But why didn't your Papá come back for you?'

'He didn't know where Ada Stracci's house was.'

Rinaldo decided that his father was not a prince, but a man like the one who lived across the road. He had two sons and he took them to the football stadium every time there was a home game. They would go off rattling their rattles and whistling their whistles, with the boys taking turns riding on their father's back. Sometimes Rinaldo lingered outside their house when he knew there was a match on in the hope that he might be taken too. He never was, but the man had taken pity on Rinaldo and given him a paper hat in Bologna's team colours.

Often Rinaldo would observe families; he'd watch parents with their children and ask himself what those lucky children had or hadn't done which had made their Mammas and their Papás decide to keep them. He wondered what he had done that had made his mother decide that she didn't want him. Perhaps he'd been very naughty, or he'd cried too much – or maybe she just hadn't liked the look of him. Once he'd overheard a mother scold a little girl and threaten to give her to the gypsies when the child had thrown a tantrum right in the middle of the pavement. He had a lot of questions, but there was nobody to answer them.

*

When Rinaldo was eight years old he lost patience with his mother. Clearly expecting her to turn up and claim him was futile. He hated living with Ada Stracci and didn't want to go back to the orphanage, so he suggested to Evelina that they should run away.

Evelina said they should go to Milano Marittima and try to find her mother's family, but she knew it was a long way away and that they would have to catch a train to get there, an obstacle which seemed insurmountable as they didn't even know how to get to the station.

'We could go and live at the Giardini Margherita until we're ready to go to Milano Marittima,' she said.

Rinaldo knew the Giardini Margherita because he had been there on a picnic organised by the orphanage. The park was vast and there were plenty of places they could shelter. It seemed like a good plan.

Evelina wanted to leave immediately, but Rinaldo said that if their escape was to be successful, preparations would have to be made. They spent a week saving food. Rinaldo did odd jobs and scoured the streets for dropped change and managed to amass five lire. Evelina sneaked two blankets from the chest outside Ada Stracci's room. They were ready.

They left Ada Stracci's after breakfast. By mid-morning they were standing before the huge iron gates at the entrance to the park.

'Did you know that when you go to heaven you have to go through big gates and they have pearls all over them?' said Evelina.

'I reckon it's a test,' replied Rinaldo.

'A test?'

'Yes. To see if you steal the pearls. If you steal the pearls, you don't get in.'

Evelina considered this for a moment. 'I hadn't thought of that. When I get there I definitely won't steal any pearls.'

Rinaldo thought that when he got there he definitely *would* steal some pearls, just not enough of them for anyone to notice, and he would do it very discreetly. The lessons learned from the *crostata* incident still played on his mind.

Freedom was a wonderful feeling. The two children explored every inch of the park. They swung on the swings. They whirled on the merry-go-rounds. They even played on the mechanical carousel, but only after it was closed because they didn't want to use their money to pay for a ride. They didn't mind that it wasn't turning. Rinaldo sat in a red aeroplane and Evelina rode a white horse with a golden mane. She said it was just like her father's horse, except her father's horse was ten times the size. Not to be outdone, Rinaldo said that his father had an aeroplane – one that could really fly.

There was an old man who came to the duck pond every day with a little hand cart loaded with bags of stale bread. Mothers, fathers, governesses and grandparents lined up to buy bread so that their children could amuse themselves feeding the ducks. The old man did a roaring trade.

'I fed the ducks when Mamma brought me here,' said Evelina. 'I'd forgotten about it until now. Mamma didn't buy bread from the man though because it's expensive. She brought some from home so I could have ice cream.'

She sat staring out across the duck pond with a smile on her face. Rinaldo sat beside her and didn't say anything. It was nice for Evelina that she had remembered something else about her mother, so he didn't want to interrupt. He imagined his own mother doing the same, except his mother would have money for both duck bread and ice cream – and even a hot *piadina* flat-bread with ham and melted cheese inside. There was a stall which sold those near the mechanical carousel.

'You know the parks full of pine trees you were talking about in Milano Marittima?' said Rinaldo.

'Yes.'

'Does one of them have a duck pond?'

'I don't know. I've never been there.'

'One of them is bound to, and I was thinking, we could earn some money there selling bread for the ducks, like the old man does.'

Evelina agreed that it was a very good idea, so they began collecting the empty bags which people had thrown into the dustbins. Some still had a little stale bread left inside, which was most welcome as their scant food supply was running out very quickly. Stale bread was better than no bread.

'When we get to Milano Marittima we must make sure everybody knows that we are brother and sister,' said Evelina. 'That way nobody will try to separate us.'

Rinaldo smiled. It gave him a warm feeling in his tummy every time Evelina said she was his sister. She linked her arm through his.

'You're my little brother, Aldino, and I'm your big sister and we'll always look after each other. Always. Forever. No excuses.'

'So who shall we tell people is our Mamma, yours or mine?'

Evelina thought for a moment. 'We should probably say it's my Mamma. We don't know anything about yours.'

Rinaldo understood Evelina's reasoning and couldn't disagree, yet somehow denying his mother felt like a bit of a betrayal.

'So I'll have to say that my name's Rinaldo Brunelli?'

'Yes,' replied Evelina.

'It sounds better than Scamorza,' conceded Rinaldo after a moment's thought. 'At least I won't get teased about cheese.'

Unsurprisingly, the intoxication of freedom wore off quickly. Sleeping on blankets on the ground was uncomfortable. Sleeping on the benches was worse. They were frightened by the rustling of the trees at night and the activity of unknown creatures in their branches. They woke to find themselves covered in bird droppings.

The second night they elected to sleep in the mechanical carousel, but were kept awake by the rain hammering on the tin roof and the chattering of their own teeth. When a stray dog came to lie with them they were able to sleep for a while, until they were woken by fleas biting their legs.

When their food ran out completely Evelina started to cry and wouldn't stop. Rinaldo was well-acquainted with being hungry, but Evelina wasn't. She said that they should go back to Ada Stracci's. Rinaldo absolutely refused.

But on their third night of freedom they were discovered. A park warden came across them sleeping in the shrubbery behind the carousel. He'd recognised them immediately as the police had put notices up about the missing children. They were returned home within the hour.

Of course Ada Stracci was furious. The Child Welfare Service did not look favourably on foster mothers whose charges escaped. Rinaldo and Evelina's stunt could have lost her the means of making a living.

She locked Rinaldo in the cellar for two days and gave Evelina to Gigio Lingua to deal with.

CHAPTER 4

Evelina's hair was so long, thick and lustrous that people would comment on it in the street. By the time the girl was twelve it had grown well past her waist.

Ada Stracci cared for it as though it were her own, washing it in bicarbonate and conditioning it with eggs and olive oil. Even if eggs or oil were in short supply, Evelina's hair would take priority. The other children were punished if they complained about going without.

Evelina was under strict instructions not to allow her hair to get dusty as this would cause it to dry out and the ends to split. Ada Stracci would braid it so tightly that the child could feel the pull on her scalp whenever she blinked.

Rinaldo arrived home one day and found Evelina hiding under a blanket.

'I've got ice cream,' he said, turning it upside down to stop the drips. 'You'd better eat it quick before it melts.'

'You have it. I'm not coming out,' replied Evelina, curling further into her blanket.

It took a great deal of encouragement to coax her from her hiding place. When she emerged, by which time the ice cream had melted, her face was red from crying. She had a bruise on her cheek. Evelina's long hair was gone. It had been cropped short and stuck out in tufts.

Rinaldo gasped. 'What happened to your hair?'

Evelina sobbed. 'Ada cut it off and took it.'

*

Ada Stracci laid out the gleaming black braid before her and ran her hand down its silky length. She had been waiting eight years for this, tending it like a precious crop. Now at last it was hers.

She sat at her dressing table brushing her own hair, which she had dyed with henna and indigo. The match with Evelina's braid was not exact, but it was close enough. She gathered her stringy hair into a bun, then twisted Evelina's long tress around it numerous times and pinned it into position. Holding her head high, she posed in front of the mirror, admiring herself from different angles, and was very pleased. She thought she looked rather regal. Then her expression soured.

She hadn't expected Evelina to put up such a fight, but when she had produced a pair of scissors with the intention of cutting the braid off neatly, the girl had made a run for it. Ada Stracci had been obliged to enlist Gigio Lingua's help, and when at last they had caught her, they had to pin her to the floor by kneeling on her in order to keep her still. She had struggled so much that a neat cut had been impossible. The silly girl was lucky she hadn't got herself stabbed. Ada Stracci had snapped three fingernails in the process and was not at all happy about it.

Unfortunately, the novelty of wearing Evelina's hair lasted only a short time. Ada Stracci found that dyeing her own hair to match was messy and time-consuming; plus she had ruined four pillowcases and several towels. Worse still, the dye had left a blue tidemark around her hairline which she had tried to scrub away, unsuccessfully, using everything from bleach to caustic soda. Not only that, the weight of the tress gave her a cricked neck. Concluding that it was more trouble than it was worth, she sold the braid to a wig-maker.

*

Ada Stracci was most displeased, and the more she looked at Evelina, the more displeased she became. The girl in whom she had invested so much time and expense, in the expectation that she would grow into a valuable beauty, was not living up to her expectations. Even once her hair had grown back a little, Ada Stracci found her to be a rather odd-looking child.

Evelina had indeed inherited La Bella Brunelli's colouring, but her mother's striking beauty had bypassed her. Aged almost thirteen she was a gawky, lanky-limbed thing. Despite the good food, she remained skinny. As for her face, there was certainly something of her mother in her eyes, but her nose had grown far too large and her mouth lacked the sensuous allure with which her mother had been blessed. Ada Stracci could not help but wonder what ugly runt of a man had sired her.

Still, she had to make something of all her years of investment in the child. Even if she wasn't quite up to standard, somebody would have her and hopefully the price would be decent on account of her pedigree. It was time to start training her, and for this she enlisted the help of Gigio Lingua.

'Where have you been?' asked Rinaldo, who had been looking for Evelina for most of the afternoon. He found her sitting up cross-legged on her bed and looking very pleased with herself.

'I've been with Ada and Gigio, learning things,' she replied, patting the space beside her.

'Learning what?'

'Did you know that men like to put their thingies in women's mouths?'

At first Rinaldo thought he had misheard. He sat down beside Evelina, turned the question over in his head and frowned.

'Why?'

'They say it feels nice. And they give girls nice clothes and money for it. Today I did it to Gigio until his thingy kind of sneezed, Gigio made a noise like he'd been punched in the belly and then that was it. Ada says I've done well and I'm still a virgin and that's important.'

'A virgin? Like the Virgin Mary? How can you be like the Virgin Mary?'

Evelina shrugged. 'I don't know. I'm not really sure what she did to be a virgin, but she was one and I am too – and one day someone will give me a lot of money because I'm a virgin.' She turned to Rinaldo and grinned. 'Ada gave me sweets.'

Rinaldo was utterly perplexed. His frown deepened and he repeated, 'Ada gave you *sweets*?' Ada Stracci never gave anybody sweets.

'Here, Aldino, have some. As many as you want.' She handed over a little paper bag.

Rinaldo looked inside doubtfully. Something felt so wrong that he didn't want to take one. It was like being offered poison.

'She gave me a cigarette too, but I didn't like it. And Ada says she's going to give me one of her china dolls. Did you see the dolls when you went into her room? Do you remember one in a pink coat with a big bow in her hair? That's the one I'm going to have. And then I'll be getting a new dress. Not an old thing like the one I'm wearing – a really nice dress, a brand new one, any dress I choose. Ada's going to take me to Via Indipendenza to buy it. And I asked whether I could have a green shawl, like my Mamma had, and Ada said I could.'

Evelina carried on talking very excitedly, almost without drawing breath – *Ada says this, Ada says that, Ada promised me this, Ada promised me that* – but Rinaldo was gripped with a feeling of unease which tied a knot in his guts. Whatever was going on, it was probably bad. He didn't trust Ada Stracci and Gigio Lingua any further than he could spit.

He looked in puzzlement at Evelina as she kept chattering, thinking that her faith in Ada Stracci had to be misplaced. The thought of Gigio Lingua's thingy was disgusting and the idea of it being in Evelina's mouth made Rinaldo want to vomit. He couldn't understand why she didn't feel the same, nor could he work out why she had forgiven Ada Stracci so easily for stealing her hair.

It was not long after this period of instruction began that Rinaldo saw a profound change in Evelina. She didn't want to go out any more, not even to San Paolo Maggiore to see the Madonna, and sometimes she wouldn't eat her supper. After a lesson with Ada Stracci and Gigio Lingua, Evelina would come down from the attic and lie on her bed, curled into a ball and facing the wall. She hardly spoke, save to say that she didn't care about having a china doll or a new dress any more.

Shortly after her thirteenth birthday, Evelina was taken away. Rinaldo never cried – not when he hurt himself, not even when Gigio Lingua whipped him – but he did cry when he knew that Evelina was gone. All the tears that he was always so careful to keep inside poured out uncontrollably. He cried all day and through most of the night, and even when he had exhausted his tears, his stomach still cramped from the effort of his deep sobs. His life had collapsed. He felt alone, powerless and detached – like Fagiolino with his strings cut.

The longing he felt for Evelina was worse than any longing he had ever felt for his mother. Evelina was the only person in the world whom he knew with absolute certainty loved him. They had promised that they would always take care of one another, but he had failed her.

Rinaldo made his way to San Paolo Maggiore. He needed to have a word with the Virgin Mary. He knelt before her, clasped his hands and began to recite his Ave Maria, as he knew he was supposed to do, but stopped halfway through.

'Evelina's gone,' he sniffed. 'I don't know where because Ada Stracci won't tell me, but I think it's a bad place and I think people are going to hurt her.' He paused, wondering whether he should mention what Evelina had done with Gigio Lingua's thingy, then thought he probably shouldn't. He knew that it was wrong and the last thing he wanted was to get Evelina into trouble with the Madonna, so he just said, 'I don't know what to do to get her back.'

He stared hard at the statue, willing her to move, or speak, or do something which might convince him she was listening, but the Madonna remained expressionless and immobile. Prayer was proving futile, so Rinaldo tried negotiation instead.

'You can stop looking for my mother, as long as Evelina comes back.'

Still there was no reaction from the Madonna. There was no sympathy or compassion in her face – just the usual passive gaze. Perhaps lighting a candle would help. Rinaldo rummaged in his pockets, but found nothing, so he tore a button from his shirt and slipped it into the offerings box.

'I didn't mean what I said about Jesus' miracles being rubbish. And if I get to heaven I won't steal any pearls. And I'm sorry about the *crostata*.' Rinaldo paused for a moment. 'I'm not sorry about taking the school smock though, because Zappatelli deserved it.'

Eventually Rinaldo gave up. The Virgin Mary felt no more available to help than his own mother.

*

Following Evelina's sale Ada Stracci filled her room with new furniture – a pelmeted bed draped in velvet, a silk bedspread, a Persian carpet, a French armoire, even a pair of canaries in a gilt cage. She also purchased a whole wardrobe of new clothes and paraded around dressed up as though she was going to a different wedding every day.

It was a few weeks after Evelina's disappearance that Ada

Stracci caught a chill. She retired to her attic bedroom, ringing her bell at regular intervals to be brought hot grappa with lemon and honey, but when her condition worsened to a full-blown cold, she summoned Rinaldo.

'Go and get me menthol cigarettes, boy. I need to clear out my chest.'

When he returned and handed her the cigarettes, Ada Stracci knocked back a large shot of grappa with lemon and honey, followed by a double shot of grappa on its own, took a further swig straight from the bottle, then lit a cigarette. It made her cough.

'Excellent,' she slurred. 'It's working.' She flared her nostrils and fired an angry look at Rinaldo. 'What are you doing, standing there gawping at me, you worthless little wretch? Get out, bastard boy! Go and make yourself useful. The kitchen stove needs cleaning. Make sure there's coal for the morning. And then go to bed.'

Rinaldo left obediently and heard Ada Stracci lock and bolt her door from the inside, but he did not head for the kitchen. Instead he remained outside the door, waiting and listening. Half an hour later Ada Stracci was snoring.

Rinaldo placed the chest and the chair under the skylight. He had grown since he had first squeezed through it and he hoped he would not get stuck. Although it took a certain amount of wriggling, he made it. He felt his way carefully across the roof in the dark.

Ada Stracci didn't flinch when the window creaked, nor did she stir as Rinaldo crossed the room to her bed. Her paraffin lamp was still lit and he stopped for a moment and looked at her open-mouthed ugliness. He could smell her breath. It was like bad eggs. He touched her arm, ready to duck out of the way if she woke, but she didn't move. Ada Stracci was soundly asleep.

The first thing he did was to release the canaries from their cage. They flew out through the open window without hesitation.

Very quietly, Rinaldo took the paraffin lamp from the bedside and tipped it onto the edge of the silk bedspread, then pulled the new Persian carpet close to the bed and doused it with more paraffin. The smell was strong, but Ada Stracci did not stir. Not even the striking and the flash of the match roused her.

Rinaldo climbed out of the window as the first flames began to lick at the edges of the bedspread. He inched across the tiles and squirmed back in through the skylight, then replaced the chair and the chest and crept back downstairs to the dormitory, where he changed into his nightshirt and got into bed.

It was no more than five minutes before the smell of burning seeped down to the dormitory. Rinaldo had expected it to be a pleasant smell, like wood-smoke and roasting meat, but it was a heavy, acrid fug which made his eyes run and his throat burn. Moments later there was urgent shouting from the street below and a hammering of fists on the door.

'Fire! Fire! Get out!' People were screaming. 'Save the children! Save the children!'

The man from the house opposite broke down the front door and rushed up the stairs to rescue the children. From the safety of the street below Rinaldo could see great tongues of flames bursting from the attic windows.

The fire died out relatively quickly and remained confined to the attic, but the neighbour had been unable to save Ada Stracci as her bedroom door had been locked and bolted from the inside. For this reason the Municipal Fire Inspector concluded that no foul play was involved. Ada Stracci had simply been the victim of an unfortunate accident.

'People really should be more careful about smoking in bed,' said the Fire Inspector, shaking his head as the woman's charred remains were carried out on a stretcher.

The neighbour was hailed as a hero for having rescued the children and was awarded a medal for bravery by the mayor.

Ada Stracci received a posthumous commendation for having dedicated her life to the care of orphans. And Rinaldo was sent to the other side of town to live with a couple called Limoni.

CHAPTER 5

Signora Limoni had been happy once, but that had changed when she had married Signor Limoni. By the time Rinaldo was placed in her care, her years of gloom far outnumbered her years of joy. Nevertheless, she knew the importance of appearances and was mindful not to seem miserable. Although she lived in a state of anguish, she wept and despaired in secret.

Her husband was a coalman for the railways. His back was bent and his shoulders were stooped. Coal dust had penetrated so deeply into the cracks of his fingers that they were indelibly black. Unlike his wife, Signor Limoni had never been cheerful. He was prone to moods as black as the coal he carried.

He had once tied a sack of coal around his neck and jumped into the river, but he had misjudged both the depth of the water and the length of the rope and had floated to the surface, still very much alive. His attempt to leave the mortal world had almost been successful, however, thanks to the passer-by who rescued him. The Good Samaritan had hauled him to shore by pulling on the rope, thus tightening the noose around Signor Limoni's neck – but only enough to make him pass out briefly.

He took this failure to be a sign that life was a punishment which he must continue to bear. Every load of coal he lugged became a symbol of his suffering. He would leave the house before six every morning and not return until the evening, when he would eat his supper in silence and retire to his dark room to think his dark thoughts.

Sometimes, Signora Limoni would encourage Rinaldo to accompany Signor Limoni to work because she thought it vital to instil a wholesome work ethic into her charges. She reasoned that once released from her care, orphans had nobody to count on but themselves. It would reflect badly upon her if they turned to crime, or became vagrants.

Rinaldo was too small to carry the coal sacks and to Signor Limoni he was more of a hindrance than a help. The man would leave him in the freight yard and tell him not to get in anybody's way. It was the longest conversation Signor Limoni ever had with Rinaldo. He never told him to mind the trains, but the boy learned this for himself very quickly. It was as he was hopping from sleeper to sleeper and balancing on the rails that a train passing on a parallel line missed him by a whisker.

Signora Limoni's home was modest, but comfortable. The food she fed her foster children was adequate. Rinaldo grew very fond of her salty bean soups. There was meat once or twice a week and milk every morning for breakfast. Often there was milk before bedtime too. Above all, the Signora's treatment of the children was fair. There were no beatings, no threats and nobody was sold.

Unlike Ada Stracci, Signora Limoni insisted that her charges should attend school, something which Rinaldo found to be surprisingly useful. He could already count and calculate and had always had a good head for numbers, but aged ten he learned to read and found to his astonishment that writing was everywhere and contained a lot of information. He had never paid any attention to it before.

He became an avid reader of advertising posters, labels, graffiti and the name-tags on people's doorbells. He also realised that the name 'Zappatelli' had been embroidered on the breast pocket of the private-school smock.

With school came the obligatory enrolment into the Opera Nazionale Balilla, the youth organisation established by Mussolini's regime. The Child Welfare Service had provided a letter stating that, to the best of their knowledge, Rinaldo was of Italian descent and therefore eligible to join the ONB.

There were weekly indoctrination meetings, sports events and summer camps. At first Rinaldo had been keen to go. He'd seen the Balilla boys in their black fez hats, green jackets and banded knee-high socks parading in military-style groups through the streets singing their marching song. The song had a line about freeing mothers, although it didn't say what their mothers needed freeing from. Before he'd been old enough for enrolment he'd sometimes marched along behind and joined in, waving an improvised flag made from his handkerchief tied to a stick.

During the first ONB meeting Rinaldo and the other new recruits were shown a film of Balilla boys being led through military-style manoeuvres by their leader, who was known as the *Caposquadra*. Each boy had his own imitation musket and the bravest amongst them were given medals. The film then showed the boys camping up in the mountains and doing gymnastics.

Rinaldo had never seen a film before and watching moving, talking images on a screen was like magic. He loved the idea of having his own imitation musket and even more than that he loved the idea of winning a medal. He would treasure it like the emerald earring. The thought of camping and gymnastics was exciting too. Fascism looked like fun.

But once the film was finished a group of bigger boys cornered him and said that it was time for his initiation. Rinaldo didn't know what an initiation was, but by the looks and stances of the boys it was going to be painful.

They crowded round him and began chanting their marching song, changing the words to say that his mother was a whore. It was only the intervention of the *Caposquadra* which saved Rinaldo from a group kicking. The *Caposquadra* punished all of them, including Rinaldo, for changing the words of the song. He administered six strikes of his stick to each of their right hands for showing such grotesque disrespect.

When Rinaldo returned home with welts on his hand and told Signora Limoni what had happened, she didn't insist that he should go back to any ONB meetings. She bathed his hand in salt water, wrapped it in a bandage and told him not to make a fuss. She said that if anybody asked, he was to show them his ONB membership card, to give the appropriate salute and to state the motto – *Libro e moschetto, Fascista perfetto* – Book and musket, perfect Fascist. Rinaldo sensed that she didn't like Mussolini very much.

Rinaldo's longing for his mother eased, perhaps because he felt a semblance of maternal protection from his new foster mother. Signora Limoni, however, insisted that under no circumstances should the boy call her 'Mamma' because she didn't want him to get attached. He should address her formally as 'Signora Limoni'. Rinaldo didn't mind. In fact, he grew rather fond of her and sensed that Signora Limoni was fond of him too, in her own way.

It was around this time that Rinaldo came to terms with the idea that his mother would never come for him. Whoever she was and wherever she was, she had no interest in him; or perhaps because so much time had passed, she had forgotten about him altogether. Signora Limoni offered words of consolation and advised that Rinaldo should pray for God to forgive his mother's wicked soul. She used words like 'godlessness', 'damnation' and 'harlotry', which were new to Rinaldo, but were, it seemed, somehow connected to the reason his mother had abandoned him.

Although the longing for his mother lessened, the wrench from Evelina was still raw. Sometimes Rinaldo couldn't sleep for worrying, and during his waking hours horrible, scary thoughts invaded his mind. His understanding of why Evelina had been taken had been vague at first, but as he grew, he became more aware of why Ada Stracci had sold her. As his awareness grew, so did his fear for Evelina's safety and his guilt for not having saved her in time. He looked out for her wherever he went, but there was no sign of Evelina.

*

One Tuesday after school Rinaldo wandered further away from the Limonis' house than was allowed. He hadn't intended to be disobedient, but had been distracted by a friendly dog. The two had meandered together for some of the afternoon, until the dog disappeared and Rinaldo realised that he was lost.

In his attempt to retrace his steps he became even more disorientated. The maze of crooked, cobbled streets and alleyways all looked the same, with their rows of old, mismatched houses all pressed together. Most were built in a reddish brick, discoloured to a dirty brown by centuries of city grime, and further stained by rusting ironwork and smoke. Some were rendered, but patches of brick showed through where the stucco had fallen off. There were so many arches – arches on the porticos, arches over the windows, arches over the doors. Rinaldo craned his neck and looked up at the windows with their wooden shutters and canvas blinds, and little balconies crammed with flower pots and washing. The top floors of the houses seemed so much closer together than the ground floors – sometimes so close together that the sky was reduced to a sliver between them.

Rinaldo walked in random circles, observing the people going about their business and catching fragments of their conversations as they passed. Sometimes, if he overheard something which sounded interesting, he would follow them for a little while, straining his ears so that he could keep on listening.

From time to time he stopped to inspect the bicycles leaning against the walls. He hoped that one day he'd be rich enough to own his own bicycle, but not a dark-coloured one, like all the others. His bicycle would be orange, firstly because orange was his favourite colour, and secondly because it would be easier to find amongst the dozens of dark ones if he left it parked against a wall.

Once he was bored with the bicycles Rinaldo occupied himself by rifling through the crates and boxes which had been left out for the rubbish men to collect. He would have continued searching for treasure, but quite unexpectedly he found himself in recognisable surroundings, in Via Farini, Bologna's most prestigious street.

Here, everything was on a grand scale. The porticos were tall, sometimes twice the height than in other places, and all their undersides were decorated with frescoes and fancy plasterwork. The pavements beneath them were made of polished marble, inlaid with geometric patterns.

Rinaldo followed the elegant curve of the street, gazing up at the ornate palazzos. He stopped for a moment in front of the building occupied by the Cassa di Risparmio bank. Its lofty arched windows were screened with the most intricate ironwork, and its front door was tall enough to drive a tram through. The boy wondered how much money they must keep in there, perhaps so much that it had to be brought in by tram.

The people who passed him were different to the ordinary folk who lived in the other parts of town. Here, fashionably-dressed couples and ladies in pairs promenaded at leisure, stopping occasionally to peruse the displays in the excusive boutiques. But haute couture and all the other accoutrements and luxurious novelties only held Rinaldo's attention for a short time. He headed for the shop which sold paintings.

Rinaldo had often stood in front of its window, many times with Evelina but more often on his own because she was bored by pictures, whereas he liked to take his time looking at them. Rinaldo was fascinated by paintings. It amazed him that someone could take blobs of paint and transform them into images which looked so real.

He wondered whether, when he was grown up, he might be a painter. He was certainly keen to have a go, but since he didn't have any money to buy paint or brushes, he didn't know whether he'd be any good at it. Usually he satisfied himself with drawing pictures in dust with his finger. Occasionally, if he was lucky enough to find a piece of dropped coal or chalk, or a piece of soft brick, he would draw pictures on the pavement.

One time, about a year before she was taken away, Evelina had dared him to go into the shop, and he had. He had crept in, ready to dart back out again if he was discovered, but once inside, it had seemed as if there was no one there. It was a beautiful place, with a shiny wooden floor which squeaked under his feet and a very high ceiling painted to look like the sky. In here, he could smell the paint. It was a strong, oily odour which made his nose prickle and his eyes feel as though he had just yawned, but it wasn't unpleasant.

There were all sorts of pictures: of flowers, of fruit, of scenes from the countryside – and even of a couple of ladies with no clothes on, which made Rinaldo giggle. One entire wall was covered in paintings of familiar places like the Due Torri, Piazza Maggiore and Piazza del Nettuno. He was particularly drawn to a painting of a balcony with white sheets hanging on a line, but as he moved closer to have a better look, he realised that the sheets weren't all white. The painter had used grey and yellow and even a little bit of green and light purple. And just as curiously, the sheets weren't square, or rectangular, like real sheets. They were no more than smudges. Perhaps being a painter was more complicated than he thought. If he was to paint sheets, he wouldn't just need white, but lots of other colours too – and how was it possible to get a smudge to look like a sheet?

It was as he stood pondering the expenses and challenges involved that he was spooked by a pretty lady in a yellow dress who must have been watching him the entire time.

'Hello, little man,' she said quizzically. 'What are you doing here?'

Normally Rinaldo would have put on his best private-schoolboy voice and said that he was looking for his mother, because that was always a good excuse for being somewhere he shouldn't be. But instead he was overcome by an attack of shyness and stood dumbstruck and rooted to the spot. The lady got up from behind the little desk where she had been working and made her way towards him.

Rinaldo was unable to do anything but stare at her, and sensing that perhaps she had scared him, she stopped. She didn't seem cross that he was there – quite the opposite, in fact. She was smiling and seemed very friendly, but for reasons he couldn't understand, Rinaldo had been assailed by panic and responded by running from the shop. Although he had gone back many times after that, he had satisfied himself with looking at the window display and had never dared to go back in.

Today the shop was closed, so he couldn't have gone in even if he'd felt brave enough. Perhaps he would next time he found himself in Via Farini. Maybe he would ask the pretty lady in the yellow dress what he had to do to become a painter, because she would know, and perhaps she would give him some sweets from the bowl on her desk.

As he knew where he was and therefore how to get back to the Limonis' house, Rinaldo thought he might as well kill a bit more time in the centre of town. The shop that sold paintings in Via Farini was less than a two-minute walk from the big church of San Petronio, where he had been countless times with Evelina.

Inside the church it was chilly and a little bit damp. Rinaldo's eyes took a moment to adjust to the dull light. The building seemed even bigger on the inside than the outside; its size further exaggerated by the fact that it was almost deserted. There were no worshippers, just two old cleaners slopping the aisle with rope mops and another straightening out the rows of straw-seated chairs.

Rinaldo thought how people's houses all smelled different – of particular cooking smells, of laundry, of the people who lived in them – but how churches all had the same smell: a combination of incense and candle wax, varnished wood and old dust. Even the brick and stone columns and the marble floors seemed to be imbued with that churchy smell. It made Rinaldo sneeze.

He made his way up one side, peering into each side-chapel in turn, looking at the statues and icons and altars festooned with artificial flowers and silverware, then stopped by one of the candle stands.

His pockets were empty apart from a sweet wrapper he'd found on the pavement. He'd picked it up because it was gold-coloured and he had reasoned that being gold it must be worth something. He slipped it into the offerings box and took two candles.

The first was for Evelina. He prayed that wherever she was, she was safe and that she would come back. He hesitated before lighting one for his mother. If, as Signora Limoni had suggested, her soul was wicked, a prayer probably wouldn't help much, so he lit the second one for Evelina too.

He stared at the flames wondering whether God really could see them from heaven. As he stood contemplating this very big question he pinched at the little globs of soft wax which were melting onto the trays. Signora Limoni had scolded him more than once for fiddling with wax in church when he should have been paying attention to the sermon, but there was something too compelling to resist about playing with wax. Rinaldo spread it across his fingertip and peeled it off to look at the impression of his fingerprint. He rolled more into little balls, squashed them together and lined them up like a row of snowmen.

He would have carried on entertaining himself with the wax had it not been for the sudden burst of *'Hallelujah!'* which cut through the quiet. At first it was a single voice, then it was joined by many more.

'Hallelujah, hallelu-hallelujah, ha-hallelu, hallelu-jah!'

The line was repeated four times, then it stopped.

There was a long pause before the voices resounded again, but Rinaldo couldn't see any singers. Their voices seemed to be coming from the sky.

'Gloria! Gloria! Gloria in excelsis Deo. Gloria! Gloria! Gloria in excelsis Deo!'

Despite not understanding Latin, in that moment Rinaldo was overcome by an explosion of devotion, as though the voices were lifting him up into the far reaches of the roof, to where the tops of the gothic arches intersected.

'Gloria! Gloria! Gloria in excelsis Deo. Gloria! Gloria! Gloria in excelsis Deo!'

Rinaldo was so mesmerised that he didn't notice one of the cleaners come up behind him.

'What are you doing, messing about down here?' he grumbled. 'You're late. You'll be in trouble with the choirmaster again.'

The cleaner ushered Rinaldo through a wooden door to the right of the altar. A sign had been pinned to it. NO ENTRY. CHOIR PRACTICE IN SESSION.

'Quick! Quick!' he said, prodding Rinaldo with the handle of his mop. 'Get up there!'

Rinaldo felt the door close behind him and found himself in a small, dim passage with one stone staircase leading up to the left and another straight ahead and down. He took the left-hand staircase. It was well-worn and twisted its way upwards until he reached the choir loft.

To Rinaldo's astonishment the choir comprised only half a

dozen boys. He had presumed there would be many more. He stood silently in the shadows, hidden behind a stack of folding chairs, listening to their rousing voices and watching the choirmaster wave his arms like a marionette. Suddenly the man held up his hands for the boys to stop.

'No, no, no!' he exclaimed. 'Gaetano, you're sharp. And you, Fausto, should know by now that it's *spiritum*, not *spirito*. As for you, Oreste, I can hear you've been smoking. How many times do you need to be told not to smoke before practice?'

The choirmaster rearranged the papers on his music stand and huffed irritably. He'd been trying to make something of the choir for six months. There had been some minor improvements, but the boys to whom he referred, not entirely in jest, as his 'rabble of delinquents' were far from performance-ready.

He'd lost the most promising boy when the lad's voice had broken after just three weeks. Two had been dishonourably discharged when they had been caught trying to leave the church with a silver pyx and a chalice stuffed into their jackets. Another had been sent to an institute for young offenders for an unrelated incident.

It had been his wife's idea to offer the boys from the orphanage of San Girolamo free musical tuition and the chance to be in the choir. She was obsessed with helping the underprivileged, which was all very noble, but potentially rather unfitting for a choirmaster of his standing. He had his reputation to think about. Still, his wife was happy that he was giving his time and expertise to help the disadvantaged, and that was important. She was pregnant again and easily upset.

He glanced at his watch as the boys ended their *Gloria* on the wrong harmony for the third time.

'All right. That'll do for today,' he said wearily. 'Same time next week, boys. 4 p.m. sharp. And try not to be late.'

Rinaldo slipped from his hiding place and made his way

quietly back down the stone staircase and out through the door by the altar. He lingered for a while behind a column and watched the boys leave, followed a few minutes later by the choirmaster, who removed the sign, locked the door and strode away, his footsteps echoing through the empty church.

Signora Limoni wasn't cross when Rinaldo arrived home a little late, just mystified by the fact that he was singing to himself in what appeared to be Latin. When she asked him where he had learned the chants he told her he had learned them in church, although he didn't tell her it was San Petronio. He said he had been to a church just a few streets away to pray for his mother's wicked soul. Signora Limoni was so impressed by Rinaldo's newly-discovered piety that she gave him an extra ladleful of bean soup.

The following Tuesday just after four o'clock Rinaldo crept back up to the choir loft and into his hiding place behind the stack of folding chairs.

'Let's warm up your voices, boys,' said the choirmaster. 'Oreste, I hope you've laid off the cigarettes this week.'

The man made several *Hmmm* and *Ahhh* sounds for the boys to copy. Very quietly, Rinaldo did the same.

'Good, good. Now, after me – *Do-re-mi-fa-sol-la-ti-do!*'

Again, Rinaldo did the same.

The choir master winced and grimaced.

'In the same key as the rest of us please, Gaetano. Let's try again, one octave higher: *Do-re-mi-fa-sol-la-ti-do!*'

After several scales and several scoldings from the choirmaster concerning mysterious things such as pitch and modulation, the boys began to practise their chants. Rinaldo joined in under his breath, wishing that he could be one of those boys and that he could summon the courage to burst from his hiding place and sing in full voice, but he was afraid of getting into trouble and not being allowed to come to choir practice at all.

Rinaldo attended choir practice every week for a month and

remained entirely undiscovered, but it was during his fifth practice, as he was reaching the last part of the *Credo*, that he was overwhelmed by the need to sneeze. He pinched his nose and held his breath, but that just made it worse. A sneeze was brewing inside him. He feared his eyeballs might pop out of his head if he held it in.

A sneeze of colossal proportions exploded from Rinaldo. It was followed by another, then another. For a few moments the boy was blinded and deafened. He was brought to his senses by a strong hand gripping his arm and tugging him with such force that his feet were lifted from the ground.

'What are you doing up here?' bellowed the choirmaster.

'Nothing,' said Rinaldo, trying to shake himself from the man's grasp.

'Didn't you read the sign? This isn't a public area. You're not supposed to be here.'

'I was only singing,' protested Rinaldo, still struggling to wrench his arm free.

'You were *singing*? So you think you can sing, do you?' The tone of the man's question indicated that he didn't hold out much hope. 'Let's hear you then. Come on!'

Up close he was an imposing man, not so much in stature but in sheer presence. The way he looked at Rinaldo made the boy feel as though he was looking right inside him.

The choirmaster was not in the most amenable of moods that day. He was worried about his wife. He had almost cancelled choir practice to stay with her, but she had insisted that he should not let the boys down.

He marched Rinaldo from his hiding place to stand before the choir. The boys sniggered. They'd all been dragged out to the front at some point to sing solo. The choirmaster considered a little light humiliation to be a reasonable punishment for most forms of misbehaviour.

'Right then,' he said. 'Show us all how it's done.'

Rinaldo swallowed hard and cleared his throat. He'd been singing all the chants to himself for weeks, but being under the choirmaster's scrutiny made him nervous. His mouth had gone very dry and for a moment he wondered whether he should just make a run for it before he embarrassed himself. Eventually he summoned the pluck, took a deep breath and burst out the first lines of the *Gloria*.

How enormous his voice sounded, echoing through the choir loft! Rinaldo sang the *Gloria* from beginning to end, then continued with the *Credo* with no pause in between.

'Good Lord!' exclaimed the choirmaster. 'You *can* sing!'

The man knew a voice with potential when he heard one – and not only was it a good voice in tone and character, but it was perfectly pitched. Perhaps the little ragamuffin could be the saviour of the choir. He now felt rotten for having tried to demean the boy, who had shown spirit as well as promise. The choir master was reminded of himself at the same age. He did his best to hide his delight behind a serious expression and pressed his lips together to suppress a smile. Rinaldo did the same.

'Well done, sonny!' he said, patting Rinaldo on the head and giving him a little wink.

Rinaldo grinned. Nobody had ever called him 'sonny' before and he rather liked it. Something about the choirmaster drew him in, and he was particularly fascinated by his clothes. Men always wore dowdy browns and greys, but this fellow was wearing a blue waistcoat over a yellow patterned shirt, and a multi-coloured handkerchief was knotted around his neck. He had been wearing a different coloured shirt, waistcoat and handkerchief every choir practice. Rinaldo hoped that one day he too would have lots of clothes, and if he did, they would all be brightly coloured.

The choirmaster dismissed the boys, but Rinaldo lingered and stood leaning over the balustrades looking down at the church below. He could see the candle-stands, set at regular intervals along the side aisles, but the flames were barely visible. He wondered whether what Evelina had said about God being able to see them from heaven could be true when he could barely make the flames out from twenty metres up. The choirmaster came to stand beside him and hooked his thumbs into the arm-holes of his waistcoat. Rinaldo wanted to do the same, but he didn't have a waistcoat, so he stretched the neck of his jumper and held onto that instead.

'Aren't you going home, sonny?'

'Not yet,' replied Rinaldo vaguely, then added, 'Can I be in your choir?'

'Well, we'll have to see. Being in a choir is a serious business, sonny. It involves dedication and commitment. Could you promise to practise at home and to attend practice here every week without fail?'

'I've been doing that already. This is the fifth time I've been here.'

The choirmaster patted Rinaldo's head again. He found his boldness endearing. His wife would like him. It was a pity she was feeling so unwell or he'd take the little lad home to meet her.

'Why do voices sound so big up here?' asked Rinaldo.

'Ah,' replied the choirmaster with the air of a man who knew things, 'it's because of the shape of the choir loft. You see what shape it is? It's like a horseshoe. It makes the sound echo, so a single voice can sound like more than one, and a small choir can sound like a big one. And if half the choir stands on one side and the other half stands facing them, which we call a *coro spezzato*, the voices reverberate from both sides. There are two organs as well, you see? One on each side. It's the same principle.'

'Does it make it easier for God to hear?'

'Of course,' the man replied, wishing that he meant it. He'd lost his faith many years before but it wasn't something he wanted made known. He hadn't even told his wife because he knew it would upset her.

'This place is very special, sonny. The Cappella Musicale di San Petronio is the oldest musical institution in Bologna, and one of the oldest in the whole of Italy. It's been here over five hundred years. There used to be a singing school here called the *Schola Cantorum*. It was established in 1436. At one time it had over a hundred choir members.'

The choirmaster shook his head sadly as he spoke. It was an outrage that such an esteemed institution was now reduced to a handful of tone-deaf, disinterested boys.

He could have continued with a long and detailed history lesson, but he didn't want to bore the boy. In any case, he was eager to get back to his wife; so instead he said, 'Do you like chocolate? I happen to love chocolate almost as much as I love music and I'll be passing Majani's chocolate shop on my way home.'

They left the church together and made their way across Piazza Maggiore, scattering the pigeons in their path. When Rinaldo took the choirmaster's hand, the man was surprised by the display of affection, but he didn't let go. He squeezed the boy's hand, looked down at him and smiled. Rinaldo had that feeling that he was looking right inside him again, except this time his expression was one of fondness.

The choirmaster slowed his pace and said, gazing at the surrounding buildings, 'Isn't this a magnificent piazza?'

Rinaldo couldn't disagree, but there was something which bothered him about San Petronio. Its towering facade was only partly and unevenly clad in marble. The rest of it was rough brick.

'When are they going to finish the front of the church?' He asked.

'Never,' replied the choirmaster. 'You see, San Petronio was supposed to be the biggest church ever built. But the Pope didn't like the idea of a church in Bologna being larger and more spectacular than St Peter's in Rome, so he held back the money for its completion. And then to make sure that it couldn't be enlarged later on, he had the Archiginnasio built right beside it.'

'What's the Archiginnasio?'

'It's a very important part of the university. It has a world-famous medical library and an Anatomical Theatre where students of medicine can learn about the human body.'

Rinaldo pondered for a moment then said, 'That's more useful than a big church.'

'You're not wrong, sonny,' laughed the choirmaster. 'And I'll tell you what else is useful. You see that building over there? It's the Palazzo d'Accursio and inside it is the Scalone dei Cavalli, which is a special staircase for horses. In times gone by the *cavaglieri* could ride all the way to the top without ever having to dismount from their horses.'

'Can we go and see it?' asked Rinaldo, eager to know more.

'Maybe another time,' replied the choirmaster. 'I'm in a bit of a hurry today, sonny. But I'll tell you about it if you like.'

Rinaldo didn't insist. He was more than happy to be out in the piazza holding the choirmaster's hand and listening to a story about horses and noblemen. He hoped that people would think they were father and son. It would be good to have a father who knew interesting things. It would also be good to have a father who loved chocolate.

Rinaldo had stood at the window of Majani's chocolate shop more times than he could remember. He had been inside once, dressed in his private-school smock, but the lady behind the counter had refused to put anything on account for him as she could not find one in the name of Zappatelli. She had also scolded him for leaving a smeary snot mark on the window where he had pressed his nose up against the glass.

It was an intoxicating shop. Shiny chocolate-brown shelves displayed lavish presentation tins and boxes. Perfect rows of chocolates were lined up on the marble counters. There were different shapes – squares, triangles and ovals – all in varying shades of chocolate. The smell was so heady that for a moment Rinaldo had the impression of his feet not quite touching the ground, as though the aroma was lifting him, just as the sound of the choir had lifted him in church.

'What's your favourite chocolate, sonny?' asked the choirmaster.

Rinaldo thought hard, but it was an impossible question to answer. It was as unknowable as whether God could see candle flames from heaven.

'My favourite's the *Scorza Nera*,' said the choirmaster. 'And as with anything, you should try it before buying it.'

He made a gesture to the lady behind the counter, who plucked a single *Scorza Nera* from the display with a pair of silver tongs as though she was handling a precious jewel. She placed it on a little paper doily and presented it to Rinaldo.

The *Scorza Nera* was quite a large chocolate, more than a comfortable mouthful for a small boy. Rinaldo bit into it, tasting the bittersweetness of the dark chocolate as it softened on his tongue. On the rare occasions that he ate chocolate, he savoured it as slowly as he could to prolong the pleasure. He closed his eyes, letting the *Scorza Nera* melt until it coated every bit of his mouth. It felt so good he didn't want to swallow it.

'You taste chocolate like a true connoisseur,' complimented the choirmaster.

Rinaldo didn't know what a connoisseur was, but judging by his companion's expression, it was a good thing to be.

'You can't come to Majani's without tasting a *Cremino Fiat*,' the choirmaster then advised him. 'They're my wife's favourites.'

The *Cremino Fiat* was a little cube of layered milk chocolate, almond and hazelnut praline. Eating it was a different experience to tasting the dark *Scorza Nera*. It was sweeter and melted in a more unctuous way, leaving Rinaldo's tongue stuck to the roof of his mouth.

'What else have you heard of which is called Fiat?' asked the choirmaster.

'Cars?' replied Rinaldo with a little difficulty as his tongue was still glued to the roof of his mouth.

'Well done, that's right. The *Cremino Fiat* was made to celebrate the launch of the Fiat Tipo motor car in 1911, and it was so good that they carried on making it.' The choirmaster stooped down so that his face was level with Rinaldo's and lowered his voice, as though he was about to say something in confidence. 'I don't know about you, sonny, but if somebody gave me the choice between a Fiat motor car and a box of Fiat chocolates, I'd choose the chocolates.'

Rinaldo frowned. Loving chocolate was understandable, but the man's choice didn't make sense.

'I'd have the motor car,' he said. 'Then I'd sell it and use the money to buy chocolates.'

The choirmaster gave Rinaldo's shoulder an affectionate squeeze. 'You'll go far in life with that spirit, young man,' he laughed.

They left Majani's with Rinaldo clutching a bag of a dozen chocolates. Having tasted several and having been unable to decide on a favourite, the choirmaster had bought him one of each kind.

'You'd better be heading home, sonny, or your Mamma will worry.'

Rinaldo nodded. He didn't want to say that he didn't have a Mamma, not a real one anyway, because Signora Limoni didn't count and reminded him all the time that she wasn't his mother.

He'd noticed that people reacted strangely if he said he was an orphan. The nice ones felt sorry for him and asked stupid questions, which he found irritating. The nasty ones called him a bastard.

During the years that he had been under Signora Limoni's supervision, he had developed a certain sense of shame concerning his mother's absence, which he tried to temper by inventing plausible lies about her whereabouts, like saying she had gone to Milano Marittima on some important business. But most of the time it was easier to say nothing at all when people asked, and to let them believe whatever they liked.

'See you next Tuesday, sonny,' said the choirmaster, ruffling Rinaldo's hair. 'Don't be late!'

He strode off towards Via Val d'Aposa humming the first lines of the *Gloria*. Rinaldo was tempted to follow him. He was curious to see where the choirmaster lived. But perhaps he shouldn't push his luck, so he made his way back to San Petronio.

*

Rinaldo stood in front of the candle-stand and thought about the story of the poor widow who made an offering of everything she had. He had four chocolates left, but was wary about leaving them all when there were no guarantees that his prayer would be listened to, let alone answered.

Eventually, and not without some reluctance, he placed two chocolates on the stand, said his usual prayer for Evelina and left, making his way back home via Via Farini and stopping for a while to admire the frescoes and the ornate iron lamps on the underside of the portico arches. He was feeling happy and confident and thought that he might try going back into the shop which sold paintings. Perhaps the lady in the yellow dress would be there again and this time he would talk to her. He was excited to tell someone that he had joined a choir. He wouldn't be telling Signora Limoni in case she forbade it. But when he got to the shop he found it closed again, so he just went home.

*

Rinaldo counted down the days to his first official choir practice. On the day in question he arrived well before four o'clock with his hair brushed and the soot scraped off his boots, but to his dismay he found a new notice on the door – *Choir practice cancelled until further notice.* Rinaldo went to find one of the cleaners to ask whether he knew why.

'It's the choirmaster's wife. She's not well again.'

Rinaldo's disappointment was overwhelming. He dragged himself round the church, scuffing the toes of his boots and sucking in his trembling lower lip, then he sat on the step of a side-altar with his head on his knees, humming the *Gloria* to himself – but not in the rousing, uplifting way that it was supposed to be sung. He hummed slowly and miserably, pressing his eyes hard against his knees to stop the tears leaking out.

He lit two candles – one for Evelina and one for the choirmaster's wife. He asked God to keep Evelina safe, but most of all to make the choirmaster's wife well again so that choir practice could resume. However, when he returned the following week he learned that the choir had been suspended indefinitely. Italy was at war.

Dreams of joining the choir faded away quickly. Suddenly everything changed. Everybody was frightened and people went about their business in a state of anxiety. Signora Limoni forbade Rinaldo from venturing any further than a five-minute run from their designated air raid shelter. She fretted every time her husband left for work because the railway network was a target. Signor Limoni's moods, on the other hand, seemed significantly less dark, even hopeful at times. Rinaldo heard him mutter that it would be a mercy if, God willing, a bomb fell on the freight yard.

Rinaldo had seen soldiers before the war, usually hanging around outside the barracks near Ada Stracci's. Someone had said that they weren't proper soldiers, just young men doing their National Service. They never looked very busy, and they certainly weren't fighting against anyone. They just stood idling in little groups, smoking cigarettes and making lewd comments at passing girls.

For a time Rinaldo wondered whether he might be a soldier one day because he liked the idea of having a uniform which was his own, but when he began to hear reports of soldiers being killed in great numbers, he changed his mind. He was glad that he was too young to be conscripted.

It was not long before food became scarce and hunger took hold. Signora Limoni's salty bean soups became far thinner and less salty. Meat was now a distant memory. There was no more milk before bed. Rinaldo didn't complain because being hungry was nothing new and he understood that Signora Limoni wasn't being mean, like Ada Stracci. There simply wasn't any food.

Rinaldo still thought of Evelina every day and hoped that she was all right. Wherever she was, he hoped that she was safe and that she wasn't starving.

When the bombing raids began in earnest, even hunger became a secondary concern. In September 1943 over a thousand people were killed not far from the Limonis' house. Rinaldo hadn't heard the air-raid sirens, but neither had anybody else. In the terror and confusion, the authorities had forgotten to sound them.

It was whilst he was on his way to work one January morning in 1944 that Signor Limoni was blown up by a stray mortar bomb. Signora Limoni took the news of her husband's death in silence. There was a small funeral service and a wreath presented by his railway colleagues, but no coffin as very little of Signor Limoni had been recoverable. What could be gathered of his remains fitted into a pot.

Rinaldo was sad. Signor Limoni had been grumpy, but he had never beaten him or been unkind. As he looked at the pot and the wreath, the boy couldn't help but think that Signor Limoni had simply got what he'd prayed for. He thought it strange that of all the prayers directed at God, He should choose to answer that one.

For Signora Limoni it was a welcome tragedy. Following an appropriate period of mourning, she cheered up significantly and became more than friendly with the local greengrocer – a jovial fellow with a broad smile and a hearty laugh. Shortly after, she announced that she was to marry him and that all her charges, including Rinaldo, would be returned to the orphanage.

However, a wing of the orphanage of San Girolamo had succumbed to the bombing raids. That, coupled with the fact that the war had caused many more children to be orphaned, meant that there was no space for Rinaldo. As he was almost fifteen he was deemed old enough to be independent. The Child Welfare Service discharged him from their care, wished him all the best and returned his mother's emerald earring to him.

Rinaldo stood outside the orphanage of San Girolamo and inspected the earring. It was a beautiful thing, with a single stone set into a gold drop, but he hadn't seen it since the age of five and it was far smaller than he remembered. He had described it to Evelina as having an emerald the size of a walnut, when in reality it was no larger than a lentil.

Still, a small emerald was better than no emerald. Rinaldo slipped the earring into his pocket and walked away from the orphanage wondering what he was supposed to do now that he was a man.

CHAPTER 6

Initially Rinaldo found work clearing bombsites and spent long days digging through the debris of the blown-out husks of buildings. It was dangerous and hard and paid very little. Great brick and stone edifices which had been standing for hundreds of years and would have stood for hundreds more were reduced to crumbling honeycomb.

There was a constant traffic of rats and cockroaches rising out of the fractured drains and buckled sewers. Stray cats and dogs fought to scavenge what they could. The smell of rot and putrefaction was pervasive. The digging teams improvised masks with strips of rag and, if it was available, dabbed toothpaste under their nostrils, but still the smell broke through.

Finding the rat-chewed corpses, or parts of them, was the worst thing. The feeling of dread whenever his pick sank into something soft made Rinaldo's guts feel as though they were turning inside out. The bodies oozed black liquid and writhed with so many maggots that sometimes they gave the impression that they were moving. Even days after the discovery of a corpse, the fetid stench still clung to Rinaldo's clothes. He didn't have the luxury of a change of clothing.

The only lodgings he could afford were squalid. There was no electricity or running water and the lavatory arrangements were unspeakable. Within a year Rinaldo found himself malnourished, physically exhausted and close to destitution. He could no longer afford to rent a room, only to rent a bed in a room which he was forced to share with other boys in equally indigent circumstances. Within a few months he was also sharing the bed, taking it in turns to sleep in shifts with his bedmates. The shared bed was lumpy and smelly and wedged between other lumpy, smelly beds, filled with sleep-talkers, snorers and farters.

Rinaldo tried to supplement his meagre income with a few black-market sales, but it was impossible to buy anything to resell when there was no money to buy it in the first place. Then, when his bag containing a few coins, some brass buttons and his precious emerald earring was stolen, Rinaldo was left with no worldly possessions apart from the shoddy clothes in which he stood.

The thief was one of his room-mates – a stupid, lumbering boy with a tongue which was too big for his mouth. Rinaldo knew it was him as he had heard him brag about the brass buttons, believing they were made of solid gold.

When Rinaldo confronted him, the boy just dismissed him with a string of obscenities and a shove. Without a second thought, Rinaldo seized him by the collar and rained blows on him, but the boy pulled a length of lead pipe from inside his shirt and struck Rinaldo with it. Rinaldo, being quicker and angrier, grabbed the pipe and struck him back. The fight ended abruptly with the dull, hollow thud of the boy's skull hitting a brick wall.

Whilst the boy was lying out cold on the floor, Rinaldo retrieved his bag. Then he took the boy's boots. They were a decent pair of hobnail boots, too big for himself, but very saleable. Rinaldo used the money to rent himself a slightly better bed in a slightly better rooming house.

There seemed to be few employment options which were legal and unlikely to kill Rinaldo prematurely through either accident or exhaustion. Hard work was no cure for poverty when there was no correlation between effort and reward. It was an incontestable fact that poor men laboured until they dropped, and when they dropped, they were still poor. It was unusual to see a poor man older than fifty. Those who looked fifty were probably considerably younger. It seemed to Rinaldo that a poor man could not go far in life on hard work.

All Rinaldo wanted was a degree of comfort in his life, the basic dignities of a hot dinner every night and a soft bed with clean sheets, but these humble aspirations seemed as out of reach as the moon.

Eventually he gave up his job clearing bombsites and found other menial work here and there – trench-digging, loading trucks, scrubbing pots. None of it was regular and none of it paid enough to live on. He tried for better jobs, but he had no specific skills and no experience. He could read, write and calculate competently, but having little formal schooling put him at the bottom of every list – if indeed he was put on the list at all.

As soon as he was old enough Rinaldo presented himself at the army recruitment office – not through patriotic duty, but in the hope that the military would, at the very least, save him from destitution. There had been a twenty-year gap between the two world wars, so he reasoned that he still had a bit of time before the next one started. However, being an orphan gave Rinaldo an automatic exoneration from National Service. He filled out a form anyway, but never received a response.

At around that time, a character of dubious reputation known as Manolunga befriended Rinaldo. Manolunga described himself as a dealer in miscellaneous goods, boasting that there was nothing he could not procure if the price was right. His preferred sources of merchandise were shops and warehouses, and his preferred time for acquiring his goods was at night when those shops and warehouses were closed.

Moonless nights were best, and it was on one such dark night that Rinaldo accompanied Manolunga on a warehouse trip along with Guercio, Manolunga's most trusted associate. Rinaldo and Manolunga would break into the warehouse whilst Guercio acted as their look-out.

Rinaldo was uneasy. Manolunga was as slippery as grease, and Guercio was blind in one eye and severely myopic in the other. Rinaldo queried how a man with such poor sight could be an efficient look-out. Manolunga assured him that what Guercio lacked in vision he more than made up for in hearing. He had ears like a bat, which was far more beneficial than eyesight in the dark.

They made their way around the warehouse looking for the best way to gain access and decided upon a small first-floor window which was conveniently positioned beside a drain pipe.

'You go up first, Mozzarella,' said Manolunga.

'Ha ha ha!' chuckled Guercio. 'Mozzarella, that's a good one, Manolunga. You're so funny!'

Rinaldo didn't react. Manolunga never called him by his name, only by a variety of cheese-related nicknames. It was nothing he hadn't heard before.

'What's the matter, Provolone? You getting cold feet?'

'Provolone! That's even funnier!' sniggered Guercio.

Rinaldo said nothing, climbed up the drainpipe and broke in. Manolunga followed. Guercio took his place under the window. If he heard anyone coming, he would whistle.

The objective of the raid was paint. Manolunga had undertaken to supply several cans to his cousin who specialised in the refurbishment of stolen bicycles.

Inside the warehouse it was pitch black. Manolunga took a torch from his jacket and shone it along a row of shelving stacked with cans of paint.

'Bingo!' he exclaimed. 'We need two blue, three black and one green. Got that, Ricotta?'

Before Rinaldo could reply, Manolunga's torch made a crackling sound and died. Rinaldo's heart sank. He'd had a bad feeling about Guercio and Manolunga and the sweep on the warehouse. He should have trusted his gut. But Manolunga was undeterred and said, 'Just grab a few cans. Never mind what colour they are.'

Rinaldo felt his way carefully through the darkness with a can of paint in each hand. Manolunga was less careful. He grabbed four, turned and headed back for the window, but in his haste he tripped and fell headlong into a bank of switches.

Suddenly rows of fluorescent tubes flickered into life and the warehouse was illuminated from floor to ceiling. Manolunga poked frantically at the switches. Lights went off. Lights came on. Lights went off. Lights came on. The warehouse flashed like a lighthouse.

'I'll jump back down and you pass the paint to me,' he instructed Rinaldo.

'No. I was first in, so I'll be first out,' replied Rinaldo, thinking that if they were discovered it would be easier to make a run for it if he was already outside. He had an escape route in mind. The river was only a thirty-second dash away and provided plenty of places to hide.

Police Constable Testoni had deviated from his designated beat that night. He didn't mind working the night-shift because most nights were quiet and he could do as he pleased. He had decided to go down to the river to eat his sandwich.

It was so peaceful on the river bank. The policeman listened to the gentle lapping of the water against the barges as he savoured the sandwich his mother had prepared for him. She made the most excellent sandwiches. His colleagues were always envious. Tonight it was a particularly delicious one – salami and pickled artichokes stuffed into a crusty ciabatta roll. He could happily have eaten two.

Once he had finished, Police Constable Testoni sat back and began scraping out the bits of salami which had got stuck between his teeth with his handcuff keys, then he lit a cigarette. It was such a lovely, quiet night. There was no rush. He had almost finished his cigarette when he saw the warehouse lights flashing.

Rinaldo shimmied down the drainpipe. As agreed, Manolunga leaned out of the window and dropped the first can for Rinaldo to catch, then the second, then the third. He was about to drop the fourth when the policeman's whistle pierced the silence.

Manolunga panicked and hurled the can to the ground. It exploded on impact, covering Guercio's feet in paint. Rinaldo ran for the river. Manolunga leapt out of the window and disappeared into the darkness.

Guercio would have made a run for it too, but he'd been startled by the crash of the paint can and he couldn't work out what had happened to his feet. He feared that perhaps he had been shot. In the commotion he forgot from which direction he had come in. He couldn't see where Manolunga or Rinaldo had gone. Blind confusion paralysed him.

Police Constable Testoni seized Guercio and pushed him up against the wall.

'Who else was with you?' he demanded.

'Nobody,' replied Guercio.

'Don't give me that! I saw a fellow run away. Did that window break itself whilst you were standing here? Did that paint throw itself out of the window? If you don't come clean things are going to get very painful for you.'

Guercio was shaking. He didn't want to get Manolunga into trouble and he feared repercussions from him far more than he feared a pasting from a policeman.

'I'll give you one more chance to tell me who else was with you.'

Guercio couldn't see the policeman very clearly, but he sensed the raising of an arm and the clenching of a fist.

'R-Rinaldo,' he stuttered.

'Rinaldo? Rinaldo who?'

Guercio's mind went blank. The name was on the tip of his tongue. He knew it was the name of a cheese, but which one? He had heard Manolunga refer to Rinaldo by so many different cheese names that he had no idea which one it was.

'Gorgonzola,' he said at last.

'Gorgonzola? Are you having me on?'

'No. That's his name. Rinaldo Gorgonzola. This was all his idea. He asked me to go for a walk with him and when we got here he told me to stand under the window and before I knew it he was chucking cans of paint out. I didn't know he was planning to steal anything.'

Clearly the policeman didn't believe Guercio. He'd heard it all before. If criminals were to be believed, the police just spent their time catching innocent people.

'What's he look like then, this Rinaldo Gorgonzola fellow?'

This time Guercio told the truth.

'I don't know,' he said. 'I can't see too well.'

Police Constable Testoni didn't hit Guercio because he reasoned that hitting a half-blind man would cause more problems than it could solve. People had got over-sensitive about that kind of thing. It could get his name into the papers and his mother would never forgive a scandal like that.

Instead he handcuffed Guercio and frog-marched him to the police station. Guercio was interrogated repeatedly, but stuck to his story. Everything was Rinaldo Gorgonzola's doing. He never mentioned Manolunga.

Guercio was sentenced to three months in prison for his part in the robbery and a further two for lying to the police. He was also ordered to pay back the cost of the broken window and the can of paint.

A warrant was issued for the arrest of Rinaldo Gorgonzola, but unable to locate him, the police eventually closed the case.

CHAPTER 7

The incident at the warehouse made Rinaldo nervous. He'd been fearing a tap on the shoulder from the law, although quite frankly the prospect of prison seemed like a comfortable option. Sometimes he wondered whether he should commit a crime with the intention of being caught – not a serious crime, just a small imprisonable offence to see him through the worst of the winter. Incarceration meant free accommodation and free food.

It was November 1948, three months since Rinaldo had been laid off from labouring on a building site. The cement-mixing and hod-carrying had ruined his only set of clothes and he hadn't had any money to buy replacements. Trying to get another regular job had been impossible. Nobody wanted to employ a man who looked as though he'd stolen his clothes from a scarecrow.

Following his lay-off he'd been evicted from his lodgings because he hadn't been able to pay the rent. Since then, he'd been sleeping outside, which hadn't been unpleasant in September, or through the earlier part of October. But once the winter had set in, it was a different matter entirely. The cold and the damp had clogged up his chest and he'd had a barking cough for weeks which was refusing to go away.

The old childhood feeling of permanent hunger returned. Now Rinaldo ate three meals a week in a soup kitchen for the homeless. The scant rations of soup were gluey and awful and full of lumpy things which were hard to identify. The rest of the time he was obliged to scavenge for what he could in the back-yards of restaurants by rifling through their dustbins after closing time, but the pickings were never very rich. As each day passed he became more aware of his bones. When he looked down at his legs, his trousers, which were held up with a length of string, appeared to have nothing inside them.

His dream of a hot dinner every night and of nestling into a soft, clean bed seemed so far beyond what was possible that he tried not to think about it. He would certainly never complain about a damp or lumpy bed again. Now luxury meant finding a doorway with a doormat and one which was deep enough to provide shelter from the wind and wide enough to stretch his legs out.

He found one such doorway in a little back street off Via Val d'Aposa and inspected it as a prospective tenant might view an apartment, assessing its size, its facilities and the amount of passing traffic. It was a pleasingly spacious doorway belonging to an insurance company office, so Rinaldo could be certain of not being disturbed there between six o'clock in the evening and eight the following morning. Its location was central, which was always a bonus, and being down a street which was too narrow for motor-vehicles, it was quiet. The doormat was a particularly thick one. Compared with other doormats he'd slept on in other doorways, it would be like floating on a feather mattress.

A little further down the street, on the opposite corner, was a cinema with the word *CINEMA* written vertically down one wall. Rinaldo hadn't paid any particular attention to it, but during his first night of residence in the insurance company doorway, as the evening drew in, the sign lit up. First it lit up in green, then it lit up in pink, then back to green and so on and so on. Rinaldo turned his back to it and tried to ignore it, but still the pulses of pink and green polluted his doorway. He hunched into his collar and covered his eyes with his sleeve in search of darkness. Eventually he managed to fall asleep.

He was woken barely an hour later by the cold of the stone floor, which bled through the doormat and leeched into his body, freezing the meagre amount of meat on his bones. He was also woken by a dream about his mother. He had found her and he knew it was her because she was wearing an emerald earring, but suddenly his dream was invaded by dozens of women wearing emerald earrings who came at him from every direction, all talking at the same time.

Rinaldo opened his eyes as a pulse of pink turned green. From where he lay he could see the bottom two letters of the flashing *CINEMA* sign. Pink *MA*. Green *MA*. Pink *MA*. Green *MA*. *MA-MA*. *MA-MA*. And his own voice in his head, some leftover remnant of his dream, calling out: 'Mamma! Mamma! Ma! Ma! Ma! Ma!'

The dream made him angry. His foolish boyhood fantasy of being reunited with his mother was long gone. He hoped that their paths would never cross because he was a son any mother would be ashamed of. Rinaldo got up, sad, raging, cold, stiff and aching, and made off towards Via Val d'Aposa. The *CINEMA* sign still pulsed behind him.

He spent the next few hours wandering the streets, trying to settle his mind, looking down and focusing only on the tramping of his feet on the pavement. He didn't want to look up because he knew what he would see, but eventually the urge became too strong.

He raised his head and glanced up into the orange and yellow rectangles of illuminated windows, catching glimpses of people in their homes, hearing fragments of tunes playing on radios, echoes of conversations, shouts, laughter, the clatter and scrape of dishes – and smelling occasional wafts of *ragú*, of frying, of after-dinner coffee.

Rinaldo wondered whether he could ever be like those people, whether one day he might have a home of his own to fill with a wife and children and those sounds of happy domesticity. Then he sighed and shook his head. A wife, children, a decent home, food on the table – these were the modest ambitions of an ordinary man, but what were the chances? He couldn't even provide for himself.

He drifted along the dimly-lit streets, using up what little energy he had, then sat on the steps of San Petronio for a while, waiting for the city to empty and watching the hands of the clock on the Torre dell'Orologio – the big clock tower – work their way round to midnight. At a quarter past he made his way back towards the insurance company doorway. The last screening had ended and the *CINEMA* sign was off. The little back street was deserted and cloaked in total darkness.

But as Rinaldo stepped into the doorway, he tripped over a pair of feet and almost fell flat on his face. The owner of the feet struck a match, which threw a brief blaze of light into the dark and illuminated his face. He was an old man with a tangled grey beard which grew right up his cheeks. He cupped the match in his hand to protect the flame, lit the stub of a candle and asked in a thick Bolognese dialect: 'You looking for a place to sleep?'

'Yes,' replied Rinaldo, 'but I'll find somewhere else. Sorry, I didn't mean to disturb you.'

'I don't mind if you want to share. There's a nice thick doormat here and plenty of room. And I've got food if you're hungry.'

Rinaldo would have refused immediately had it not been for the mention of food, but he hesitated before accepting because surely there had to be a catch. Although he was now by definition a vagrant, he steered clear of other vagrants because they were usually mad, or drunk, or both.

He stepped closer, assessing whether the old man smelled of drink, and ascertained that he smelled of other things, some not particularly pleasant, but alcohol was not one of them. Evidently the old man shared the same concerns.

'Not a drinker, are you?' he said.

'No.'

'Do you smoke? If you do, I'd rather you smoked outside.'

Rinaldo replied that no, he didn't smoke, and wondered how, if he did, he would have any option but to smoke outside.

'Good, good. Come on in then if you want. Make yourself at home. Would you mind taking your boots off?'

Again, Rinaldo hesitated. The last thing he needed was to have his boots stolen, but he took them off anyway, thinking that he would tie them to his wrists overnight to keep them safe. The old man seemed satisfied that all his conditions had been met and said, 'I'll light another candle if there's going to be two of us.'

The old man lit another stub, which cast a second pale patch of light in the doorway. Quite clearly he was a veteran of rough sleeping and was very well-equipped with blankets, candle stubs and a large haversack. Two brooms were propped up in one corner, beside his boots.

'Where's your blankets?' asked the old man.

'I haven't got any,' replied Rinaldo.

'You shouldn't be sleeping outside with no blankets. I've got lots of blankets. Good, warm ones. I already had plenty enough, but the nice lady in Via Val d'Aposa who gives me socks gave me two new ones the other day. I don't mind sharing those either. The blankets, I mean, not the socks.'

Rinaldo sat down beside him with his boots tucked safely by his side, drew his legs up and rested his chin on his knees, but he was still uncertain whether he should be suspicious of the apparent show of charity.

'What's your name?' the old fellow asked.

'Rinaldo.'

'Ha! Well, blow me down! So is mine.' The old man patted his chest as though to emphasise the point. 'I'm called Rinaldo too. Rinaldo Rossi. Have you eaten?'

'No.'

Rinaldo Rossi reached into his haversack and took out a battered tin lunch box and several paper packages, which he laid out with deliberate care.

'I've got *tagliatelle* with *ragú* and some *tortelloni*. They're in the same tin so they're a bit mixed together, but it's not a bad combination. The tortelloni are from the trattoria in Via Val d'Aposa. They do good *tortelloni* there, but the restaurant in Via Carbonesi puts more ricotta in the filling. The *tagliatelle* are good too. Not too *al dente*. They don't soak up the *ragú* properly when they're too *al dente*. And I've got some bread and garlic sausage and some cheese. The cheese is a bit hard, but you're young so you've probably got the teeth for it.' Rinaldo Rossi then took out another package and sniffed it. 'There's some cake in here. It's from yesterday, so it's gone a bit dry, but it's still good. It's got cherries in it, or it might be plums. Could even be apricots. I'm not sure. And I've got milk too.'

Rinaldo stared wide-eyed at the selection, amazed that he was not only being offered food, but a full menu. His mouth was watering so much that he had to lick away the spit from the corners of his mouth.

'Don't you want it?' he said.

'No,' replied Rinaldo Rossi, patting his belly. 'I don't sleep well if I'm too full. I already had two dinners.'

'*Two* dinners?'

'I have two dinners most nights. Some days I have two lunches. Sometimes I have two dinners and two lunches. The trattorie and the restaurants round these parts are good to me. They always give me what's left after closing time. And because they give me food, I sweep for them.'

Rinaldo Rossi pointed at the two brooms in the corner, then knitted his bushy brows in concentration. He seemed to be performing some sort of complicated calculation in his mind.

'Do they give me food because I sweep for them, or do I sweep for them because they give me food?' He repeated the question several times, but seemed unable to reach a conclusion, so he shrugged and said, 'Hmm, not sure which way round it's supposed to be. So I had *passatelli* this evening and then I had *cannelloni*. Or was that yesterday? It might have been yesterday. I might have had *lasagne* and *risotto*. I confuse things sometimes. Anyway, this was extra leftovers and you can have it if you want it.'

'I can't pay you. I haven't got any money,' said Rinaldo, whose stomach was making a noise like a train.

'Pay me? Well, it's kind of you to offer even though you haven't got any money, but I don't get on too good with money. I can't really make out how it's supposed to work. Why is a bit of paper worth more than a piece of metal? Makes no sense to me. Sometimes people give me money, even though I don't ever ask for it. I just put it in the church offerings box. They collect for the poor, you know, the church. So I'm happy to let the poor have it if they need it. And when I put money in the box the church give me candles. But they don't let me take the candles away, well, not the new candles. They let me have the stubs. The new candles have to stay in the church because dead people like them. So I give my candles to my mother, Giuseppina. Except I don't really give them to her because I can't because she's dead, so I just say they're for her when I light them.'

'Giuseppina? My mother was called Giuseppina too.'

'Do you light candles for her?'

'I haven't for a long time.'

'Then next time I've got some money I shall light a candle for her and say the money came from you.'

Rinaldo pinched himself, wondering whether everything he was experiencing was real, or a freakishly vivid hallucination brought on by hunger. He was overcome by a strange, mystical kind of feeling. There he was, sitting beside another Rinaldo, the son of another Giuseppina. They were both homeless and broke. Was this a vision of himself in the future? Was this a premonition of how his life would be when he grew so accustomed to poverty that he would no longer see it as poverty?

This dismal thought was interrupted by Rinaldo Rossi asking, 'So, you having any of this food then?'

Rinaldo nodded eagerly. The old man wiped a spoon on his sleeve, passed the tin lunch box to him and wished him *buon appetito*.

Rinaldo dug the spoon into the congealed, rubbery pasta, which had set into a single mass in the tin. It took some chewing. Twisting *tagliatelle* around a spoon wasn't easy, and made all the more difficult by the fact that his fingers were numb with cold. Nevertheless, Rinaldo ate with a feeling of great pleasure, savouring each mouthful. He could have eaten the lot and another portion on top, but he stopped just short of half. He would have been grateful just for that, but Rinaldo Rossi passed him the package of cake, apologising for the fact that it was a bit squashed.

'How long have you been sleeping on the streets?' Rinaldo asked him.

The old man thought hard.

'I can't be sure,' he said. 'I've never been very good at counting things and years are long things to count. I did have lodgings once, but it was a long time ago. I had my own room just round the corner with things in it. There was a bed and a table and a stove and a sink. I had dishes too and spoons. I kept it all nice. I was never any trouble. I had a job in a brush factory back in those days. I was assistant night-watchman. It was a nice job. I liked it. It was back then that I learned to be good at sweeping.'

He reached across to the brooms which were propped against the wall and held one in the glow of the candlelight for Rinaldo to inspect.

‘See this broom? I’ve had it since I was a boy. It belonged to my father, and to his father before him.’

Rinaldo peered at the broom through the semi-darkness. Although he was no expert, he thought it looked rather new. But he didn’t want to question the old man, or query the origins of his heirloom, so he made a noise of admiration and said, ‘It’s in very good condition.’

‘Ah, yes. I look after it well. I’ve had to change the handle many times, and the brush, but it’s the best broom I’ve ever had. They don’t make them like this any more.’

Rinaldo smiled to himself, amused at the old man’s skewed logic. Rinaldo Rossi then turned his attention to the second broom.

‘See this one? This is my inside broom for when I sweep indoors, although mainly I sweep outdoors. But inside brooms are different. The bristles are softer and they’ve got more spring in them. The handles are thinner and lighter.’

‘You certainly know your brooms.’

‘Ah, well,’ replied Rinaldo Rossi with the air of a man who knew what he was talking about, ‘I’ve been sweeping a long time, and when you do something for a long time you get to know it well,’

The old man continued with an earnest address on the subject of brooms, but the more he talked, the more disjointed and muddled his discourse became. He would start a sentence on one topic and jump onto another, then start again with something else, but Rinaldo didn’t mind. He felt strangely soothed by the old man’s rambling, gruff voice and meandering dialect.

As the food settled in his belly, Rinaldo felt himself growing drowsy. With the old man still talking, he forgot about securing his boots to his wrists, curled up and drifted off to sleep.

When he awoke at first light, feeling that he had slept better than any other night he had slept in a doorway, Rinaldo Rossi was gone. Rinaldo realised that the old man had not only covered him with a blanket, but had also tucked him in. What was more, he had left him half a bottle of milk and a package wrapped in newspaper. Rinaldo opened it and found that it contained a bread roll and a whole smoked Scamorza cheese the size of his fist. His boots were still there, exactly where he had left them.

Over the days and nights which followed, Rinaldo looked out for Rinaldo Rossi. He would happily have spent another night sharing a doorway, and not just because of the food. He had felt comforted by the old man's company and kindness, and thought it would be rude not to offer to return his blanket.

Yet despite searching the area around Via Val d'Aposa and further beyond, there was no sign of Rinaldo Rossi. He hoped that the old man was all right, but he was concerned, so he called in at the trattoria which had provided the *tortelloni*.

'I'm looking for Rinaldo Rossi. I think he sweeps for you sometimes. Have you seen him?'

The owner of the trattoria shook his head sadly. 'Last I heard, he'd been taken to hospital. He'd suffered a stroke.'

'Is he all right?'

'I don't know. But it wasn't looking good.'

It was a long walk across town to the hospital, but Rinaldo felt compelled to go and visit. Despite having known him only a few hours, he'd felt an unusually deep connection to the old man.

When at last he reached the hospital and found the right ward, the duty nurse refused to let him in, primarily for reasons of hygiene, but also because Rinaldo Rossi already had a visitor. After a certain amount of pleading and the promise that he wouldn't touch anything, sit on anything or lean on anything, she conceded that Rinaldo could look through the small pane of glass of the door, on condition that he did not fog the glass with his breath.

Rinaldo Rossi was either unconscious, or asleep. It was impossible to tell from a distance. His visitor was a lady who was sitting by his bedside holding his hand and talking to him. She had her back to the door, but Rinaldo could see that she was well-dressed. He thought that perhaps she was a charity worker, or some sort of hospital volunteer.

'Who's the lady?' he asked.

The nurse shrugged and said, 'That's the woman who had him brought in. She's been here every day.'

'Can I speak to her?'

The duty nurse replied with a very firm 'no' and continued hovering around to ensure that Rinaldo was doing as he was told and was not contaminating anything with his filthiness. She kept casting looks in his direction, with her mouth twisted into an expression of exaggerated distaste and her eyes narrowed to a pair of little slits. She might as well have been holding her nose.

'Will he recover?' asked Rinaldo.

'It's in the hands of God,' replied the nurse, which Rinaldo considered to be a rather inadequate answer from a supposed medical professional.

'Is somebody looking after his brooms?'

The nurse looked at Rinaldo as though he was not only repulsive, but also deranged.

'*Brooms?*'

'He would have had brooms with him. And blankets. And a haversack with all his things in it.'

'I expect it's all been incinerated. We don't keep things which are a contamination risk.'

The sadness that Rinaldo felt for the plight of the kind old man was so profound that he couldn't bear it, so he didn't question the nurse any further. He turned and hurried away, wiping his eyes with the backs of his dirty hands.

When Rinaldo returned to the hospital the following week, Rinaldo Rossi was no longer there. The same nurse informed him that the old man had been taken to live out the final few days of his life in the care of the good Sisters of Santa Caterina.

*

As Christmas drew near, Rinaldo spent his days wandering without destination through the centre of Bologna, watching people going about their business. It was such ordinary business to people in comfortable circumstances, with their shopping, Christmas preparations, meeting with friends and family to drink hot chocolate and exchange festive wishes – *Buon Natale! Buon Natale!* – but to Rinaldo it was all extraordinary in its unattainability.

He watched well-to-do families bustling out of shops laden with gifts and packages. Families of more modest means restricted themselves to looking at the window displays, or haggling over the statuettes of Jesus, Mary and Joseph on sale at the little stalls lined up under the porticos.

Rinaldo stood before the window of a high-end grocery shop, casting his eyes over the extravaganza of luxury foodstuffs, especially the *certosini* – Bologna's very own Christmas cakes – crowned with candied oranges and cherries, which gleamed like jewels. He saw jars of the fruit conserve called *mostarda,* and of *salsa verde.* Hanging above were lines of salamis, *zamponi* – stuffed pigs' trotters – and a whole *prosciutto* ham on the bone. And in the background, wrapped in Christmas-patterned paper and secured with giant ribbons, was a pyramid of boxes as tall as an average man containing the sweet, raisin-filled seasonal cakes called *panettoni.*

But when he shifted his gaze from the bounty of food to the glass which separated him from it, Rinaldo caught a reflection of himself which merged with the display, and for a moment he appeared to be standing in the very midst of the splendour. His dismal image was made worse by the lighting in the window, which illuminated his poverty-stricken state. His jacket was patched. His trousers were frayed. He didn't have a coat or a hat. He needed a haircut.

Rinaldo felt a rush of disgust for his life. He could not shake off the feeling he had, as if he was still the small boy in broken boots who gazed longingly at the cakes in the pastry shop.

'*Buon Natale*,' he muttered bitterly to himself, stamping his feet, partly in frustration and partly to try to warm them, before moving on.

The cold aggravated his hunger and his hunger was aggravated by the cold. For a while he lingered by a stand which sold roasted chestnuts, absorbing the heat from the brazier and hoping to satisfy his hunger with the smell. Every spit and crackle fired a burst of scent into his nostrils. But being so close to the delicious aroma just made it worse. Rinaldo's stomach protested at the deception and his legs began to tremble. He had to lean against a wall to stop himself from keeling over.

As the afternoon light faded, the smoky dampness in the air grew heavier and a wet sleet began to peck at the nape of his neck. Icy trickles seeped into his shirt collar and ran down his back. Rinaldo hunched into his jacket, which was more holes and patches than jacket, and cursed the wretched cold. It was no weather to be outside and under-dressed. But he was obsessed with the chestnuts. He visualised the chestnut-seller scooping a generous portion into a paper cone and twisting the top to keep them hot. He imagined how the little package would warm his hands, how he would sink his teeth into each husk, splitting it open to pop out the chestnut. Again, Rinaldo's stomach protested.

He reached into his pocket and felt for the emerald earring.

It would make sense to pawn it, or just sell it and be done with it. There had been times when he was certain that he should get rid of the earring – that it was jinxed and the cause of all his misery. Other times he felt guilty for even thinking such a thing. As long as he had the earring he could never truly say that he had nothing.

It was then he realised that the chestnut-seller was eyeing him suspiciously. Rinaldo sighed and moved on. He looked up as he passed the church of San Petronio. For a moment he wondered whether he should go in and shelter from the cold. He could warm his hands by the candle-stands – then he thought better of it. Since leaving Signora Limoni's care he hadn't been into any church at all. He'd stopped praying too. Hoping for some sort of divine intervention was nothing but a waste of time.

He made his way towards Piazza del Nettuno and stopped by the fountain. Neptune's muscular bulk shimmered with an icy sheen and little sharp stalactites dripped from his trident. The flow of the water had slowed to a trickle. The spouts were icing up.

A drunk had been found dead in that fountain on All Saints' Day. Some reports said he'd climbed in, slipped, hit his head and drowned. Others conjectured that he had drowned himself on purpose. He had left behind dependent parents, a wife and seven children. Opinions on the tragedy were mixed. Some were disgusted at the man's feckless behaviour. Others said it was hardly surprising that a man burdened with so many responsibilities should seek a desperate solution.

It struck Rinaldo then that if he died, there would be nobody to miss him. He had grown from an unwanted infant to an unwanted child, and then to an unwanted young man. Perhaps he had no place in this world and was not meant to be here. It was a morbid, yet comforting thought. Being dead seemed so much easier than being alive.

He shivered at the thought of the cold water soaking through his clothes, but other than that he could think of no reason why he should not drown himself. He would have to wait until the crowds had cleared though, or some wannabe hero would drag him out, just like Signor Limoni had been dragged out of the river. Perhaps it would be more effective to jump from the top of the Torre Asinelli – the taller of Bologna's famous Two Towers – although knowing his luck he'd probably land on somebody and kill them instead.

It was then that he noticed there were coins in the water. They didn't amount to much, but certainly enough to purchase a portion of chestnuts. The thought of ending his life left Rinaldo as quickly as it had arrived.

He leaned into the basin of the fountain, trying to give the impression he was making a wish rather than fishing for coins. As he braced himself to dip his hand into the icy water a man shoved him, almost knocking him off his feet and shouted, 'Get a job, you thieving toe-rag!'

Then the man strode away, his long camel overcoat billowing behind him.

A rush of great indignation overcame Rinaldo. Two things offended him. The first was being barged into and insulted. The second was the way the man wore his coat. He wore it open, like an advertisement for the fact that he had on so many warm clothes that he didn't even need to do up his coat.

The man crossed the road and headed down Via Rizzoli. Rinaldo followed twenty paces behind and watched as the fellow made his way into a swanky bar by the Due Torri. It was the sort of fashionable establishment where waiters in white jackets and bow ties served Vermouth cocktails with fancy names off silver trays, and gave a complimentary glass of sparkling water with every coffee. The man shook himself out of his overcoat and hung it on the stand by the door. Rinaldo slipped in behind him and took the coat before the man had reached the bar. He also took his hat.

Oh, the sumptuous warmth of a proper coat! It was a finely-tailored garment made of camel-coloured cashmere. Its rabbit-fur collar was imbued with a pleasantly manly cologne. The garment was a few sizes too large, but Rinaldo felt like a bigger man in a bigger coat. The hat was also too big, but a bit of newspaper folded into the inside band would solve that. At least it covered his shaggy hair. Rinaldo's luck was turning. He could feel it as he nestled into the comforting warmth of the coat.

He checked the pockets in the hope of finding a nice fat wallet, but all he found was half a bar of chocolate and a pair of leather gloves. It was better than nothing. Rinaldo put on the gloves and stuffed the chocolate into his mouth, then hurried back down Via Rizzoli at a brisk pace, thinking it best to put some distance between the man and his coat and hat now that they weren't his coat and hat any more.

Wearing such a splendid overcoat changed Rinaldo's gait and his gestures, even the tone of voice in which he spoke to himself. He assumed the affectations of a gentleman of status, untroubled by his precarious situation, his homelessness or his hunger. He turned into Via Indipendenza and sauntered along with his head held high. When he caught sight of himself in another shop window he had that old private-school smock feeling again – that being well-dressed made him different.

Rinaldo amused himself window-shopping, gazing at the array of inaccessibly costly things in each shop and enjoying his reflection in the elegant overcoat and hat. He gave himself an imaginary budget, envisaging how he would spend it, and became so caught up in his fantasy that before he knew it he was not outside a shop looking in, but inside a shop browsing goods.

It was a shop filled with unnecessary things – fancy ornaments, scented stationery, decorative candles and a thousand other expensive, absurd and superfluous items.

'Good afternoon. Can I be of assistance, Signore?' asked a young shop girl. Rinaldo remarked that she had addressed him formally, as one would address a person of importance.

Rinaldo stated in the most bourgeois voice that he could muster that he was seeking a gift for his mother. The girl brought out an array of possibilities for his perusal, laying them out on the counter in a deliberate, ceremonious manner. There were hand-painted boxes, embroidered tablecloths, decorative dishes.

'Perhaps your mother would appreciate a piece from our Murano glassware collection, Signore? Or a fine lace centrepiece from Verona? Or might I suggest an English tea set? They're rather fashionable this year.'

It felt so good to be treated with such courtesy, to make small-talk about the form, the colour, the craftsmanship of each object; or even to assume an air of dissatisfaction with a particular item, claiming that it was too big, too small, too gaudy, or that his mother already possessed something similar. Rinaldo imagined how it would feel to have to make such decisions as to what to buy without the slightest concern of how much it cost.

As the girl disappeared behind the counter to fetch more possibilities Rinaldo was distracted by a peculiar sound – the kind of sound somebody might make if they were trying to attract the attention of a cat.

'Psst! Psst! Psst!' called the voice from behind him. 'Is that you, Mozzarella?'

It was Manolunga, who had followed him into the shop. At first Rinaldo ignored him.

'Psst! Psst! Provolone!'

'What do you want?'

'I could use your help.'

'I'm not helping you. You'll get me into trouble.'

Undeterred, Manolunga came up beside him. 'I just need you to talk to a few people.'

'Talk to a few people?'

'Yes. That's all. You strike up a conversation, or ask for directions, or something like that. Keep 'em distracted. I'll do the rest. There'll be a nice bit of money in it for you.'

Rinaldo shook his head. He wasn't getting involved in that old pickpockets' trick and he certainly wasn't going to get involved with Manolunga again.

'Your loss,' said Manolunga. 'Anyway, good to see you, Pecorino. Best of luck to you, mate. Nice coat, by the way.'

He patted Rinaldo on the shoulder and made his way out of the shop. It took Rinaldo a few moments to realise that Manolunga had taken the emerald earring from his pocket. Rinaldo sprang off to find him, leaving the surprised shop girl holding an armful of brocade cushions.

Manolunga was not difficult to locate. He was waiting for Rinaldo outside. He grinned and dangled the earring at him, then threw it for Rinaldo to catch.

'I wasn't going to keep it, Bel Paese. Just wanted to show you how good I am at what I do.'

Rinaldo felt like giving Manolunga a slap, but he steeled himself. It wasn't worth the trouble. So much for thinking that his luck had changed. He turned and made his way back down Via Indipendenza, his mood significantly soured.

'Look in your other pocket, Parmigiano!' Manolunga called after him as Rinaldo walked away. Rinaldo stopped and felt in his other pocket. Inside was a 1,000-lire note, neatly folded in four.

'That's just a little sweetener, Mascarpone. Plenty more where that came from. Go and buy yourself some dinner. You look like you need it. And think about what I said. See you later, mate. You'll find me round here. I'll be counting my money!'

With that, Manolunga dissolved into the crowd.

Rinaldo stood looking at the note, knowing that he should give it back, but somehow his stomach had detected that there was the possibility of being filled and it pleaded so loudly that he could not ignore it.

He found a modest little workmen's restaurant down a back street. It was nothing fancy, but Rinaldo didn't want fancy. He wanted good, wholesome food at a reasonable price, and plenty of it. The other diners were mainly eating alone. Some looked up from their meals and their newspapers as Rinaldo walked in. Their gazes lingered on the elegant overcoat. Rinaldo knew better than to leave it on the hat stand, so he found a place at a corner table and sat down with his newly-appropriated coat and hat tucked safely by his side.

'What can I get you, fella?' asked the proprietor.

'Everything,' replied Rinaldo.

Rinaldo ate with absolute concentration, his knife and fork firmly gripped in his hands, utterly engrossed in satisfying his appetite. He forgot about eating slowly and savouring each mouthful. In less time than it would normally have taken him to make his way through a bowl of soup, he polished off half a pound of pasta and wiped his dish clean with half a loaf of bread. He even wiped the grease from around his mouth with the last piece of crust. Boiled tripe and beans followed, then cheese, vanilla custard (twice), coffee and a glass of *digestivo*.

He sat back and stretched, then rested his hands on his paunch. His stomach was so swollen that it hurt and he had to loosen the string which held up his trousers, but he hadn't felt so good in months. He sighed with full-bellied contentment and began to inspect his new clothes.

Much to Rinaldo's delight the fedora hat was lined in purple silk and looked as though it had hardly been worn. Rinaldo turned it over in his hands, stroking the felt delicately with his fingertips, then he took a discarded newspaper from a neighbouring table, tore off the sports page and folded it into a strip, which he tucked into the inside band. With the newspaper in place the fit was perfect.

He then directed his attention to the overcoat, running his hand over the soft cashmere and combing the rabbit fur with his fingers as he inspected the perfectly-joined seams. Clearly the overcoat was a garment which had been made to the highest standard of workmanship. There wasn't a stitch out of place. He couldn't begin to imagine how much it had cost.

When he turned the overcoat to inspect the lining, he discovered a hidden pocket. Inside it, loosely rolled up, was a striking red and blue tartan neck scarf. How fortunate Rinaldo felt to have been insulted by such a stylish gentleman!

As he unfurled the scarf something fell out of it, bounced, rolled in a circle and settled by his foot. It was an old, tarnished coin of some sort. All Rinaldo could make out of the writing around the edge were the letters *TI*. A man's head in profile featured on one side and a seated woman featured on the other. Rinaldo guessed that it must be a lucky charm for its owner. He gripped it tightly. He could feel the good luck seeping into his hand.

Perhaps he could help Manolunga a little, he thought, just enough to buy a few more decent dinners and rent himself a bed for a couple of nights. Adding another misdemeanour to his day's thefts wouldn't be the end of the world as long as he wasn't caught, and the chances of anyone suspecting a richly-clothed gentleman of being a thief were very slight.

He left the restaurant with a case of indigestion and enough change for several more meals, but as he stepped outside he found that the weather had worsened. The sleet had thickened and drove down diagonally. A stinging wind whipped needle-sharp shards into his face, slicing into his cheeks. The wires which stretched between the buildings and across the streets were clad in sleeves of ice. The *strillone* who manned the newspaper stand announced that it was to get even colder.

Rinaldo searched through the thinning crowds, but there was no sign of Manolunga. He'd missed his chance. Maybe the coin wasn't a lucky talisman after all and the curse of bad luck was still upon him.

It was then that he saw two policemen heading straight for him. Rinaldo panicked and ducked into a dark doorway, with his head hunched into the fur collar of the overcoat and his face half-hidden by the hat. He held his breath as he watched the policemen pass. A few moments later they passed again, escorting Manolunga between them.

Rinaldo clutched the coin in his pocket. Perhaps bad luck had saved him from worse luck.

CHAPTER 8

The Tognazzi family had been scrap merchants since the early 1800s. Their yard in Via del Pratello had been a lucrative business for several generations, but when Benito Tognazzi inherited it from his father he was to be the last of the Tognazzi scrap dynasty, albeit through no fault of his own. The business was dealt a blow during the Great War and never recovered. By 1920 Benito Tognazzi the scrap-merchant had become Benito Tognazzi the ex-scrap-merchant.

His wife, Ardilla, who also happened to be his cousin, had inherited a large house which backed on to the yard. The Tognazzis were astute and money-minded, and realising that they would never be able to revive the scrap business, they had decided they should make something of the house. Thus they had opened a brothel in 1922 and named it 'Madama Gioconda's'.

It had been no small undertaking. Opening a brothel required licences and bribes to expedite them. The government insisted on certain standards.

It had taken the Tognazzis two years of hard work to get the whole thing up and running. Benito Tognazzi had toiled day and night installing modern plumbing, an electrical system and partitioning off rooms. Ardilla Tognazzi had worked hard too, ensuring that their very finite budget was judiciously spent and that the establishment was comfortably appointed. She had scoured the city for good quality furniture, negotiating the best possible prices. She had made all the curtains and even stuffed the mattresses herself.

Madama Gioconda's was by no means the only brothel in the area, but the Tognazzis decided that it should be the best by offering value for money, pleasant décor and above all, hygiene. The patrons who lived around Via del Pratello could not afford an establishment as fine as the silk-lined salons of Via dell'Orso, which were frequented by gentlemen of means, but the Tognazzis were determined that their brothel should be a far cry from the squalid, lice-filled syphilis pits like those around Vicolo del Falcone.

Via del Pratello was not new territory for Rinaldo as it was only a few streets away from Ada Stracci's old house. It was a shabby street where rents were relatively cheap, lined with little shops which sold anything and everything, most of it second-hand. There was a jail at one end, where Gigio Lingua had ended up, and three official licensed brothels, including Madama Gioconda's.

Following his fortunate escape from Manolunga and the police, Rinaldo had thought it sensible to lie low for a while and to keep away from the centre of town, so he had been camping out in a disused cellar just around the corner from Madama Gioconda's. His quarters were far from luxurious, but he'd slept in worse places, and now that spring was in the air once again, he had less to complain about than he'd had during the winter. It was too warm to wear the camel overcoat and hat now, so he had stashed them away securely in a corner of the cellar, wrapped up in a cotton sheet with a bagful of salt to stop them getting damp.

By the time Rinaldo met the Tognazzis, Madama Gioconda's had been a thriving business for a quarter of a century and had become something of an institution in Via del Pratello. Benito and Ardilla Tognazzi were considered respectable business-owners. They even paid some of their taxes, some of the time.

'I hear you're looking for a job, boy,' said Benito Tognazzi. He was a short, over-fed man with thinning, slicked-back hair and a mouthful of teeth so straight, white and perfect that they were probably false. His little fat fingers were covered in rings, and on his wrist was the biggest gold watch that Rinaldo had ever seen. He could have read the time on it from across the street.

'I need an errand boy,' Benito went on. 'What's your name?'

'Rinaldo.'

'Rinaldo what?'

'Rinaldo Scamorza.'

'What? Like the cheese?' Benito Tognazzi guffawed as though it was the funniest thing he'd ever heard. Rinaldo gave his customary jaded nod.

'Go and talk to my wife, Cheese-boy. She'll tell you what needs doing.'

The doorway into Madama Gioconda's was plain. Only the opening times and a sign which read *No loitering outside the premises* gave any indication that it was something other than an ordinary residence. The door was always closed, as was required by the law.

As Rinaldo stepped inside, his path was blocked by a man of quite remarkable ugliness. All brothels had a doorman to keep out or eject the drunk or disorderly, or the time-wasters who only came in to gawp at the girls with no intention or means to pay for services. Madama Gioconda's doorman had a face which was purplish and pox-marked and a nose which looked as though it had been punched more than once. He was of short stature and was almost as broad as he was tall. He stood squarely, with his arms folded and his weight on his heels. He looked impossible to knock over. He was a man of few words and even fewer thoughts. Everybody called him Buttafuori.

'I'm here to see Signora Tognazzi about a job,' said Rinaldo.

'Back door. Through the yard. Wait in the kitchen,' grunted Buttafuori and closed the front door.

Rinaldo made his way around the back through the old scrapyard, which was empty apart from a row of dustbins and a brand new Lancia motor car. The kitchen door was open, so he went in.

A lumpish young woman was seated at the table peeling an industrial quantity of potatoes very slowly. She was the Tognazzis' daughter – a ponderous girl with a vacant expression, a low, flat forehead and eyebrows like moustaches. Rinaldo introduced himself. The daughter said nothing. She just made a growling noise and nodded in the direction of another door. Rinaldo thanked her and went through.

He found himself in a large, low-lit, smoky room, adorned with velvet curtains, mirrors and couches, where a handful of men sat talking to a collection of women who were dressed in high heels and scant underclothes. Some of the women lay draped over the arms of the couches. Others stood leaning against the walls.

A woman with extravagantly rouged cheeks caught Rinaldo's eye and gave him a provocative glance. She sat back, gripped her knees with her hands and opened her legs wide. Another, who was perched backwards on a chair, whistled at him before dropping her camisole to expose her breast, then cupped her hand underneath it, to show off its shape and volume. Rinaldo wasn't sure where to look.

Seated on a podium behind an elegant wooden counter was Benito Tognazzi's wife, Ardilla, who was so similar in appearance to her husband that she might have been mistaken for his sister, with the exception of her teeth, most of which were gold.

'You can't be here unless you've got money and you intend to spend it,' she said sharply.

'I've come about a job,' explained Rinaldo. 'Signor Tognazzi sent me.'

Ardilla Tognazzi looked him up and down. 'Can you read and count?' she asked.

'Yes.'

'Can you ride a bicycle?'

'Yes.'

'You'll run errands,' she said, seemingly satisfied that Rinaldo was sufficiently qualified for the job. 'You'll fetch things from the market and you'll collect laundry. Sheets get changed once a day. Towels get changed after each client. One towel per client. The girls put the used towels in the baskets outside their rooms. It'll be your job to take them down to the laundry in the basement and bring the washed laundry up. You'll also take the rubbish out. Don't talk to the girls in the public areas. Never speak to the clients. If someone asks you a question, don't answer it. Tell them to come and ask me. No stealing. No spitting. No shirking. One week's trial period. Got all that?'

'Yes, Signora Tognazzi. Thank you,' affirmed Rinaldo, very meekly.

'Oh, and another thing. Keep your hands to yourself and your pecker in your trousers. If I catch you trying to get your end away with any of my girls, you're out.'

Rinaldo found himself busy within minutes of his appointment. The Tognazzis provided him with a three-wheeled bicycle, equipped with a large box on the front, on which to run their errands. His first day was over fifteen hours long and by the end of it his puny legs felt as though they might fall off, but Rinaldo didn't complain because running errands was far more pleasant than any of the jobs he'd done before. The Tognazzis did not complain either, which was high praise indeed. They even offered him accommodation in the basement. It was no more than a camp bed wedged between laundry baskets, but it was a significant improvement on all of his previous lodgings. He didn't mind the fishy smell of the unwashed sheets too much, even though it prickled his nose and made him sneeze, like the sacred incense in church.

Madama Gioconda's was open from 9 a.m. until midnight

every day except Sunday. It would have been open seven days a week if the law had allowed it. The stream of clients was constant and turnover was quick.

Once they had passed Buttafuori's inspection, patrons would be invited into the salon to choose their service and their companion. They were discouraged from engaging any of the women in conversation until they had paid. Ardilla Tognazzi was very strict about it. For the regulars, of which there were many, she had just one word: 'Usual?'

She would then exchange their payment for a ticket.

The small pink tickets were the cheapest and most popular, and bought ten minutes in a room just off the main salon which was divided into cubicles by a system of curtains. Ardilla Tognazzi referred to it rather pompously as the 'antechamber'. The women who worked there called it 'the suck and spit room'.

Clients who required further stimulation were sold a green ticket which entitled them to a quarter of an hour in one of the upstairs bedrooms. The blue and brown tickets were larger owing to the fact that the clients had a greater choice of services, which would be written precisely on the back. They purchased half an hour and an hour respectively.

The ticket system was devised to ensure that there were no misunderstandings. Clients got what they paid for, no more and no less. Tips paid directly to the women were absolutely prohibited. Instead, they were collected by Ardilla Tognazzi, who divided them in a way which she considered fair – allocating three quarters to the establishment and the remaining quarter to be distributed between the women.

The Tognazzis were sticklers for the regulations which the government imposed. The working women underwent regular medical examinations. All the bedrooms were fumigated and whitewashed in lime once a year. They kept the required stocks of disinfectants, insecticide, soap and prophylactics.

Policemen in plain clothes came in regularly to check that things were in order. Ardilla Tognazzi would give them a green ticket free of charge so that they could carry out their investigations thoroughly.

The women worked in shifts with only short breaks for meals. It was also the proprietors' legal obligation to provide them with a wholesome diet. The government insisted upon it as they were providing an important service. The Tognazzis followed all the dietary guidelines to the letter.

'You can have the same food as the girls,' said Ardilla Tognazzi to Rinaldo.

'Do you need me to give you my ration card, Signora Tognazzi?'

Ardilla Tognazzi snorted, made a hissing sound through her gold teeth and pulled an expression of disgust.

'*Ration card?* We wouldn't touch that pigswill! We have proper food here.'

Rinaldo could hardly believe the Tognazzis' generosity. There was always pasta or rice on the stove and even meat and fish. The cold store was well-stocked with milk and cheese. Fresh fruit and vegetables were plentiful, despite the fact that ordinary households were still constrained by rationing.

And just when he thought that things couldn't get any better, Ardilla Tognazzi added, 'You look like a vagrant. Don't you have any other clothes?' to which Rinaldo replied that he did not. The only smart things he owned were the camel overcoat, fedora hat and tartan scarf. But it was far too hot to wear those and the overcoat wasn't appropriate for riding a bicycle anyway.

'Go to the market and get yourself something decent to wear,' she said. 'I don't want you running my errands looking like that. You give a bad impression.'

Ardilla Tognazzi stuffed 2,000 lire into his hand and told him to be quick.

'Thank you!' exclaimed Rinaldo. He was so grateful that he could have hugged her, but he wisely refrained.

That night, Rinaldo lay in his bed with his lucky coin clutched in his hand and his new second-hand clothes hanging on a hook on the wall by his side. Working as an errand boy for a brothel wasn't a job he'd ever envisaged, but at last now he had a secure income, decent clothes, a warm, dry bed and guaranteed food. Luck could come from unexpected directions, he thought.

Brothel life was an education for Rinaldo. At first he was embarrassed, but he quickly grew accustomed to the panting and grunting and the blasphemous cries of ecstasy. Sometimes he saw things which he would have preferred not to see, other times he glimpsed things which made no sense to him.

There were around twenty women working at Madama Gioconda's, all of whom lived on site. The Tognazzis prided themselves on being able to cater to most tastes – as long as those tastes fell within the parameters of the law.

Ardilla Tognazzi had rigorous standards when it came to her girls' appearances. Every morning before opening time, the women would be lined up in the kitchen for her inspection. Hair was checked for lice, teeth and fingernails were checked for cleanliness. Ardilla would also sniff the women to ensure that there was no trace of the previous day's sexual activity. If any was found, she would spray them copiously with an antiseptic cologne which smelled like a combination of alcohol, naphthalene and violets.

Kohl pencil, rouge and lipstick in copious quantities were obligatory. Rinaldo couldn't understand why the women were obliged to plaster themselves with so much make-up, and he was mystified as to why some of them shaved their eyebrows off and then drew them back on. He thought that most of them would have looked a lot prettier in their natural state. He was reminded of Fagiolino's wife, Brisabella, from the Burattini puppet shows.

Their attire was inspected too. Ardilla Tognazzi would buy cheap satins in bulk from the market and sell them on to the women for a modest profit. Most didn't own their own shoes, but instead would rent them from the brothel at a daily rate. Extra charges were sometimes applied for wear and tear, and always for damage.

Any bitching, bickering or behaviour which might disrupt the smooth running of the establishment was not tolerated. Although there was no question that Ardilla Tognazzi was in charge, she was happy to assign peace-keeping responsibilities to her most trusted girls, Fifi la Française and Carlotta.

The French girl, Fifi la Française, had not always been French. She had been born to Italian parents and had grown up just outside Reggio Emilia. Originally she had come to Bologna to make her fortune as an actress, but when that didn't happen, she had found work at Madama Gioconda's instead. Her acting skills were used in assuming a reasonably convincing French accent which was said to drive gentlemen wild with excitement. Nobody minded that her French vocabulary was limited to '*Oui, oui, Monsieur,*' and '*Oh là là!*'

Of all the ladies at Madama Gioconda's, Carlotta was the friendliest and most popular. She was a generously-upholstered creature – all hips and bosom and well-distributed flesh. It was not uncommon for Benito Tognazzi to visit Carlotta on Saturday afternoons when his wife was at the hairdresser's. Ardilla Tognazzi was well aware of it and it didn't bother her. She was a busy woman. She employed a charwoman to clean her house, a washerwoman to do her laundry and a gardener to keep the grounds in order. There was nothing wrong with delegating chores.

Then there was Esmeralda, a long-legged, green-eyed beauty with lustrous hair which fell like a black waterfall down her back. Something about her had caught Rinaldo's eye, but Esmeralda had ignored him, as she did most people. Esmeralda was more likely to greet her clients with a sneer than a smile. Whatever colour of ticket was presented to her she would give a resigned nod. She never spoke to the men who bought her services. Most women led their clients off by the hand, but not so Esmeralda. Sometimes Ardilla Tognazzi would reprimand her for dawdling and for not showing an adequate level of enthusiasm.

It was whilst Rinaldo was eating his lunch alone in the kitchen during his first week that Esmeralda came in. She closed the door behind her, lit a cigarette, then stopped and took a long look at him.

'There's plenty more in the pot,' said Rinaldo, not looking up from his lunch. 'It's still warm.'

'Thanks,' replied Esmeralda, then added, 'Scamorza. Is that your name?'

'As far as I know,' replied Rinaldo, fully expecting a quip about cheese.

'Rinaldo Scamorza?'

Rinaldo stopped eating and looked up. 'Yes.'

Esmeralda leaned across the table and looked straight at him, with her face close to his. It was a strong-featured, compellingly beautiful face. Suddenly Rinaldo recognised it from under the thick mask of make-up.

'My, how you've grown, little Aldino!' she murmured.

Rinaldo bounded from his seat as though he was on springs and threw his arms around Evelina, crushing her with a hug and clasping her so tightly that he almost choked them both. Then he almost cried. Evelina took his embrace stiffly, then pulled away.

It was ten years since Rinaldo had seen Evelina. The grown-up Evelina was very different to the child he had known before. Her expression was hard. Her green eyes were guarded. It looked as though a great deal of time had passed since she had last smiled. But Rinaldo was so overcome with joy that he felt his head spin and his temples pound. His heart beat so fast that he could feel his chest vibrating.

'Are you all right?' he asked.

Evelina shrugged. 'All right enough, I suppose.'

'What happened to you when you left Ada Stracci's?'

'I was sold,' replied Evelina in a slightly weary way.

'I know that. But who bought you?'

'Just some people,' she said matter-of-factly, and looked away.

'Where did they take you?'

'Different towns, different cities. I'm not really sure which ones. I must have lost my virginity five hundred times. It didn't take me long to realise that everything Ada Stracci had promised about fine clothes and money was a load of rubbish. The fine clothes and the money were for her. Then the war broke out and I ended up here. And here I am. Still alive, unlike Ada Stracci. I heard about the fire. I'm glad the old bitch roasted.'

You're welcome, thought Rinaldo, although he didn't say it out loud.

He had so many questions for Evelina, but before he could ask any more they were interrupted by Ardilla Tognazzi entering the kitchen.

'Esmeralda, get your arse back in the salon right now! Don't think I'm not counting your cigarette breaks. That's the fourth one today.'

Evelina rolled her eyes, tossed her unfinished cigarette into the sink and did as she was told. Ardilla Tognazzi turned to Rinaldo.

'Is that your second helping?' she asked sharply, narrowing her eyes and scrutinising the enormous pile of food on his plate.

'No, Signora Tognazzi,' replied Rinaldo politely, which was true as it was his third.

'You've got two minutes to finish your lunch, then I need you to go to the market for castor oil and a large aubergine.'

Rinaldo couldn't finish his lunch. He was too overcome with joy for having found Evelina. Yet his relief at finding her was overshadowed by the anger he felt for the way she had come to be at Madama Gioconda's. He thought that if he ever came across the vile virgin-mongers who had bought Evelina at the age of thirteen, or any other individual who dealt in young girls, he would send them the same way as Ada Stracci. Rinaldo held his breath to stifle the murderous impulse he felt. It was just as well for Gigio Lingua that he had ended up in jail. It was a lucky escape for him compared with the fate Rinaldo thought he deserved.

But there was no changing the past. At least now Evelina was safe and he knew where she was, and knowing that, he could help her get away.

He began to hatch a plan for a new life together, where they could look after each other like brother and sister, just as they had pledged to do as children. Rinaldo began doing sums in his head, thinking that they could both continue working at Madama Gioconda's for a time – he didn't know how long for – perhaps a year or so, less if they were really careful. He thought they could save up all their wages and they could leave, get a little home that they could share, find jobs they liked. It didn't necessarily need to be in Bologna. Perhaps they could go and start a new life in Milano Marittima, close to Evelina's family. Although he had never been out of Bologna, he'd seen pictures of the seaside and thought how nice it looked.

But it was difficult for Rinaldo to speak to Evelina in private as they both worked such long hours. Even when they managed to steal a few minutes, Evelina wasn't much given to conversation because invariably she was either tired, or had a headache, or a stomach ache. She was also cagey about others knowing their connection because she said people couldn't be trusted.

She certainly didn't want the Tognazzis to know. Fifi and Carlotta were aware, but that was all right because they knew when to keep their mouths shut. Rinaldo couldn't see what the problem was, but he respected Evelina's wishes.

Rinaldo passed his week's probationary period and found himself an official employee at Madama Gioconda's, having impressed the Tognazzis with his hard work and reliability. He was feeling energetic, well-fed and healthy. During the first few days it had felt as though the bicycle box had been filled with lead and rocks, even when it was empty, but now that muscles were popping up on his legs, fetching and carrying all the Tognazzis' provisions was becoming easier.

He struck up good relationships with shopkeepers, market traders and suppliers, and even moonlighted a little now and then, delivering things which weren't for the Tognazzis for a few extra lire, but very discreetly because he wasn't sure Ardilla Tognazzi would approve. He didn't want to get on the wrong side of her.

The working women liked him and were friendly. Some ribbed him for being a virgin, whilst others offered to unburden him of his virginity. Despite the offers, Rinaldo was not tempted to accept. In private the women ridiculed most of the men who bought their services. He didn't ever want to become one of those men.

They mocked the gouty old ones, the pimply young ones, the fat ones, the thin ones, the married ones who said their wives didn't understand them, the mummy's boys and the ones who thought they were God's gift to the fairer sex but couldn't find their way around a woman's body if you gave them a map. Sarcastic remarks, humiliating jibes and disparaging assertions of their virility abounded.

Evelina never joined in with these conversations. She didn't seem to see the funny side to any encounter.

Rinaldo suggested to Evelina that they could go out into town on Sunday when Madama Gioconda's was closed. They could look around the places they used to visit as children and he could tell her about his plan, but Evelina refused to go.

It was unusual for any of the women to leave the premises, so on Sundays they would congregate in the salon to chat and pass away the time. If it had been a good week, the Tognazzis would provide a tray of pastries for them.

Fifi would often entertain her fellow workers by reading magazines and the past week's newspapers out loud.

'Listen to this!' she said, without her French accent. 'Senator Lina Merlin's on a mission to close all brothels down.'

Carlotta was plucking the hair from her big toes and immediately put down her tweezers.

'Close us down?' she scoffed. 'Like we haven't heard that before. Unless men stop wanting to get their legs over, they'll never close us down.'

'It's serious this time,' continued Fifi. 'She's getting a petition signed by other senators.'

'Hah! I'd bet my fanny most of those senators spend more time in brothels than in the senate,' said Carlotta.

'Carlotta's right,' said one of the other women. 'You should see the punters in some of the bordellos in Rome. Those places stink so bad of power and money you can hardly breathe in there.'

Carlotta shook her head and resumed plucking, then looked up again and said scornfully: 'Anyway, what does someone like Senator Lina Merlin know about women like us? She's just some rich do-gooder. What does she suggest we do if they close the brothels? Who'd give us jobs? The men who fuck us wouldn't even employ us to scrub their floors. We can't walk down a street without getting abused or spat at.'

Undeterred, Fifi continued reading.

'It says here she's talking about prostitution not being a crime, but its exploitation being a crime.'

'What? What does that mean?'

'It means we could still work, just not in brothels, and anyone making money off us would be breaking the law.'

Carlotta laughed like a clucking hen and shook her head again.

'So she'd turn people like the Tognazzis into criminals and us all into street-walkers? How does that improve anything? At least in here we've got a roof over our heads, food in our bellies, the government protects us and we're relatively safe.'

Another of the women nodded in agreement and chipped in with, 'Carlotta's got a point. Those two street girls who were killed near the station last month didn't even make the news.'

'And what about health checks?' continued Carlotta. 'We get checked and our health cards get signed off every other month. Street girls don't. There's already so much clap and tuberculosis amongst the street girls that there'd be a country-wide epidemic within a month. I might be uneducated, but I'm not stupid. Merlin's educated and stupid.'

Evelina said nothing and didn't seem to be listening. She just sat, mute and distant, blowing smoke rings and picking at her bitten fingernails. She seemed utterly detached from everything.

'I might write to Senator Lina Merlin,' said Fifi. 'It says here that hundreds of women have already written to her asking for help and explaining how things could be improved.'

'You go ahead and write to her – and good luck to you if the Tognazzis find out. You're wasting your time. This will all blow over and nothing will change,' stated Carlotta, turning her attention back to her toes.

*

Rinaldo had hoped to be paid weekly, but Benito Tognazzi informed him that the accounts and wages were worked out monthly. Nevertheless, Benito Tognazzi had been so pleased with Rinaldo that as his second week drew to a close, he took him aside.

'You've done well, Cheese-boy,' he said, patting his shoulder. 'You've earned a bonus.'

'Thank you, Signor Tognazzi,' replied Rinaldo, thinking that a little bonus would be very handy as he was in need of a razor. Perhaps it was owing to the fact that he had been well-nourished that whiskers were finally beginning to make an appearance on his upper lip.

'I know who you've got your randy little eyes on,' smirked Benito Tognazzi. 'Hey, Esmeralda, come here! Give young Cheese-boy his bonus.' He glanced down at his enormous gold wristwatch and added, 'Hand-relief only. Ten minutes – no longer. It's twenty past now. I want you done by half past.'

Rather than giving the customary resigned nod reserved for her clients, Evelina looked awkward. Nevertheless, she did as Benito Tognazzi asked and led a horrified Rinaldo into one of the rooms.

'How old are you now, Aldino? Nineteen?'

'Yes.'

'Is it really true you've never done it?'

'Yes.'

'Is it what you want?'

'No!' exclaimed Rinaldo, backing away. 'It's *not* what I want. And definitely not with you. You're my sister!'

Evelina lit a cigarette, took a long, thoughtful drag and said, 'You'll never hear the end of it if Tognazzi thinks you haven't had a go. And nor will I.'

'Can't we just pretend then?'

Evelina giggled and for an instant the hardness melted and

Rinaldo saw a glimmer of the old Evelina. For the briefest moment they were children again, Aldino Fagiolino and Evelina Sganapina, plotting, scheming and conspiring against the world.

'You'll have to make a bit of a noise, so pant like you've just run up the stairs,' she whispered. 'As it's your first time a minute will be enough. In fact, a minute would be quite impressive. And on my signal make it sound like you're being strangled.'

Rinaldo made appropriate noises, trying not to laugh, just in case Benito Tognazzi was listening at the door, as it was something he liked to do sometimes. Once the charade was over, Evelina lay back and took the last few drags of her cigarette, blowing the smoke out through her nose and laughed. 'I wish it was always as easy as that.'

But then her good humour vanished, she withdrew back into her own head and her habitual expression, which was something between indifference and bitterness, returned. Rinaldo could feel that she wanted to be alone, to have just a few moments away from everybody, even him.

'I'm dead tired,' she sighed, stretching and rubbing her back, 'and every bit of me aches. It's like someone's taken a mallet to my kidneys.' She yawned and stubbed out her cigarette on the bedpost. 'You'd better go, Aldino. I'm going to bag this bed for the night and I'm sharing with Fifi. I've had to share with Carlotta the last few nights and she snores. I need my sleep as there's a group of apprentices from the sock factory coming first thing tomorrow morning.'

But the next morning Evelina didn't make an appearance in the salon, and when clients asked for her they were informed that she was unavailable. Carlotta told Rinaldo that Evelina was unwell and that she was up in the infirmary.

Legislation concerning the women's health was strict. An establishment's reputation could be tarnished by an outbreak of something contagious. The Tognazzis had been forced to close for a whole week in 1932 owing to an outbreak of pubic lice – although at the time they had claimed that it was gastric influenza – a claim which they continued to maintain.

The infirmary was a small room in the attic where any girl considered to be an infection risk of any kind would be quarantined until she was better. Rinaldo found Evelina sitting on a little narrow bed with her chin on her knees, taking long, hard drags of a cigarette and aiming smoke rings out of the window. She glanced up as he came in, but didn't seem pleased to see him. The look she gave him was more one of annoyance, as though his arrival had interrupted something important.

'Are you unwell? I can go and get you medicine from the pharmacy if you need me to.'

Evelina shrugged and said, 'There's no medicine to cure me. I'm just having one of those days.'

'What do you mean?'

Evelina blew a smoke ring, followed by a smaller one which tucked itself neatly inside the first, then stared towards the window with an inexpressive gaze.

'Just one of those days when I don't want to be here,' she sighed. 'So Ardilla sent me up here because she says I create a bad atmosphere when I'm like this.'

'That's good of Ardilla.'

Evelina made a spitting sound and swore in dialect.

'Good of Ardilla?' she snapped, then swore again. 'There's nothing good about Ardilla Tognazzi. She's a mean bitch. Being up here isn't a free pass. I'll have to make up for the lost time plus some more. And Ardilla will do her best to give me the worst punters when I go back down, just to teach me a lesson. She'll give me the ones with sewer breath. And then tonight she'll make me collect up and wash the spit bowls from the suck and spit room.'

She spoke with such contempt that Rinaldo couldn't think of anything to say which might be helpful, or which might console her. He just sat down at the foot of the bed and watched the smoke rings dissolve. Evelina stubbed her cigarette into a coffee cup which was already overflowing with spent butts and immediately lit another one, then offered the packet to Rinaldo, but he declined. Cigarettes set his teeth on edge.

'It's good you don't smoke,' she said. 'It's bad for you.'

'Why do you do it then?'

'Because I don't care and I can't stop.' Evelina turned her gaze back towards the window and continued with, 'You don't understand, do you, Aldino? I'm not like the other girls here. I'm not like Carlotta. She's always smiling and joking and everybody loves her. Benito Tognazzi buys her things all the time and even takes her out some Sundays in his car. And I'm not like Fifi either. She's clever. She keeps her punters talking. Sometimes she doesn't even need to take her knickers off. But I can't do that. I hate them all and that's why I don't ever talk to them.'

She blew two streams of smoke out hard through her nostrils and looked down at her cigarette, which she had buckled between her fingers. She tossed it onto the windowsill and watched as it smouldered a little black burn mark on the paint, then squashed the glowing end with her thumb. She seemed to be gleaning some sort of satisfaction from the pain of the burn. When she spoke again, it was with undisguised self-loathing.

'Doesn't it disgust you that I'm a whore?'

Rinaldo was taken aback by the abruptness of the question and the harsh tone of Evelina's voice.

'No, of course I'm not disgusted. I'm just worried about you,' he replied soothingly, which was true, but rather than placating Evelina, his answer seemed to provoke her. The pitch of her voice rose, and as if to shock him, or to underline the hatred that she felt for herself which she wanted him to feel too, she began to describe, in graphic detail, all the *services* that she was made to provide.

These were not the mocking, sarcastic accounts he had heard exchanged between the other women. Evelina spat her words out viciously.

'All it takes is a few lire to buy me. What do you reckon I'm worth, Rinaldo? Twenty pink tickets a day? Ten green ones? Sometimes I feel I'm just one of those tickets – paid for, then torn up and thrown away. *Men* don't think about that. *Men* think about nothing but fucking and don't care how or who it's with. All *men* want is a place to stick their dick.'

Men – every time she said the word a look of utter contempt flashed in her eyes. She glared at Rinaldo. Maybe it was a warning not to become one of them, or the suspicion that he was already, or would become one simply by the nature of his biology.

Then she turned her vitriol towards the Tognazzis. With all that money, they pretended to be oh-so-respectable – all airs and graces, gold jewellery, gold teeth, fine clothes, flash cars. What had they ever done to earn it? Benito Tognazzi had never had to sell his hairy arse. The last time Ardilla Tognazzi had had to spread her legs was to push out that mongrel daughter of theirs. The Tognazzis were scum. She called them 'cunt-peddlers'.

Rinaldo sat and listened without interrupting, overwhelmed by the venom of Evelina's words. He feared that if he said one wrong word she might jump from the window. Eventually, when she stopped, breathless with hatred, he spoke as softly and calmly as he could.

'Why don't you leave? You don't have to live this life, Evelina.'

'Leave? Leave and do what? You heard what Carlotta said. We can't even walk down the street minding our own business without getting shouted at, or worse. What sort of life do you think a girl like me is going to have? I've been ridden by half the city.'

'You could go somewhere new where nobody knows you. Start a completely new life.'

'How? I'd need money for that.'

'But you earn money here.'

Evelina stared at him in bewilderment, astonished by his stupidity, and gave a scornful laugh.

'Oh Aldino, you're a sweet boy, but so naïve! Do you think the money I make here goes into my pocket? Once the Tognazzis have taken their cut, charged me for use of the rooms, washing sheets, towels, food, toiletries, cigarettes and the rest, there's nothing left. In fact, most of the time there's less than nothing left. Unless I've turned at least twenty tricks a day every single day I end up in debt. I've been in debt since I got here and it keeps on growing. I wouldn't even have a decent set of clothes to leave in, or a pair of shoes of my own. I have nothing. What am I going to do, leave here in stockings and rented heels with my bare arse showing, walk into some nice dress shop and ask for a job?'

'I'll do it then. I'll get some money together for you. I just need a few weeks—' but Evelina didn't want to listen to his plan. She cut him off with, 'Go, Aldino. I want to be alone. Forget everything I've said,' and made a gesture which was something between a wave good-bye and a signal of dismissal, then leaned back against the wall and closed her eyes as though he was already gone.

But Rinaldo couldn't forget anything. Evelina's words were stamped into his mind. He had to get her away from Madama Gioconda's – and quickly.

CHAPTER 9

The pawnbroker inspected Rinaldo's lucky coin under a magnifying glass.

'It's a Roman Denarius,' he said. 'See here where you can make out the letters *TI*? That's the Emperor Tiberius. It's Tiberius' head on the front and his mother, Livia, is on the back.'

'How old is it?'

'About two thousand years, give or take.'

Rinaldo had expected the coin to be old, but not that old.

'What's it worth?' he asked eagerly.

The pawnbroker shook his head and said, 'Not a lot. Coins like this are quite common and I've seen others in much better condition. Some people do collect them and it's got a value to the right collector, probably enough to get yourself a new necktie, but don't go making any plans to buy a palazzo in the centre of the town.'

The coin wasn't worth pawning, or selling, so reluctantly Rinaldo took out the emerald earring instead.

'Ah, now that's a lovely piece,' said the pawnbroker, biting the gold to check its purity. 'But there's only one. Obviously if it was a pair I'd give you more. You'd be better off taking it to a jeweller who'd remove the stone and melt the gold down.'

Rinaldo knew that, but the whole point of pawning the earring was that he intended to buy it back. It would take two months' wages and a bit more, but it was the only way he could think of to find money for Evelina quickly.

With the money from the pawned earring in his pocket he headed to a tailor's in the centre of town. He waited until the tailor was in the back room with a customer, leaving a doltish shop-boy in charge. It was time to enlist Zappatelli's help again.

'I've come to fetch Signora Zappatelli's garments,' announced Rinaldo in a tone which indicated that the matter was urgent.

The boy knitted his brows with such concentration that they met over the bridge of his nose. He thought very hard and echoed the word in syllables. 'Zap-pa-tel-li?'

'Yes,' confirmed Rinaldo impatiently. 'Signora Zappatelli has sent me and she's in a hurry. She's due to leave for her holiday villa in Milano Marittima within the hour.'

The boy began to look through the garments on the rail behind the counter, taking a very long time to read each label.

'Zappatelli?' he asked again. 'Zappatelli with a "z"?'

'Of course,' replied Rinaldo. 'How else would you spell it?'

The boy kept looking.

'With a double "p"?'

'Yes. And a double "l". Now please hurry or Signora Zappatelli will miss her train for Milano Marittima.'

The boy had come to the end of the rail of clothes.

'I'll have to go and ask the boss,' he said, although he didn't seem too keen on the prospect.

'Would it be easier if I looked?' suggested Rinaldo with an irritated tut. 'I'll recognise the garments.'

'Oh, if you wouldn't mind. The boss doesn't like being disturbed when he's measuring a client and I've been in enough trouble already this week.'

Rinaldo made his way behind the counter and picked out a skirt, a blouse and a jacket which was a rather nice match for both.

'Signora Zappatelli says she'll send the maid to settle the account before the end of the week,' he told the lad.

The shop-boy thanked him enthusiastically for his help as he left. Rinaldo hoped he hadn't cost him his job and pledged to make it up to him some day.

'What's this?' Evelina asked as Rinaldo handed her the bundle of garments.

'Clothes that you can leave in. And some money. You can start a new life somewhere else.'

'Where did you get this money?'

'I pawned the emerald earring.'

'Your mother's earring? No, Aldino, you can't do that! I can't take this money!'

'Too late – it's done. But I'll get it back.'

'How?'

'When I'm paid, so don't worry about it. Just leave town. Find somewhere to live and find a job.'

At first Evelina seemed angry. She paced across the room and stood at the window with her back to him, but when at last she turned, Rinaldo saw it was not anger, but fear.

'You must tell no one what you've done,' she said under her breath. 'The Tognazzis will kill you if they find out. And what about you?'

'I don't have the life you have, Evelina. I can leave whenever I want.'

'I'll go to Milano Marittima. Maybe my mother's family, or someone who knew my mother will take me in and help me get settled.'

Still, there was fear in Evelina's eyes.

'Come with me, Aldino,' she pleaded, grabbing Rinaldo's hands. 'I'm too afraid to go by myself.'

For the briefest moment Rinaldo thought he would, but he couldn't leave the earring with the pawnbroker. He couldn't leave before he had bought it back.

'I will come, just not straight away. I have things to do here.'

Evelina nodded, although she still seemed uncertain.

'I'll send for you,' she said finally. 'As soon as I'm settled I'll let you know where I am.'

Two days later, Evelina was gone.

The Tognazzis were furious. Evelina was one of their better earners, despite her unfriendly attitude. A lot of men preferred women who didn't waste time talking. They didn't have another girl with legs as good as hers either. And she had left taking with her a pair of nearly-new shoes, the audacity of which had particularly incensed Ardilla.

'Did she say anything to you, Cheese-boy?' demanded Benito Tognazzi, cornering Rinaldo in the kitchen and jabbing an accusatory finger at his chest.

'No, Signor Tognazzi.'

The man scowled and eyed Rinaldo suspiciously.

'I saw you two looking a bit chummy if you ask me,' he growled, baring his fake teeth. 'You're sure she didn't tell you she was going to leave, or where she was going?'

Rinaldo shrugged. 'She didn't say a thing, Signor Tognazzi.'

'Well, she won't get far. It won't surprise me if she begs to come back,' he grunted. 'Once a whore, always a whore. You can't change 'em, the stupid bitches.'

Rinaldo's fists were clenched in his pockets. It took all his self-control not to remove one and knock Benito Tognazzi out with it.

That evening as Rinaldo was getting into bed Carlotta and Fifi came to find him in the basement, demanding to know where Evelina had gone. They didn't ask whether he had anything to do with her disappearance; they knew without having to be told. Their furious painted faces loomed so menacingly in the semi-darkness that despite Rinaldo's protests, eventually he confessed.

'You've sent her somewhere she's never been, to try to find people whose names she doesn't even know, in the hope that they'll take her in? Rinaldo, how could you be so stupid?' Fifi exploded. 'That poor girl's got no idea how to look after herself in the outside world. She wouldn't know that she was being tricked if someone charged her 1,000 lire for a glass of water! Don't you know what kinds of people are out there, Rinaldo? There are people who can smell a helpless girl coming a mile off.'

'You didn't see her when she first came here,' added Carlotta. 'The Tognazzis took her in out of pity. When Evelina got here she was a mess. She wouldn't eat, she wouldn't even speak. The Tognazzis might be money-grabbing pigs, but as money-grabbing pigs go, they're decent ones. They looked after her until she was fit to work. Evelina would have died in the gutter if they hadn't helped her.'

Fifi was looking at Rinaldo and shaking her head. Rinaldo was staring at his feet.

'We've put the word out that if she's found working on the streets she's to be brought straight back here,' said Fifi. 'If there's one little bit of hope in all of this it's that the Tognazzis have still got her documents. She won't get far without those.'

As they were leaving, Fifi turned and added, 'If anything happens to Evelina, on your head be it, Rinaldo.'

Rinaldo didn't need to be told. He was well aware of that.

*

When at last pay day came, Ardilla Tognazzi handed Rinaldo an envelope. He knew it would not be enough to buy back the earring, but he planned to leave it with the pawnbroker as a deposit. The pawnbroker was a reasonable fellow. But when Rinaldo opened his envelope it contained a fraction of the pay that he had been expecting.

'Where's the rest of my money?' he demanded. 'I've been working fifteen- and sixteen-hour days six days a week for a month.'

'Yes. And you've been eating like a buffalo and using a bed, not to mention the facilities. That money's your pay minus your food and board,' replied Ardilla Tognazzi.

'And what's this? You gave me 2,000 lire for clothes and you've deducted 3,000 lire from my wages!'

When Ardilla explained why, Rinaldo learned a new term – *Interest.*

Clearly Ardilla Tognazzi cared nothing for Rinaldo's complaints. She waved him away like a bothersome insect, saying, 'That's the way things work here. If it's not good enough for you, go elsewhere. I can find another errand boy in less time than you need to take a shit.'

Rinaldo could have left. He could have tried to seek less exploitative employers, but on balance he considered that what the Tognazzis offered in food and lodgings was the best that he could do at the time. In any case, he needed to be somewhere where Evelina could find him. He hoped that despite Fifi and Carlotta's misgivings, it wouldn't be long before she sent for him. The Tognazzis took his lack of protest as a sign of weakness and increased their demands upon him.

*

There was no word from Evelina during the month which followed her escape. Two months passed. Three months passed, then four, then five, then six. Rinaldo grew increasingly concerned. Fifi and Carlotta were still very angry with him.

Rinaldo fluctuated between acute anxiety and tentative optimism. Sometimes he was so consumed with worry for his friend's safety that he couldn't think straight. Other times he tried to convince himself that the fact that Evelina hadn't come back, or been brought back, was a good sign. He wondered whether perhaps she had sent word of her whereabouts, but her letter, or letters, had been intercepted by the Tognazzis. The postman always handed the mail directly to Ardilla.

When Rinaldo asked the postman whether anything had arrived addressed to him, the man had said no, but Rinaldo doubted whether he could trust him. Ardilla Tognazzi gave the postman pink tickets at half price, so the boy knew where the fellow's loyalties lay.

Aside from grave concern about Evelina's safety, Rinaldo fretted that he would not be able to buy back the emerald earring. The brothel provided limitless easy opportunities to steal. Rinaldo lost count of the number of wallets left in coats whilst clients were far too occupied to notice. But however tempting, he left each wallet, watch and any other valuable untouched for he knew that if a theft was reported, suspicion would fall first upon the women, and he didn't want to cause them any trouble. He needed to come up with another plan.

The Tognazzis did not live on-site and none of the women knew where exactly they lived, not even Fifi and Carlotta. Rinaldo made discreet enquiries, but to no avail. He decided that he would find out, but it was easier said than done as he was so busy. He followed Ardilla Tognazzi whenever he could, but she didn't go home. He had ended up following her several times to the milliner's, twice to the perfumery and once to the chiropodist's. Following Benito Tognazzi was even harder as he had a motorcar and never seemed to drive off in the same direction. Trying to keep up with a car on a three-wheeled bicycle was impossible.

In the end, it was the Tognazzis' daughter who led him to a stylish townhouse in Via Audinot. It took a while as she moved so slowly, went by a circuitous route and often stopped to talk to pigeons. She looked over her shoulder on more than one occasion, but she didn't spot Rinaldo on his bicycle. She probably wouldn't have noticed if a herd of trumpeting elephants had been pursuing her.

Via Audinot was only a fifteen-minute walk from Via del Pratello, but it was a very different kind of road. It was situated outside the old city walls in a well-to-do residential district of broad, tree-lined avenues and large private houses.

The Tognazzis' home was a pink Liberty-style house with a turret and little blue tiles set into its frontage. It had an ornamental garden and a fishpond. A gardener was busy raking paths and clipping shrubs.

Once he knew its location, Rinaldo returned to the Tognazzis' house whenever he could, but gaining access was problematic. Sometimes the gardener was there. A charwoman came to clean three mornings each week. When the house was empty, it was securely locked. Rinaldo knew better than to break in and risk attracting attention. He'd learned that lesson with Manolunga at the warehouse.

He concluded that if he was to gain access it would be easiest when the daughter was there. The Tognazzis' daughter went home every day after lunch, at around 2 p.m. From the safety of the garden shrubbery, Rinaldo would watch her. She would eat a second lunch, usually biscuits and milk, then she would go to the sitting room and take a nap on the couch.

Rinaldo peered in through the sitting-room window. The room was lavishly furnished, but silk-covered couches and crystal chandeliers were useless to him. His attention was focused on a huge carved credenza which displayed a vast collection of silverware. Rinaldo waited many times, hoping the girl would forget to lock the door before her nap, but she never did. He needed to come up with some way of distracting the Tognazzi's daughter, preferably some way of making her go upstairs.

As he crouched in the shrubbery, considering what to do, something scurried past his foot, spooking him and almost making him blow his own cover.

'Damned mouse!' he muttered, settling himself again. Then

he paused. *Mouse!* Suddenly, he had an idea. He slipped out of the Tognazzi's garden and made his way back to Via del Pratello.

There was a rat-catcher by the name of Nando – a red-eyed fellow who had trouble breathing. He had quarters just around the corner from Madama Gioconda's in a dark, filthy space with a low vaulted ceiling hung with traps. At the back was a big cage of live rats ready to be released into the neighbourhood if business was slow.

As he entered, Rinaldo was almost asphyxiated by a thick miasma of ammonia and the stench of decomposing rats.

'Could I have a rat?' he asked, covering his mouth with his sleeve. 'A live one?'

Nando coughed, wheezed and cleared his throat. 'What d'you want one for?'

'As a pet.'

'As a *pet*?' Nando squinted mistrustfully through the dimness. His face seemed unable to twist itself into a pleasant expression.

'Yes. I'm told they can be trained to be very affectionate.'

Nando coughed and spat a glob of green phlegm onto the floor which just missed Rinaldo's foot.

'You got money?' he said, rubbing his thumb and forefinger together.

'You want me to *buy* it? They're vermin. I know you throw them into the river.'

'Well, you want one, so it's got a value.' Nando came closer, scrutinising Rinaldo's face.

'What's it worth to you?'

Rinaldo had no money in his pockets, but he did have almost half a packet of *Nazionali* cigarettes which he had found outside Madama Gioconda's. He had been intending to give it to the women on Sunday.

'This is all I've got,' he said. 'Surely it's worth a rat?'

Nando thought about it and scratched his chin.

‘Are they real *Nazionali*?’

‘As far as I know.’

‘Give ’em here. Let’s have a look.’

The old rat-catcher took the cigarettes and inspected each one in turn, assessing its length and its weight, then smelling it to ensure he was not being offered cigarettes which had been cut down, or rolled with sawdust instead of tobacco.

‘That’ll do,’ he said and beckoned Rinaldo over to the cage. It was writhing with rats.

‘I’d like a female, please. A pregnant one.’

‘She’ll have a lot of pups,’ rasped Nando.

‘Then I’ll have a whole family of pets!’ grinned Rinaldo.

Nando looked at him as though he was mad, then reached into the cage, pulled out a rat and held it up by its tail.

‘This one’s full. Fit to burst. So I’m not just selling you one rat, I could be selling you up to a dozen. That’ll be extra.’

‘I only have the cigarettes to give you.’

‘Then you can’t have this one.’

Rinaldo rummaged in his pockets again and found a book of matches.

‘How about I add these matches to the cigarettes?’

‘Not damp, are they?’

‘They shouldn’t be. They’ve been in my pocket and my jacket hasn’t got wet.’

‘How many are there?’

‘Eighteen left out of twenty-four.’

‘Strike one so I can see they’re still good.’

‘But then there’ll only be seventeen left. You’re not going to make a fuss about that, are you?’

Rinaldo struck a match and it seemed to meet with Nando’s approval. The deal was sealed.

‘How long before she has her pups?’ asked Rinaldo as Nando stuffed the rat into a bag.

'She's a few days off. Three or four, I'd say.'

Having the rat made Rinaldo uneasy. He didn't want to keep her in his basement room, so he put her in a wooden crate in the yard, which he lined with rags, and fed her bread and kitchen scraps. He named her Ardilla in honour of Ardilla Tognazzi. But time was ticking. He could see the pups wriggling in her swollen belly and he didn't want to be stuck with a crate of rats.

It was a Tuesday, which Rinaldo knew should mean no gardener and no charwoman at the Tognazzis. He undertook his duties quickly that morning, then made off towards Via Audinot with Ardilla the rat tucked into a bag in the front box of his bicycle. She was making a lot of noise. Rinaldo hoped she would keep hold of her pups long enough for him to execute his plan.

The Tognazzis' daughter lumbered home at the usual time, let herself in and sat in the kitchen eating biscuits and drinking milk. She had locked the door as she always did, but the window was ajar. As soon as Rinaldo released Ardilla the rat onto the windowsill, the creature shot inside. The almost instant screech, followed by the clatter of a chair falling onto its back and the slamming of the door let him know that the Tognazzis' daughter had seen the rat.

He climbed in through the window. Ardilla the rat had gone straight for the biscuits on the table and was gorging on them. The Tognazzis' daughter could be heard screaming from upstairs.

Rinaldo headed for the sitting room and stuffed two sacks with silverware from the credenza – dishes, platters, candelabras, a very heavy coffee set on a tray, a collection of fancy cigarette cases and snuff boxes. There were also a dozen silver bowls, all shaped like different sea shells and filled with sweets. Rinaldo slipped the bowls into his sack and stuffed the sweets into his pockets.

He then noticed that Benito Tognazzi had been kind enough

to leave his enormous gold wristwatch on a side-table. It would have been rude to refuse such a generous donation, so Rinaldo took that too. It weighed as much as a bag of flour.

He concluded his business in under a minute and left through the kitchen window, wishing Ardilla the rat well in her new home. The box on the front of his bicycle was so crammed with silver that he could barely close the lid.

Rinaldo knew that disappearing straight after the theft would put him under suspicion, so he carried on with his errand-boy duties normally for several more weeks. He stashed the silver in the disused cellar where he had slept before moving into Madama Gioconda's.

The Tognazzis had been in a highly agitated state ever since the burglary. Benito Tognazzi had been absent for several days, overseeing the fitting of bars to the windows of his house. Ardilla Tognazzi sent Rinaldo out to buy rat poison, but as he couldn't bear the thought of Ardilla the rat and her litter being poisoned, he replaced the lethal white powder with flour and salt. He knew the swap was unlikely to be discovered as nobody would be crazy enough to taste it.

News spread about the burglary at the Tognazzi residence, so trying to sell or pawn his loot locally was too risky. However, Rinaldo had heard of a fellow who lived in another part of town, a shady silversmith called Ringhiera who asked no questions. When things had settled a little, he went to seek him out. Rinaldo found himself face-to-face with a man of an alarming colour. Years of smelting silver had turned Ringhiera's skin mauve. Even the whites of his eyes were mauve.

The fellow laid out the Tognazzis' silverware before him.

'Nice pieces,' he said, exposing his purple gums and making an appreciative whistling sound through his teeth. 'These aren't cheap trinkets. Seems a shame to melt them, but I'm guessing you'd rather they disappeared.'

'Probably best,' replied Rinaldo.

'When I melt them down you can have a third of the silver, or the equivalent value in cash, minus ten percent for the exchange.'

After a modest amount of haggling, it was agreed that the silver would be halved and Rinaldo would take the cash with only a five percent commission.

'All right then,' said Ringhiera. 'Meet me tomorrow night at the sports bar by Porta San Donato and I'll have your money for you. And once we're done we both agree we've never met.'

Ringhiera was true to his word and although he didn't show it, Rinaldo was astonished at the amount of money which was passed to him. The very next day he went to buy back the emerald earring from the pawnbroker and still had a large amount of cash to spare.

He never returned to work for the Tognazzis at Madama Gioconda's, but he kept the three-wheeled bicycle.

CHAPTER 10

It was mid-February when Rinaldo took the train to Milano Marittima. But instead of the idyllic seaside resort he had imagined it to be, he found a small, grim, closed town. There were no tourists, just locals going about their out-of-season business. It was hard to imagine it as a place where anybody would want to spend a holiday.

Rinaldo called in at every bar and shop which was open with the same question.

'I'm looking for my sister. Her name's Evelina Brunelli. She's twenty-four years old. Quite tall. Long black hair. Have you seen her?'

The answer was always the same.

'No.'

'Do you know anyone called Brunelli?'

'No.'

Once he had exhausted the shops and the bars, he began stopping people in the street, but the answer was no different.

Rinaldo scoured every part of town, passing lines of locked-up holiday villas, hotels and boarding houses. The promenade was deserted. All the little ice-cream and novelty kiosks were boarded up. There were boats with pedals, like bicycles, as Evelina had described. They were stacked up under makeshift shelters and tarpaulins, all bound with lengths of chain and padlocked.

Rinaldo had never seen the sea before and he didn't think much of it. He had expected it to be blue, like on postcards, but instead it was a dull, dirty grey. It stretched out before him, rolling and foaming. The sharp, stinging wind whipped the waves into white-crested curls and made his nose run. Rinaldo hunched into the fur collar of his camel overcoat and thrust his hands deep into his pockets, but he was still cold. When the wind slapped his hat off his head, he chased it down the promenade, but a second gust caught it and blew it into the sea. Rinaldo stood amongst the fluttering litter watching helplessly as his precious fedora hat with the purple lining bobbed away.

The parks full of pine trees of which Evelina had spoken were dark, even during the day. Rinaldo sat on a bench which was scarred with graffiti – mainly lovers' names – some encircled in crude heart shapes, some crossed out. He scratched his own name into the seat hoping that Evelina might find herself sitting there. She would read his name and she would know that he had come here to look for her.

After a fruitless three-day search Rinaldo took the train back to Bologna, but it was a painful journey, wracked with worry and guilt. He could sense that something bad had happened to Evelina. Why had he let her leave alone? Why hadn't he listened when she'd said she was too scared to go by herself? Why had he put more importance on buying back that damned earring than ensuring her safety?

He had lost Evelina again, and this time it really was his fault.

*

The fact was that Evelina had not made it to Milano Marittima. She could read a little, but not well. Ada Stracci had thought it unnecessary that she should learn. The arrival and departure boards at the station had baffled her – so many letters, so many numbers, and always changing. She had been too afraid to ask for help in case somebody recognised her and word got back to the Tognazzis.

She had misunderstood the notice on the platform and the

train she boarded was not bound for Milano Marittima, but for Milan. The place names were similar, but the places were very different. When she finally got off the train, Evelina found herself in a run-down, densely-populated part of the big city.

She hadn't known who to talk to, or whom to trust. Men had howled and whistled at her and made comments which were both obscene and flattering. Women's gazes had followed her with a look of loathing in their eyes. They had pulled their children out of the way, as though even glancing at her might in some way infect them with her filth and immorality. How did they know? she wondered. How did they know what she was? She might as well have had her profession stamped on her forehead.

When two thugs had dragged her into an alleyway and ripped at her good clothes she'd given them both what they wanted because they'd threatened to cut her face if she didn't. Soon after this incident, a woman who had shown her apparent kindness had stolen the last of the money Rinaldo had given her and then made off with her shoes.

Evelina thought about trying to stow away on a train to get back to Bologna, but she couldn't face Rinaldo. In the space of three days she had lost all his money and so he would never get his precious emerald earring back. Surely he would never forgive her. Finding herself penniless, hungry and barefoot, she knocked at the door of the first brothel she found and went back to doing the only thing she knew.

The proprietor couldn't believe his luck when Evelina came begging to be taken in. She appeared at his door looking as though she'd been living on the streets, but it wasn't difficult to see that there was something special under the dirty clothes and dishevelled hair. What a beauty! The girl could have been in the movies. She was enough to empty any man's wallet.

The proprietor had been in the trade for long enough to know

Evelina's type. She was the sort of girl who couldn't look after herself in normal society and developed a dependency on being confined. She was perfect brothel-fodder. Life would be so much easier if all girls were like that.

He summoned a doctor, who checked Evelina for tuberculosis and venereal diseases and inspected her teeth. The doctor declared that Evelina was clean, so they both tried her out personally and concluded that she was a little surly, but experienced. In the right hands, the girl could be a gold mine. The proprietor put her to work immediately.

At first Evelina was relieved to be back within the confines of a brothel. The brief time she had spent fending for herself had been a frightening ordeal, but the relief wore off very quickly. Evelina hated the new brothel. It wasn't run well, like Madama Gioconda's. It was a cheap-end grimy place and the beds stank. The other women resented her looks and were spiteful towards her. As for the clients, they were the kind of men who didn't mind stinking beds, or stinking girls for that matter. There was no proper bathroom, just a sink in the corner of Evelina's room. The hot tap didn't work. The cold tap dribbled rusty water. There was never any soap.

The proprietor was unfussy about the calibre of clientele he allowed into his establishment. As long as they had money it didn't matter how unsavoury they were. Unlike at Madama Gioconda's, there was no communal salon or ticket system. Men were sent directly to the rooms.

Evelina's room smelled as though something had died under the floorboards. The window could be opened, but the shutters had been nailed shut. Everything was peeling, grubby and stained. Even after their fortnightly wash, the sheets felt greasy.

The use of prophylactics was not enforced, as it had been at Madama Gioconda's. Sometimes Evelina worried that she would go the same way as her mother; at other times she prayed for it. Why, oh why, had she listened to Rinaldo? She should have known better than to go along with his hare-brained plan. Her escape from Madama Gioconda's was as stupid and ill-thought-through as when they had run away to the Giardini Margherita together as children.

Evelina was aware of always feeling sad. Even on good days she felt it like a heaviness in her head. When it was really bad, that heaviness overcame her body, sometimes to the point where she couldn't move. But over the years at Madama Gioconda's it had become manageable. Carlotta and Fifi had always looked out for her. They had been there to pick her up when it all became too much. Even Ardilla Tognazzi, for all her many faults, had understood that sometimes life overwhelmed her.

In the new brothel there were no good days – just bad ones and worse ones. Evelina woke every morning in a state of paralysis and feeling more tired than when she had gone to sleep. Sometimes the surge of sadness came the moment she opened her eyes; other times it took a little longer, but it always came. There were days when she would question whether she was actually alive, and usually she would be disappointed to find that she was. She often held her breath for a long time, hoping that her heart would stop, but it never worked. Starving took too long – she'd been trying that for years. Once she'd tried drinking bleach to make everything go away, but she hadn't been able to keep it down and her stomach had never been quite right since.

Evelina knew that she was somewhere in Milan. She had heard of Milan, but she didn't know how far away it was from Bologna or whether, if you looked for it on a map, it was above Bologna, or somewhere down in the heel or toe of the boot of Italy, or to one side of it. This feeling of complete disorientation compounded the fear she felt. If ever she mustered the courage to run away she had no idea in which direction she should run.

It was the same fear she'd felt after she'd been taken from Ada Stracci's and moved to countless different places, staying in each one just long enough for her virginity to be sold a dozen times. She remembered asking where they were going and they would always tell her – Parma, Piacenza, La Spezia, Novara, Genoa. None of it meant anything to her. If they'd told her they were going to the moon it would have made more sense. At least she could see where the moon was.

Whenever the nightmares came she was thirteen all over again, sold to men with a taste for unripe flesh and rewarded with sweets for her trouble. At first she had fought them. She had lashed out, bitten and scratched, but fighting just made things worse and resistance took energy. Evelina learned quickly that it was less painful if she let her body go limp and her mind go numb; to focus on a spot on the ceiling, or a crack in the wall, until everything around her disappeared, and eventually, until she disappeared too. She had become so good at deadening her body and her mind that she couldn't remember any details of any of those first encounters. The men just blended into a single mass of sour sweat, slobbering mouths and big, heavy hands which gripped her so tightly she thought she might snap.

There were other things that she did remember very clearly. They travelled around all the time. Sometimes they'd only drive for a few hours to get to the next place, other times they'd drive for days. Usually they'd sleep in the car, but occasionally they would stay overnight in a shabby hotel, where she was always told to pretend to be somebody's daughter, or niece. Nobody asked any questions, but she had never asked anyone for help. She was too afraid to speak. Evelina trusted no one.

She recalled the little roadside stands where they'd stop for sandwiches. There had been a time when she had been permanently hungry, because they wouldn't let her eat a whole sandwich. They said she was growing too quickly, so she shouldn't have too much food. They gave her cigarettes instead. At first they had made her sick, but after a time she found that she couldn't do without them.

Thoughts of her mother often occupied her mind, although so many years had passed since her death that to Evelina her mother was more of a feeling than a physical person. Evelina had made up so many stories about her to make herself and Rinaldo feel better that now it was hard to know what was real and what she had invented. Her mother had been a shared illusion created to comfort them both. Rinaldo had never questioned her stories, not even the far-fetched ones. It was wrong to lie, but Evelina reasoned that making up a story with good intentions wasn't really telling a lie.

She remembered that Mamma had dark hair and wore a shawl, like a Madonna, except hers was green. She couldn't recall her face, but presumed that it was not dissimilar to her own. Hers was one of those strong-featured faces that could be very beautiful, or very ugly, depending on the day, on the light, or on her mood. Perhaps her mother's face had been like that. But she could never quite fix the image of her mother's face in her mind. It was like trying to see something through running water.

What she did remember very clearly was sitting at a little table set for two and tracing her finger around the outlines of the flowers on the wallpaper as she waited for her supper. Mamma was standing at the stove with her back to her whipping eggs and heating broth to make *stracciatella*. Evelina loved that dish, always looked forward to it, and there was usually plenty of day-old bread to soften up in the soup because the baker would bring a bag of it every time he came to see Mamma. Sometimes he would bring big, fat *grissini* too. They were a little bit stale, but Evelina could remember the oily taste and the way the grains of salt felt on her tongue.

Evelina thought that memories were strange things. Why

could she remember *stracciatella*, the flowers on the wallpaper and the taste of stale *grissini*, but not her mother's face?

She had also forgotten about the pot shaped like a strawberry until she had seen it in Ada Stracci's room during a lesson with Gigio Lingua. She knew it was the same pot because it was chipped from where she had accidentally knocked it off the table whilst fishing the money out to count it. But the money had gone. Ada Stracci used the strawberry-shaped pot as an ashtray.

She didn't know whether Ada Stracci had taken her, or whether her mother had given her away willingly. If she had given her away willingly, had her mother known what future Ada Stracci had in store for her? But it was no secret how La Bella Brunelli made her living. Perhaps if she had not died, Evelina's fate would have been the same anyway.

Sometimes Evelina fantasised about an ordinary life and about doing everyday things like decent people did. She had never eaten in a restaurant, or been to watch a film at the cinema, or gone out to look at the displays in the shops, let alone bought anything with money of her own.

She struggled to understand money. She knew that at Madama Gioconda's ten minutes in the suck and spit room cost 200 lire and half an hour in a bedroom cost between 500 and 900, depending on the service; but in the outside world she had no idea of the value of anything. She didn't know the price of a loaf of bread, or a kilo of sugar, or a pat of lard – or how much milk, if any, could be bought for 50 lire.

How strange and wondrous it would be, she thought, to know these things and to be able to walk down a street and not be afraid – nobody would whistle, or cat-call, or shout abuse, or spit. She tried to imagine how it would feel to have a respectable job. Perhaps she could be a nurse, or she could look after little children. It would be nice to care for others. She thought that she could be good at that.

Evelina would comfort herself with thoughts of this made-up life. But the reality was that it was impossible to imagine how her life could ever change, so she learned not to hope for anything better.

As one week rolled into the next, Evelina agonised about whether to try to send word to Rinaldo. She knew he must be worried about her, but he would be so angry knowing she had not only lost all his money, but landed herself in a worse situation than before. And how would she send word, anyway? Even if she'd known how to write, she didn't have a sheet of paper, or an envelope, let alone any money for a stamp, and she couldn't tell him exactly where she was because she didn't know. She didn't trust anybody to help her.

Eventually she convinced herself that she would not try to contact Rinaldo at all – ever. He would be better off without her. She was nothing but trouble. Lots of people had told her that. And she wasn't right in her head. Lots of people had told her that too. The best thing was to keep silent and disappear, and eventually he would forget her.

The proprietor of the brothel grew very dissatisfied with Evelina very quickly. The girl had not turned out to be profitable. Her good looks were not enough to override her bad attitude. At best she was aloof; at worst, she was hostile. Clients had complained and some had demanded their money back. When Evelina wasn't working she spent her time lying immobile on her bed, curled into a ball and facing the wall. Tempting though it was to slap some sense into her, the proprietor knew better than to damage the goods.

And then, to top it all, she got herself knocked up, and not just once. Pregnancy was a pitfall of the profession. Evelina had fallen pregnant more times than she could count during her years spent being a virgin. Usually the problem could be resolved with strong infusions of parsley tea and concoctions of bitter herbs. Despite the fact that the remedies made her vomit and gave her cramps which made her bend double, they no longer had their intended outcome. Evelina seemed to have grown immune to their effects. It was astonishing that she could conceive at all after all the assaults on her womb, and nothing short of a miracle that she had never succumbed to the blood loss after each abortion.

There was only one other way to overcome this inconvenient fertility, and that was to call upon the 'plumber' to perform an intervention – but the regular interruptions to Evelina's work vexed the proprietor. Every abortion meant extra costs and at least a week's convalescence, sometimes more if the bleeding was bad.

Evelina fell pregnant four times in ten months, and that was unacceptable to the proprietor. The last thing he needed was a breeder.

'You're going to have to be more careful,' he said.

'How can I be more careful? You're the one who doesn't insist they use a rubber. And there's no bathroom. I can't even wash myself out.'

'Use your imagination then. Give yourself an enema and do it the French way. There are plenty of men who'll pay more for that.'

Evelina recoiled at the thought of 'the French way'. She knew that she couldn't get pregnant that way because Ada Stracci had explained how things worked. It was probably the only truthful thing that Ada had ever said to her. Gigio Lingua had never got her pregnant, so that was proof enough.

When Evelina fell pregnant for the fifth time the 'plumber' recommended sterilisation and the proprietor agreed. Evelina was not consulted. She woke after the operation in a blood-soaked bed feeling as if she had been sawn in half and with her brain throbbing as though it was about to exploded inside her skull. Her only recollection of the weeks that followed was pain and pills and the feeling that something had gone very badly wrong.

There were pills for everything – pills for pain, pills to go to sleep, pills to wake up – but the best ones were the yellow pills. They numbed her body, but better than that, they dissolved the sadness in her head. They were like little yellow miracles which bathed her every thought in sunshine. Everything was light and clear and filled with wonder. The nightmares stopped and were replaced by dreams which she could guide at will.

She could make herself small – so small that she was no bigger than a speck of dust – and weightless, as if she was made of nothing but light and air. She could fly anywhere she wanted. Sometimes she would take herself to Milano Marittima, although she had never been there in real life. She would fly through the parks full of pine trees and into the shops which sold things made of sea shells. Best of all, she would fly to her mother.

At last Evelina could see her mother's face in full, radiant detail. She was so beautiful, like the Madonna in San Paolo Maggiore. She could feel the roughness of the green shawl. She could smell it.

'Will you come and get me, Mamma? I want to be in heaven with you.'

Her beautiful mother smiled and said, 'Yes, my darling. Soon we'll be in Milano Marittima. We'll have a pretty little house with a garden and a view of the sea. We'll have *stracciatella* every day.'

'Can Aldino come too?'

'Of course! He's your little brother and so I'll be his Mamma too.'

In that moment, suddenly and from nowhere, Evelina experienced an unfamiliar burst of true, profound joy. She was ten years old, watching the Burattini puppet show with six-year-old Aldino. They had both laughed themselves helpless. And from that, another happy memory came, of holding hands and skipping in time to a song they had made up.

'Aldino-Fagiolino, Evelina-Sganapina, Aldino-Fagiolino, Evelina-Sganapina, Aldino Fagiolino ...'

Then they were sitting together on somebody's doorstep, cuddled close and sharing a jam-filled *raviola* which Rinaldo had managed to swindle out of a shopkeeper. One by one, lots of instances of happiness popped back into her head – little snapshots of moments with Aldino, like photographs but made of feelings. If only she could hold on to them, she thought, but it was like grabbing soap bubbles.

How Evelina had missed Rinaldo after she had been taken from Ada Stracci's, and how afraid she had been that he would get into trouble if she couldn't protect him any more. She had never told him that sometimes, when she knew that Ada Stracci was going to have him beaten, she would take Gigio Lingua aside and negotiate. There was never much to the negotiation. Gigio Lingua had shown her what to do to buy his leniency, even before the official lessons had started.

Come here, Evelina. Come to Gigio. Kneel down. His dick stank of piss. It stuck up, swollen, purplish and shiny, like some freakish creature that belonged in the sea. *Grip it tight.* The low growl under the cartoon moustache. *Good girl, good girl. You know how.* Then his spidery hands crawling all over her, tangling in her hair, pushing her head down. *Open wide. Deeper. Deeper. Deep as you can.* That growl again. The gasp that was almost a laugh, but there was nothing funny. *Yes, that's the way. You like that, don't you?* Evelina didn't like it, but even though it burned her throat, even though she wanted to gag, even though the piss stench made her eyes water, to save Rinaldo from a beating she would reply, 'Yes.'

But that was something that Rinaldo could never know, or he would realise how bad she was, how disgusting she was and how she had brought it all upon herself. Everything was her fault. That thought tormented her.

Evelina had recognised Rinaldo as soon as he had arrived at Madama Gioconda's, but it had taken her three days to pluck up the courage to approach him. She'd been ashamed of what he would think, finding her reduced to working in a brothel. She thought he would be angry with her, but he had shown her nothing but kindness. It had reminded her why she loved him so much. He might have grown up, but he was still her little brother, Aldino.

She wished she'd been nicer to him when he'd come to see her in the infirmary, and she wished she hadn't said all those things and upset him with her crude words. She regretted not having been warmer towards him, but it was difficult to remember how to be warm and she had been afraid of the questions he might ask. When he had wanted to know what had happened to her after she'd left Ada Stracci's, she had glossed over her life, as though her travels from city to city had been pleasant sightseeing excursions.

She hadn't given the names of the people who had taken her away because when she had learned about the fire which killed Ada Stracci she'd had a feeling in her bones that Rinaldo had had something to do with it. That feeling had been confirmed when she'd mentioned the fire to him. He'd said nothing, but the look on his face had said, 'You're welcome.'

The pills made time pass differently. Evelina knew that she had been sterilised in November and when she asked the proprietor how long it was until Christmas he informed her that it was already February.

It was clear to the proprietor that Evelina was in no fit state to work and probably wouldn't be for some time. She'd lost a lot of weight and with it she'd lost her looks. He made her strip off so that he could take a good look at her. She stood before him with her arms crossed over what remained of her breasts. She was a wreck – all xylophone ribs, jutting hips and armpit hair. Her legs, which had been her most marketable feature, were reduced to a pair of knobbly sticks. She reeked so strongly of tobacco that it seemed to be exuding from her pores.

The proprietor told her to get dressed again. Looking at her was making him queasy. Evelina got back into her bed, curled into a ball and faced the wall. She smiled to herself. It was a relief to look ugly. Her beauty, which was supposed to bring her such success and such wealth, had done her no favours.

Despite the proprietor's efforts to get Evelina back on her feet, Evelina wasn't complying. She wouldn't eat anything beyond a few mouthfuls. He was concerned that she would die and that was the last thing he needed. If the authorities got involved it would mean the certain closure of his establishment and ruinous fines, or even prison, because he didn't conform to all the regulations. The policemen who turned a blind eye in return for cash and sexual favours couldn't turn a blind eye to a dead woman, even if she was just a whore.

Eventually he concluded that he'd done his best for her. He couldn't help Evelina if she wouldn't help herself. He tried to sell her to other brothels, but nobody would take her in her condition. He was well within his rights to put her back out on the street, but he needed to recover some money; at least enough to cover all the medical costs he'd incurred.

He made a telephone call of last resort. The conversation comprised three questions:

Did the girl have family, or close friends?

Would anybody look for her if she disappeared?

How much?

A car was sent in the middle of the night to fetch Evelina. The proprietor had given her a few extra yellow pills and enough sleeping draught to make her compliant. She put up no resistance as they carried her out. All she did was chant some nonsense song.

'Aldino-Fagiolino, Evelina-Sganapina, Aldino-Fagiolino, Evelina-Sganapina, Aldino-Fagiolino ...'

He closed the door with an overwhelming sense of relief. That damned crazy girl had been a liability. He wasn't sorry that he would never see her again, nor that, in all likelihood, nobody would ever see her again.

CHAPTER 11

Rinaldo turned around before the mirror inspecting his stylish new suit. It was the fashionable, loose-fitted kind with broad shoulders and sharply-creased trousers. It wasn't some second-hand or cheap market suit, but a made-to-measure garment tailored especially for him.

Initially he had been undecided about whether to choose a plain fabric or a pinstripe, but in the end had gone for a bold dogtooth check in a vibrant mustard shade. The suit made a clear statement. It said that Rinaldo was doing all right. Perhaps next time he would go for the pinstripe. Perhaps he would go for both the pinstripe and the plain. Perhaps he would buy socks to match his favourite red spotted tie. Having money made the possibilities endless.

Rinaldo gave himself a nod of approval. He considered himself to be reasonably handsome and had reached a perfectly respectable height of one metre sixty-six, or one metre seventy-nine in his new shoes and hat if he stood up straight. Recently he had also grown a rather splendid moustache, which he felt gave him an air of distinction.

'I trust everything is to your satisfaction, Signor Scamorza?' inquired the tailor, brushing a stray thread from Rinaldo's shoulder and signalling to his assistant to help the customer into his coat.

Rinaldo took a step back and consulted the mirror again. The camel overcoat looked particularly fine over the new suit. The style was a little out-dated now that it was 1959, but Rinaldo had turned down the tailor's offer to alter it to a more fashionable cut because he loved it just as it was – and now it wasn't too big any more. Rinaldo felt that he'd grown into the overcoat, and not just physically.

'Perfect!' he declared, then turned to the tailor's assistant, took out his wallet, peeled the top five notes from a wad of money and said, 'A little something extra for your trouble.'

The assistant was stunned by the generosity of the tip. He hadn't recognised Rinaldo as the young trickster who had made off with several garments for a mysterious Signora Zappatelli ten years previously.

Rinaldo checked his inside pocket for his lucky Roman coin and made his way out, thinking that he would take a little stroll. He paused for a moment and glanced at his watch. It was too early for lunch, but it was mild for the time of year and he was eager to take his new suit for a walk.

He found himself wandering down Via del Pratello, where he passed Buttafuori and Nando the rat-catcher talking together, but neither recognised him. The last time they had seen him he had been a skinny, shabby boy. Now he was a robust young man dressed in a snappy dogtooth check suit and sporting a splendid moustache.

Madama Gioconda's was no longer in business. Following a decade-long crusade, Senator Lina Merlin had achieved what she had campaigned for – the closure of all brothels. For some it was a victory – the end of exploitation and of government-sanctioned immorality. For others it was regressive and short-sighted and made life worse for the women whose lot it was intended to improve. The majority of women ejected from the brothels ended up working on the streets. The new law changed everything whilst simultaneously changing nothing. Rinaldo hoped that the ladies from Madama Gioconda's had found alternative employment.

He supposed that the Tognazzis had retired. As he passed the former brothel he stopped for a moment and gave them a little ironic nod of gratitude. It was thanks to their three-wheeled bicycle and their silver that he had started his delivery business, and the sale of Benito Tognazzi's weighty gold watch had kept him in food and board for quite some time. But the days of petty thefts and scratching out an existence with menial jobs were a long way behind Rinaldo. Now he boasted the title of 'entrepreneur'. He ran his business by the book and paid his taxes. Signor Rinaldo Scamorza was an upstanding citizen.

At that very moment one of his delivery boys rode past dressed in his smart blue uniform, called out, 'Morning, boss!' and gave a little salute.

Rinaldo returned the greeting and continued walking, taking no particular direction and crossing paths with several more of his delivery boys. He was very proud of his fleet of brightly-painted orange bicycles, each with its large box fixed to the front and onto which a copy of his lucky Roman coin had been painted above the words *Denarius Deliveries*. Although the sign-writer had done a sterling job and the image was a perfect reproduction of Tiberius Caesar's profile, everybody always assumed it was Julius Caesar. Rinaldo had given up on correcting them.

His business was based on a simple idea. People would telephone or mail their order through to any shop in Bologna, or directly to Denarius Deliveries, and one of the boys would be sent out to collect and deliver it. Customers could order anything, as long as it was available and could fit into a bicycle box. It hadn't gone unnoticed by the shopkeepers and market traders that people bought more if they didn't have to carry it themselves. The speedy service meant that customers could get whatever they wanted, usually within the hour, without ever leaving the comfort of their own homes. Rinaldo reckoned that it was the future of shopping.

In the evenings the boys delivered food from restaurants to

people's homes. Busy working people, or those who had no wish to cook, could telephone a restaurant and have any dinner they fancied brought straight to their door, piping hot and ready to eat. This new service was still in its early stages, but Rinaldo was certain that it would take off.

Rinaldo was considered a good and fair employer. The previous year he had even received a commendation from the Chamber of Commerce. He ensured his delivery boys received a decent wage and let them keep all their tips, reasoning that the more they thought they could make in tips, the better the service they would provide and the better that would be for his business. The system worked well. Denarius Deliveries had an excellent reputation, providing both punctuality and politeness at an affordable price.

There was still plenty of money for Rinaldo to pay himself a very comfortable salary every month and enough to put aside for future investments. He'd already been to the Piaggio showroom to have a look at their new range of Ape models, and to inquire about staged payments. The Ape, which meant 'bee', was a three-wheeled vehicle, based on a Vespa scooter, but with an enclosed cab and a platform at the back, like a little van – the perfect commercial vehicle for Bologna's old, narrow streets and also for deliveries further afield, or deliveries of goods which were too heavy or bulky to fit in a bicycle box. The prospect of a little fleet of Apes, all buzzing around town and all painted in their orange livery and with Emperor Tiberius' profile on the side gave Rinaldo a flutter of excitement.

As he ambled along enjoying the early spring sunshine, his thoughts turned from commercial vehicles to lunch. He was undecided about which of his favourite restaurants to choose. Perhaps he would go to the Nettuno, which served the best veal *cotolette* in Bologna. Or maybe he would go to Tonino's for a succulent *Fiorentina* steak. Then again, he hadn't been to

Nonna Franca's for a dish of freshly-made *tortellini* for a while – but perhaps he should go easy on the pasta, he thought. He didn't want his new trousers to feel too tight.

Eventually he decided that he would try somewhere new. He'd heard excellent reports about a place near the Montagnola Park. Apparently it was a little pricey, but there was nothing wrong with treating himself, especially as it was nearly his birthday. It was March the 20th 1959 and there was only one day to go before he turned thirty.

Rinaldo didn't have any plans for a celebration. Although he had a wide circle of acquaintances and business associates with whom he was on good terms, he had no close friends. He was not averse to meeting up for a beer, or a game of cards and to exchange a bit of friendly banter and a few off-colour jokes, or watch a football match on the television in a bar, but he had found himself to be not gregarious by nature. Mostly he went along when invited just to be polite, and more often than not, he made his excuses early.

The truth was, Rinaldo preferred to keep himself to himself.

As for women, being a very eligible bachelor, over the past few years many of his acquaintances had introduced him to their sisters, cousins, and a whole selection of nubile and marriageable Signorinas. Some had been very lovely women. Although Rinaldo had skirted around the edges of a few romantic interludes, he had talked his way out of committing to any serious relationships.

Each time such an opportunity arose, Rinaldo was overcome by the feeling that any woman he cared for would disappear from his life. Either she would abandon him, like his mother; or she would drop him if a better prospect came along, as Signora Limoni had done when she took up with the local greengrocer after the death of her husband; or he would lose her forever through his own carelessness, like Evelina.

Rinaldo was so lost in his thoughts that he was paying no attention to where he was going. He had turned off in entirely the wrong direction in Piazza San Francesco and unexpectedly he found himself standing in front of the orphanage of San Girolamo.

Although questions concerning the murky circumstances of his birth still frequently occupied his mind, he had never been back to the orphanage since being released from its care. He had thought about it many times, supposing that the Child Welfare Service must have a file on him which could contain some information about his mother, even perhaps some detail of his abandonment which had been missed, or which hadn't seemed important at the time. Yet each time he had considered asking to look at his records he had found more reasons than were necessary to avoid doing so.

But today he felt different. Perhaps it was the new suit which gave him such confidence. Lunch could wait. If he didn't look at his file, he would never know if there was any useful information, and he reasoned that it would be better to know some part of the truth than to carry on making assumptions based on assumptions.

He stepped through the orphanage doorway, passing under the Latin inscription *In Loco Parentis*, which he had been told meant 'In the Place of Parents' – something which he had always considered to be a rather optimistic claim – and was directed to a back office where an elderly lady with ivory-coloured hair was sitting working at a desk.

'My goodness, it's Rinaldo Scamorza!' she exclaimed once Rinaldo had introduced himself. 'How marvellous to see you all grown up. You look as though you're doing very well for yourself. I don't suppose you remember me, but I remember you very clearly. You were the boy with the emerald earring. I used to let you look at it when you'd been good.'

Rinaldo had no recollection of the lady. He had very few orphanage memories apart from over-crowded dormitories where most of the boys rocked themselves to sleep, and being told off for drawing on a wall. But when Rinaldo asked to see his records the lady looked uncertain and said, 'It's a long time since you were in our care and many of our records were destroyed during the bombings. I'm not sure if we still have anything, but I'll see what I can find.'

She left him waiting for a long time before finally coming back holding a thin file and a small box.

'I'm afraid I haven't got very much to show you,' she said, leafing through the scant paperwork. 'I have your mother's name, but you know that already. I also have the address where you were found.'

'The address where I was found? I thought my mother left me here.'

'No,' said the lady. 'You were reported abandoned in Via Val d'Aposa, at number 7b. It was a rooming house.'

'Are you sure?'

'I couldn't be more certain. I was sent to collect you myself and I remember it very clearly. You'd been left in a vegetable crate wrapped in a yellow blanket. You were very poorly. It was just as well you were found in good time. You probably wouldn't have survived much longer.'

The new information winded Rinaldo. It was like being punched in the chest, but from the inside.

'Who found me?'

The lady scanned the documents in front of her and said, 'Apparently it was a Signor Rossi. He was another tenant in the rooming house. The landlord alerted the police, who in turn alerted us. I have a copy of the police report here, but that doesn't say much either. Just that nobody was aware of your mother's pregnancy, or who she was, or where she'd come from.'

'Is there any other information about my mother?'

'She's described as a young girl.'

'How young?'

'I'm sorry, Rinaldo. I have nothing beyond that description and her name. But having her name is an important piece of information. You could search the public records. Scamorza is a very unusual name, so if she's still living in Bologna officially, she should be easy to find.'

'And if she isn't living in Bologna officially?'

'Then you'd have to search further afield.'

'But she could be anywhere. I'd have to search every public records office in every city, town and village in Italy! Did nobody try to find her at the time?'

'No. When children are abandoned we work on the assumption that their mothers don't wish to be found, so we don't look.'

'But the landlord must have spoken to my mother at some point. Did he say how long she'd been living there? Was she living there alone? Did he say what she looked like? Do you remember anyone saying anything about her, perhaps something which wasn't in the report? Anything at all?'

The ivory-haired lady thought for a moment, then said, 'Come to think of it, I do remember a brief conversation I had with the landlord. Your mother had never caused any trouble, but she'd disappeared owing rent. She'd also left the stove on and he wasn't very happy about that, although just as well that she did, because that probably saved your life. If you'd got cold, that would have been the end of you. You were very weak and suffering from jaundice.'

'Jaundice? I didn't know that.'

'Oh, it's not uncommon in newborns,' said the ivory-haired lady with a dismissive gesture, 'nothing a bit of sunlight didn't sort out. But you were suffering from convulsions too.'

'Convulsions? Aren't those rather serious?'

'Yes, they can be fatal. In fact, as I was on my way to have you baptised, you suffered a convulsion, stopped breathing and turned blue. You gave me quite a fright! I had to turn you upside down and shake you.'

Being turned upside down and shaken was exactly how Rinaldo felt in that moment; except it also felt as though he had been dropped on his head, then kicked down a staircase for good measure. Beads of sweat were trickling down the back of his neck.

'But after a good feed and a few days in the clinic, you were right as rain,' smiled the ivory-haired lady.

'How about Signor Rossi? Did you talk to Signor Rossi?'

'Not that I can recall.'

'Do you know his first name?'

The lady ran her finger along several lines of writing and shook her head. 'Sorry. No. No Christian name is mentioned.'

'And what about the room I was found in? What do you remember about that?'

'It was a long time ago, Rinaldo, and I was only there very briefly. I do remember that the room was on the first floor overlooking the street and that it was quite basic, but it was clean. If it's any comfort, you were clean too. We could never be sure exactly when you were born, but for the brief time you were in your mother's care it appeared that she'd done her best to look after you.'

'You couldn't be sure when I was born? You mean that my birth date isn't actually my birth date?'

'You were presumed to be under a week old, so you were assigned the birth date of the day you were found. It's normal procedure when we can't be sure.'

Rinaldo couldn't move. It was as though the weight of the new information was pinning him to his seat. The two truths of which he had always been certain – that his mother had left him at the orphanage and that his date of birth was the 21st of March

1929 – were false. What else was false? Was his mother really called Giuseppina Scamorza? Was he really Rinaldo Scamorza? If not, who was he?

'I'm sorry I can't be more helpful, Rinaldo, I really am,' the woman said kindly, 'but we still have this. It's yours to take if you want.'

She reached into the box and took out a small, yellow woolly bundle.

'This is the blanket you were found wrapped in. I'm surprised we still have it. Things like this are usually disposed of.'

The blanket was a crudely-crocheted square, slightly moth-eaten, but very soft.

'Do you think my mother made this for me?'

'I would say it was highly likely. It's not something shop-bought.'

Rinaldo held the blanket close to his face, hoping that some trace of his mother might still be discernible, but the little yellow blanket just smelled as though it had been in storage for thirty years.

The ivory-haired lady reached forward, rested her hand gently on his arm and said gravely, 'Rinaldo, whilst I understand your wish to find out about your mother and possibly even to locate her, it would be wrong of me not to ask you whether you are prepared for her *not* wishing to be found? A long time has passed. There is a very high probability that she has a husband and has other children, and if that is the case it's possible that her family are not aware of your existence. Your sudden appearance might cause acute distress for all concerned, including you.'

It was kind of the lady to forewarn him, but over the years Rinaldo had gone through every possible scenario. His mother had never come looking for him so he knew that if he did find her, he was likely to face a second rejection. He understood that he was probably a dirty little secret.

Nevertheless, that was not enough to cancel out his curiosity, and not just about the circumstances which had led to him being left in a crate in a rooming-house in Via Val d'Aposa. He couldn't help but be intrigued to know something, *anything*, about his mother. He would be curious to see her, even unbeknown to her and from a distance, just to know what she looked like. Did he have his mother's eyes, or his mother's nose? Where had his curly hair come from? But it wasn't just the inheritance of physical traits which fired his curiosity. He was intrigued to know what parts of his character were learned and what was inborn.

And what of his father? Was he a man whom his mother had loved? He hoped that he had been conceived in love, but was not blind to the possibility that he might have been conceived in violence. Had the circumstances of his birth been different, on what kind of man might he have modelled himself?

Then there was the fundamental question – did his father even know of his existence?

So many questions ricocheted around his mind, but didn't collide with any answers. The only person who held the key to unlock all the mysteries was Giuseppina Scamorza.

His thoughts were interrupted by the woman who smiled warmly and said, 'Whatever you decide to do and whatever path your search takes, I hope you find something which brings you comfort. I'm so pleased you came here today, Rinaldo. I've known hundreds, no, *thousands*, of children during the forty years I have worked for the Child Welfare Service, but once children leave our care it's very rare for me to cross paths with them again. Seeing you here today, and seeing what a fine young man you've become, has touched my heart. I'm due to retire at the end of this month. I should have retired years ago, but my work here has been more of a calling than a job. Meeting you today feels like a sort of closure.'

She put her arms around Rinaldo and kissed his cheek lightly. As far as Rinaldo could recall, it was the first gesture of affection he had ever received within the walls of the orphanage of San Girolamo.

'Can I keep my file?' he asked.

'Hmm ...' pondered the lady. 'Normally that wouldn't be allowed. But after all this time, I don't see why not. It's of no use to anybody but you. And I can't lose my job over it.'

Rinaldo left the orphanage with his file wrapped in the yellow blanket, thinking that he would make a start with the Public Records Office, but his inquiry revealed nothing. There was no record of any Giuseppina Scamorza, or anybody else called Scamorza in Bologna, apart from Rinaldo himself.

The only other lead was the tenant who had found him, Signor Rossi, but it was pointless searching for him as there was no first name in the police report. Rossi was such a common name. Trying to find someone called Rossi in Bologna was not so much like looking for a needle in a haystack, more like looking for a needle in a stack of needles.

As he walked back towards Piazza San Francesco, the question of his date of birth played on his mind. If March the 21st was not his real date of birth, but simply the date on which he had been found, he must already be thirty years old. He wondered whether his mother ever thought of him on his birthday, whichever day that might be. He wondered whether, in fact, she ever thought of him at all.

Rinaldo took a roundabout route towards Via Val d'Aposa, along Via Carbonesi and past Majani's chocolate shop until he reached the church of San Paolo Maggiore. For a moment he wondered whether he should go in, then thought better of it. Going back in would only make him think of Evelina – and now wasn't the time to be thinking about all that. None of his fourteen trips to Milano Marittima had yielded any answers. Anyway, churches were for people who believed in God, and he had dismissed religion as nonsense a long time ago.

He stood in the piazzetta in front of San Paolo Maggiore looking down Via Val d'Aposa. It was an ordinary but well-kept little cobbled street of brick and terracotta-coloured buildings, all slightly different, but joined together in a continuous row, and most three or four floors high. Some dwellings opened straight onto the street, others had porticos. A concrete bollard stood at the entrance to stop vehicles from entering and getting stuck where the buildings pinched together.

Rinaldo had known Via Val d'Aposa since childhood. Number 7b was a narrow house – three storeys high but just two windows wide. There was a shoe shop on the ground floor. Nothing about it was remarkable. Rinaldo had passed the building countless times without paying it the slightest attention, but as he stood looking up at the first-floor windows he was overcome by an oddly settled feeling. Knowing that his mother had lived there and had kept him in the room with her, even just for a short time, gave him something tangible. It was a small scrap of certainty amongst all the unknowns, and that certainty was a great comfort.

It took Rinaldo a while to summon the pluck to knock on the door of number 7b, but when at last he did, the door was answered by a man who informed him that the property had changed ownership several times since 1929. He had no knowledge of a baby ever having been abandoned in the house, or of any Giuseppina Scamorza or Signor Rossi who might have lived there.

'Could I see the room?' asked Rinaldo.

'You can if you want,' replied the new owner of the house. 'But it's nothing like it was when I bought this place. It was a hovel. No proper plumbing, dodgy electrics. And don't get me started on the dry rot and the rats.'

He led Rinaldo up a narrow staircase to the first-floor room, skirting past paint pots, tools and scaffolding planks. Clearly the room was very different to the way it might have been in 1929. It was no longer a bedroom, but a dining room. The walls smelled recently plastered and the floor was paved in modern ceramic tiles.

Rinaldo stood at the window and surveyed the street below. The only traffic was on foot, or bicycle. The view probably hadn't changed at all since his mother had rented the room. He wondered how many times she had stood at that window. Maybe she had stood there holding him in her arms. For a few moments Rinaldo felt something of her and of them together, as though part of them had remained in the room. He could imagine her standing there. If he stepped back he could even discern her features and her expression, but when he tried to get closer, the image blurred. It was like looking at that picture of white sheets on a washing line in the shop which sold paintings in Via Farini. From a distance the objects in it were clear, but up close all the details blended into a mess of brush-strokes where all the forms were lost and even the colours made no sense.

Suddenly Rinaldo was overcome by the understanding that he had not been recklessly abandoned, but left somewhere safe where his mother knew he would be found. It was as though through being in that same room he could see the situation from her point of view for the first time.

Rinaldo shut his eyes tightly, imagining his young, frightened mother. He could feel her desperation. Bitterness and resentment faded and became meaningless, and he felt deeply protective of her. He thought of her without hostility and understood that leaving him was not some selfish, callous act, but the only choice for a young girl in impossible circumstances. Perhaps his mother had been deceived, or abandoned, or both. But as he stood at the window looking down over the heads of the people passing in the street, his hope that she had loved him at some point, even briefly, finally felt like a certainty. As the orphanage lady had said, in the short time that he was in his mother's care she had done her best to look after him.

Now even the mystery behind the emerald earring felt different. His mother wasn't the rich lady dripping in jewellery and gems whom he'd imagined as a child. She was a poor girl who had disappeared owing rent for a little shabby room. It was impossible to say how she had come about the emerald earring. It wasn't beyond the realms of possibility that she had stolen it. But knowing that despite her precarious circumstances she had left something so valuable made the earring all the more precious.

Perhaps the ivory-haired lady's advice was wise. Maybe it was better not to look for his mother. His appearance would be like throwing a hand grenade into her life and the last thing he wanted was to distress her, especially if she had found happiness, which he hoped with all his heart that she had. Rinaldo didn't want to be the reminder of a difficult and painful part of her life.

Of course he would like to know the whole truth with nothing hidden, but maybe he should be content with believing that she had done her best for him: just knowing that eased his longing and filled the void to a certain extent. Although he hadn't found her, he had found something *of* her, and he could learn to be satisfied with that.

If one day she decided to look for him, it wouldn't be such a challenge to locate him. All Giuseppina Scamorza would need to do was to make an inquiry with the Public Records Office.

With this new feeling of peace, Rinaldo stood looking down at the street below until a lady in a yellow beret came out of the doorway opposite. She looked directly up at the window, held Rinaldo's gaze for a moment, then hurried off down Via Val d'Aposa.

*

Over the weeks that followed, Rinaldo found himself gravitating more and more towards Via Val d'Aposa. He would walk its length every day, often several times. It gave him a sense of originating from somewhere, as though finally he had some roots. Every time he would stop in front of the shoe shop and look up into the windows of number 7b. He would send his mother, Giuseppina Scamorza, whoever she was and wherever she was, good wishes. It was strange, he thought, that he could feel love for someone he didn't know, and that he could feel it so deeply.

Rinaldo had been in a position to afford to rent a flat of his own for quite some time, but he had been so busy with work that he'd had neither the time nor the inclination to go looking. The shared accommodation where he'd been living for the past few years was more than adequate. He had his own heated room with a comfortable bed. His fellow tenants were decent – all professional young men with good jobs – and his landlady kept the place spotless, changed the sheets every week and provided evening meals on request. But Rinaldo was sick of living under other people's house rules and having to queue for the bathroom every morning. He was feeling the need for a place of his own, and since the disclosure of the new information from his orphanage file he had experienced a compulsion to live as close as possible to the spot where he had first come into the world.

He had also become a regular patron of the bar situated on the corner of Via Val d'Aposa and Via Carbonesi. The barman was a friendly fellow who liked to keep his ear to the ground and was always happy to chat. Yet despite being a mine of information about the neighbourhood and not averse to sharing a bit of local gossip, he didn't know anything about any abandoned babies going back as far as 1929.

One day as he was serving Rinaldo his mid-morning coffee he said, 'Are you still looking for a place to rent round here?'

'Yes,' replied Rinaldo.

'I've heard of an apartment that's just come up. Central heating. Fully furnished. All mod cons. Sounds like just what you're looking for.'

'Is it in Via Val d'Aposa?'

'No. It's in Vicolo Chiuso, at number 3.'

Rinaldo thought for a moment. He knew the area well, but didn't think he'd heard of a street by that name.

'Vicolo Chiuso? Where's that?'

'Ah,' said the barman, tapping the side of his nose as though he was about to reveal something highly secret, 'you'd have to know it's there to find it. About halfway up Via Val d'Aposa you'll see a big arched doorway opposite the shoe shop. It looks like the doorway into a building, but it's actually the entrance to Vicolo Chiuso. It passes underneath a house.'

As soon as Rinaldo heard the words 'opposite the shoe shop' his ears pricked up.

'Do you know the apartment? What's it like?'

'I haven't seen it myself, but I would imagine it's very nice. It belongs to Miranda Fiorelli. She's a lovely lady. Her husband, Alberto, was a music teacher. He used to stop by here for his coffee every morning and sit exactly where you're sitting. He's been dead a few years now ...'

Undoubtedly the barman would have continued with a long and detailed description of the Fiorellis, but Rinaldo downed his coffee in one mouthful, thanked him and hurried off to find Vicolo Chiuso.

As the barman had said, the enormous brass-studded door opposite the shoe shop looked like the entrance to a house. It was the door through which Rinaldo had seen the lady in the yellow beret come out. He pushed it open to reveal a short, dead-end alleyway, no wider than two metres at its opening and tapering to less than a metre at its narrowest. It was like a ravine hewn between the buildings. Rinaldo was intrigued by the secrecy of the place. He had passed its entrance a thousand times without the slightest inkling of what lay behind it.

The doors were numbered from one to four. He paused for a while outside number 3 and took a moment to read the nameplates on the letterboxes. *Dottore Saudelli, Ingeniere Michellini, Avvocato Malaguti* – and right at the top, *Professore Fiorelli.* Announcing your occupation on a letterbox wasn't the sort of thing you saw in the more modest parts of town, where there was never anything to announce that a dwelling might be occupied by Pozzi the road-sweeper, or Bianchi the railway clerk, or Martini the ironmonger.

Rinaldo hesitated for a moment, wondering whether being a delivery company owner would be a sufficient pedigree to live in such a place. Nevertheless, he was curious to see the apartment because of where it was, and by viewing it he was under no obligation to live there. As the main door to the building was ajar, he stepped inside.

The first thing he noticed was how clean it smelled, as though the floors and staircases had been washed that very morning – and not with cheap bleach, which more often than not was used to disinfect and disguise the smell of urine – but with the more expensive products, scented with pine and lemon.

The place was utterly quiet, unpolluted by the noise of the city, or the doctors, engineers, lawyers and professors who inhabited it. Rinaldo stood listening to the silence, until the sound of a door opening and closing on one of the upper floors echoed down the stairwell. It was followed by the brisk tip-tap of a lady's footsteps descending the stairs.

Rinaldo felt a flush of nervous agitation, a strange combination of panic and excitement, where he could feel his pulse through his temples. The only time he had felt anything similar was when he had stood in the shop which sold paintings in Via Farini as an eight-year-old boy – the feeling that although he had no dishonest intentions, he would land himself in trouble for being in a place he shouldn't be, a place where someone like him didn't really belong. He turned to make his exit, then caught his breath and pulled himself together. He had as much right to be there as any prospective tenant looking for a flat.

As he rounded the first bend of the staircase he came face-to-face with the lady in the yellow beret, who stopped the moment she saw him and stared at him in a rather disconcerting way. Rinaldo pulled his camel overcoat closed, hoping she wasn't disturbed by his mustard check suit. He'd quickly realised it wasn't to everybody's taste.

She gave him a searching look, and keeping her gaze firmly fixed on him, asked whether they had met before.

'No, I don't think so,' said Rinaldo, which was true. Seeing somebody come out of a doorway didn't count as meeting them, and he wasn't going to tell a stranger the circumstances which had led him to be standing at the window above the shoe shop.

'Funny,' she mused, still scrutinising his face, 'you're definitely familiar.'

'I'm looking for Miranda Fiorelli.'

'Oh,' replied the lady, 'that's me. And who might you be?'

'Rinaldo Scamorza. I've come about the apartment for rent.'

Miranda Fiorelli smiled. 'Would you like to view it now?'

'Only if it's convenient, Signora,' said Rinaldo, aware that in his effort to appear suitable, he was talking in his best Italian and without a hint of dialect. He lifted his chin and reminded himself to pronounce the letter 's' correctly.

'Certainly. I was on my way to run a small errand, but it's nothing urgent, so I'd be glad to show you. The apartment is on the second floor – I live above it. If you'll give me a moment when we get there, I'll pop upstairs to fetch the key.'

They made their way up the staircase together, passing apartment doors with polished brass name-plates. There was a doormat and an umbrella stand outside every door. This was the kind of genteel place where people who were conscientious enough to wipe their feet could leave their umbrellas unattended without the fear of them being stolen.

'Do you have a motor-car, Signor Scamorza?' Inquired Miranda Fiorelli, and Rinaldo was caught by surprise, uncertain where the question was leading. Was ownership of a motor-car some sort of condition to judge his eligibility as a tenant? He had forty-seven bicycles and would soon boast three Ape vehicles, but he had no motor car. Aside from affordability, he couldn't drive and he didn't need one.

Before he could decide why Miranda Fiorelli wanted to know, she continued with, 'The reason I ask is that the previous tenant, who vacated the apartment last month, left due to the issues with parking. He was obliged to leave his car at the far end of Via Carbonesi, or sometimes even further away, and I'm sorry to say that it was damaged twice. Parking is becoming more and more of a problem. It's something which wouldn't have crossed anyone's mind a few years ago.'

Rinaldo replied that no, he did not own a motor-car and did not envisage purchasing one any time soon, but inwardly he was buoyed by the fact that Miranda Fiorelli considered him potentially able to afford one. He must have made a good enough first impression.

They reached the second floor, where Miranda Fiorelli asked Rinaldo to wait for a moment whilst she went upstairs to fetch the key. Rinaldo stood looking at what might become his front door. It was freshly varnished, with a round, polished doorknob which turned his reflection upside down. The obligatory umbrella stand stood on one side and on the other was a big, ornate pot containing a leafy green plant. The doormat appeared to be brand new. He considered how fine a shiny brass plate engraved with the name *Rinaldo Scamorza* would look – or should that be *Signor Rinaldo Scamorza*? Or might another title be appropriate?

Miranda Fiorelli came back down the stairs a few moments later holding the key.

'We have a few general rules in the building,' she informed Rinaldo. 'No open umbrellas are to be left out to dry in any of the communal areas. No bicycles, laundry or other items are to encumber the landings or main entrance. And of course, no refuse is to be left outside the doors – that goes without saying. The closest municipal dustbins are situated in Via Val d'Aposa, just across from the Oratorio dello Spirito Santo. Also, the volume of radios and suchlike is to be kept at a level which will not disturb the neighbours. The same applies to any social gatherings.'

Miranda Fiorelli paused and a little wry smile twitched at the corners of her mouth. 'The lady on the ground floor is rather militant about these rules and is not shy about voicing her grievances.' She then dropped the tone of her voice as though she was about to divulge something rather indiscreet and added: 'Between you and me, Signor Scamorza, I would discourage you from engaging in lengthy conversation with her, or disclosing any personal information, as she is a most terrible gossip and rather prone to elaboration.'

Rinaldo warmed to Miranda Fiorelli very quickly. Despite being the owner of not only one, but two apartments, there was nothing haughty or snobbish about her. In fact, he thought her a particularly nice lady – warm, friendly, without the airs and graces he would have expected. She made him feel at ease and not at all conscious of his lower status. He stood a little straighter with his shoulders back and crossed the threshold with a feeling of increasing self-confidence.

'My late husband's family have owned this apartment and the one above since the 1830s,' continued Miranda Fiorelli as they made their way inside. 'Alberto's mother was the last of the

Fiorellis to have lived here, but she passed away some twenty years ago. My husband and I didn't have any children, so it's been rented out to various tenants since.'

The barman had predicted that the apartment would be nice, but it was more than 'nice'. The rooms were generous in size, with high ceilings and black and white marble floors polished to a mirror shine. It wasn't some generic rental place, kitted out with functional furniture, but instead was elegantly appointed, full of antiques and paintings in thick gilt frames. It had a solid, moneyed smell, of heirlooms and beeswax polish. If this was the apartment Miranda Fiorelli chose to rent out, Rinaldo could hardly begin to imagine how luxurious her apartment upstairs must be.

The place was so imbued with Fiorelli family history that Rinaldo could feel it like a presence. Every piece of furniture had a story behind it. The dining table and chairs had belonged to Alberto's grandmother, he learned. All the furniture in the larger bedroom had been part of Alberto's mother's dowry. Many of the paintings had been purchased by Alberto who was, Miranda Fiorelli explained, a keen collector of works by Bolognese artists.

As he took in his opulent surroundings Rinaldo lost himself in the fantasy that it was his own family history. He imagined how it would feel to be born into a situation where everything was already in place; to inherit a home filled with things passed from generation to generation; to enjoy a sheltered childhood, well-nourished with good food and affection and where his greatest concern would be only how to make the most of the advantages afforded him by birth.

As Miranda Fiorelli showed him around he found himself inexplicably at ease amongst the antiques and the paintings. The sensation was a magnified version of that feeling he had experienced when he had first tried on Zappatelli's school smock, or the camel overcoat.

'May I inquire what you do for a living, Signor Scamorza?'

'Bicycle deliveries,' replied Rinaldo vaguely. He had been distracted by a spectacular painting of Neptune's fountain where the jets of water had been rendered so expertly that he could almost hear the splashes and trickles.

'You deliver bicycles?'

'No, no. I deliver things *by* bicycle. Well, not me personally any more. I employ delivery boys. You've probably seen them around town. Denarius Deliveries.'

'Oh yes!' exclaimed Miranda Fiorelli. 'The orange bicycles with the image of Tiberius Caesar on the front box.'

'Yes, that's right!' Rinaldo was delighted. Miranda Fiorelli was the first and only person to have named the correct Roman Emperor. It made him like her even more.

He was shown the three generously-proportioned bedrooms, the kitchen with its row of fitted cabinets and modern refrigerator, and the bathroom, which was something of a revelation. It gleamed with floor-to-ceiling tiles and chunky chrome fittings, and was the only bathroom Rinaldo had ever seen where you could walk all the way around the bath-tub. And what a tub! It was the type you could lie down in, not one of those mean little sit-up ones where you couldn't even stretch your legs out.

Rinaldo had never had a bathroom entirely to himself and as he circled the tub he imagined the luxury of bathing at leisure, without restrictions on the number of baths he could take each week, or how much hot water he could use, or how long he could lie and soak for. How marvellous it would feel, stepping into a tub without having to scrub away the previous bather's ring of grease, body hair and soap scum, or of clearing the drain of detritus of dubious origin.

He felt that it was not accidental that he was shown to the sitting room last, as it was so spacious, open and bright, furnished with velvet couches and carved furniture. Set into each of the four corners of the ceiling was an intricate stucco motif with curly tendrils, all pointing inwards towards the central ceiling rose, from which hung a fine alabaster chandelier. Rinaldo could see how many lights there were in the room – not just the chandelier with its dozen candle-shaped bulbs, but table lamps too, and a tall standard lamp with a silk shade. There were probably more light bulbs in that single room than you'd find in three poor men's homes combined.

The walls were adorned with yet more paintings. In fact, in some places there were more paintings than wall. Rinaldo stood entranced in the middle of the room, bewitched by the landscapes, the cityscapes, the still lifes and the portraits, careful not to be seen staring for too long at a rather alluring nude.

'Your husband collected all of these?' he asked in wonder. It stunned him that someone could have so much spare money to spend on paintings.

'Many of them,' replied Miranda Fiorelli. 'The rest are unsold stock from the art gallery I used to own in Via Farini. When I closed it I kept what I hadn't been able to sell. I'd happily have some of them upstairs, but being an attic apartment there are very few walls sufficiently vertical to hang pictures.'

Rinaldo hesitated at the mention of the art gallery in Via Farini. Could that be the shop which had so fascinated him as a child? He looked at Miranda Fiorelli, trying to remember the pretty lady in the yellow dress who'd smiled at him and called him 'little man'. Could it be her? Miranda Fiorelli was certainly very attractive and probably about the right age. Maybe that was the reason she'd asked whether they had met before. Perhaps she had recognised something about him, something that had struck her as familiar. But then Rinaldo dismissed the notion as ridiculous. She couldn't possibly have recognised him from having glimpsed him once when he was eight years old.

For a moment he wondered whether he should mention the

encounter, then decided against it. There was no reason for Miranda Fiorelli to know that he'd been an urchin, particularly as he felt he was making such a good impression as a well-turned-out young man.

Miranda Fiorelli gestured to Rinaldo to follow her through the French doors, saying, 'Do come and have a look at the view from the balcony, Signor Scamorza.'

Stretching out below them was a magnificent garden belonging to a most beautiful building; an unexpectedly green and open space in the centre of the crowded city. There were trees, flower beds, gravel paths and little shrubs clipped into perfect spheres – no traffic noise and no bustle of humanity, just rustling leaves and birdsong.

'That's a former Jewish palace dating from the early sixteenth century,' said Miranda Fiorelli, indicating the elegant building with its arched apertures and intricate brickwork. 'Although you wouldn't know it from the street side. It has a deliberately plain façade – all wall and hardly any windows. But the back of the building is quite superb, isn't it? Of course, it's not a palace any more. It was divided into apartments after the Jews were expelled from the city in 1597. This area was once Bologna's Jewish ghetto and used to be known as the *Jewish Cage*. The city authorities would lock the Jews in between sunset and sunrise. That's why Vicolo Chiuso is closed off by a door.'

Rinaldo took in the information, pretending that he had some notion of the plight of the Jews and the history of the area, when in reality he had none. The only fact that he knew about Jewish people was that they weren't Catholic, like everybody else was. He didn't want to ruin the good impression he felt he was making, so he said with an air of feigned understanding, 'Terrible thing, locking them up like that.'

'I couldn't agree more, Signor Scamorza. And it is truly appalling that mistreatment and atrocities have continued to be committed.'

As Miranda Fiorelli was in agreement with his vague, uninformed opinion, Rinaldo thought that it was probably best to leave it at that. He didn't want to dig himself into a hole and make himself look like an uneducated idiot.

Miranda Fiorelli made no further comment and turned her attention to practical matters, explaining something about the central-heating boiler as they made their way back inside.

Rinaldo thought back to all those noisy, disordered places in the down-at-heel parts of town, where he'd slept in dormitories, in shared quarters and in bedrooms with paper-thin walls. For a moment his confidence left him and suddenly the prospect of living in such a quiet, genteel apartment seemed so implausible that he had the impression of being outside of his own body; as though he was a spectator in the room, observing himself and the antique furniture, the paintings, the big, soft sofas. The man he looked at could not possibly be Rinaldo Scamorza. He was dressed too well. The surroundings were too opulent. He felt like an imposter. At any moment he would wake up and find himself back in some grubby little room with a lumpy bed and peeling walls. There would be no green, leafy scent wafting in from the palace garden – just the stale smell of mildew and mouse droppings.

He regained his senses as Miranda Fiorelli's tone became business-like. She named the monthly rental price, and the terms and conditions, such as deposit amount and notice, and almost without consideration, Rinaldo heard himself say, 'That all sounds fine to me. When can I move in?'

'At your earliest convenience, Signor Scamorza. If you're certain that you'll take the apartment I won't take any further viewings.'

'In that case I'll move in today.'

'Today?'

'I've only got a few bits and pieces back at my lodgings. I'll ask one of my delivery boys to bring them over. I can come back at five o'clock with the deposit and the first month's rent. Is that all right, Signora Fiorelli?'

'Of course.' Miranda Fiorelli smiled and reached out her hand to shake Rinaldo's. 'And please, as we are to be neighbours, call me Miranda.'

PART II

MIRANDA AND ALBERTO

CHAPTER 12

Miranda's attic apartment was a quirky, irregularly-shaped space with sloping ceilings which touched the floor in some places. It had a slightly shabby, well-lived-in kind of look to it and was casually furnished with nothing that matched, but somehow fitted together. Shelves crammed with books took up any space which was not needed for essential furniture. Miranda knew it would be sensible to give some away to the university library but she couldn't bear to, knowing that Alberto had touched every one of them.

People were often surprised that with such a grand spread of rooms available to them downstairs, she and Alberto had chosen to remain in the modest attic flat. Had they been blessed with children, undoubtedly the couple would have moved into the far larger apartment below, but they were very attached to the attic. It was their love-nest. They adored its higgledy-piggledy bohemian feeling and the illogical arrangement of the rooms. The terrace was cut into the roof and was not overlooked by any of the neighbouring buildings. In her younger days Miranda had sunbathed there naked and completely unobserved.

The dining table had not been used for dining for some time. It was piled with what Alberto referred to as his *magnum opus* – his life's work – but it had come to an untimely end, just as his life had. Miranda had made a commitment that she would finish transcribing Alberto's research and would prepare it for publication. There was an awful lot of it though. She was quite overwhelmed by it, and to be perfectly honest, thoroughly bored. There were so many technical words, so many translations of archaic Italian and so much Latin text to decipher, for which her schoolgirl Latin was proving woefully inadequate. Although she always had a declensions chart and dictionary to hand and checked and double-checked her translations, Miranda was frequently plagued by the doubt that she might be typing nonsense.

Sometimes she would question whether giving up her beloved Galleria Fiorelli in order to dedicate herself to Alberto's work had been a good idea, then she would remind herself how important his research had been to him – and if it was important to Alberto, it was important to her.

Miranda rolled a fresh sheet of paper into her typewriter, sighed and set to work. Just a few more weeks and she would be done with the fifteenth century. Only four and a bit more centuries to go after that. At her current pace she had ten more years of translation and typing ahead of her.

Five years had passed since Alberto's departure. At first being without him had been unbearable, but gradually, as one year slid into the next, Miranda had settled into her widow's routine and learned to fill the void with other things – a very select few friendships, charity commitments and of course, the preparation of his research.

Despite his physical absence, Miranda still felt Alberto's presence in their home. In an odd way Alberto was *more* present since his death. He was no longer at work, or out on choir business, or engaged in his research and not wanting to be disturbed. Miranda could talk to him whenever she wanted and about whatever subject, however whimsical, and he was always available to answer.

In the evenings she turned on the standard lamp beside his red leather armchair because a good light was important for reading. Alberto always had his nose in a book. He maintained that one could never learn too much. Miranda's own armchair was still positioned in the same place, opposite Alberto's with the footstool they shared in between.

She still bought him birthday gifts, anniversary gifts and sometimes just spontaneous gifts if the fancy took her, or if she saw something she knew Alberto would appreciate. Recently she had bought him a beautiful mother-of-pearl tie clasp and had pinned it onto his favourite red spotted tie.

There were three photographs of Alberto on the dining table. Miranda had angled them so that he could see her as she typed. It was always better talking face-to-face.

The Alberto in their wedding photograph liked to reminisce. He had an excellent memory. The Alberto receiving his professorship was her advisor in all matters pertaining to his research. The Alberto in the third photograph, taken whilst he was sitting in his red leather armchair, with a broad smile on his face and his thumbs hooked into the arm-holes of his waistcoat, was her counsel in all other matters. Miranda always enjoyed his affectionate chatter.

She contemplated the wedding photograph, taken in 1930 on the steps of San Paolo Maggiore. How young they both looked! Alberto still had all of his hair and none of it was grey. He would be nearing his sixtieth birthday now. As for Miranda, she knew she hadn't aged too badly. In fact, she was rather well-preserved considering her vintage. It was difficult to say whether she looked her age. How was one *supposed* to look at forty-nine?

Miranda turned her attention back to her typing, then looked up at the Alberto receiving his professorship and muttered, 'I really wish you'd taken a bit more care annotating this section, my love. Your handwriting's even worse than usual.'

Alberto apologised, saying that if he'd known his death was imminent he'd have ensured his handwriting was more legible. There would have been other things he would have done too, like going back to the island of Capri, where they had first met and fallen in love. Miranda had been wanting to go back for years.

She worked for a couple of hours, then decided it was enough for the day. Typing numbed her fingers and the click-clatter of the keys and the ping of the end-of-line bell made her ears ring. It was also very tedious. Little and often was best.

'That's all for today, my love,' she said. 'Our new tenant is due here at five, so I'd better make myself presentable. I know you'll like him. He's a charming young man. I took to him straight away.'

Alberto raised an eyebrow.

'I don't mean it like that, for heaven's sake! You've nothing to be jealous about.'

Alberto didn't mind really – not that he hadn't had his jealous moments in the past. What man with a pretty wife didn't feel the rise of the green-eyed monster from time to time?

Miranda laid out her English tea set. She hadn't been much of a tea-drinker before Alberto had bought it for her. Cold lemon tea was refreshing in the summer, but the thought of putting milk into hot tea like the English were purported to do had seemed very counter-intuitive. Surely the milk would react with the lemon? It was only when Alberto had handed back his cup of curdled tea and explained that it should be *either* milk *or* lemon, not both, that the English quirk had made sense.

Still, Miranda had never been able to pronounce the name of the tea set. How was one supposed to pronounce a mouthful like *Wedgwood*? English was so awkward. Alberto had explained that the idiosyncrasies of the English language were due to a mixture of linguistic influences. He'd given so many examples that by the time he'd finished, his tea had gone cold.

*

Rinaldo arrived at five o'clock precisely with his deposit and first month's rent. Miranda took his overcoat from him. The overcoat was the first thing she'd noticed when they'd met on the stairs earlier that day. It was identical to the one Alberto had had stolen from the bar in town all those years ago – the same soft camel-coloured cashmere, the same thick rabbit-fur collar.

Alberto was certain that he knew who had taken it. He'd stopped a beggar from stealing coins from Neptune's fountain. He said that the thieving toe-rag must have followed him and helped himself to his overcoat. He'd also had the gall to take his brand new fedora hat with the lovely purple lining. Miranda wished that Alberto had given the poor fellow something. Trying to fish a few coins from a fountain was the act of a desperate man, and her husband's lack of charity had cost him far more than parting with a bit of spare change.

It was then that Miranda realised she was still holding the overcoat. More to the point, she was holding it close to her face so that she could breathe in its smell. But of course it wasn't Alberto's overcoat and it didn't smell of him, or his cologne. She also realised that Rinaldo was standing awkwardly, waiting to be invited to sit down.

'May I ask what you're typing?' he asked, looking across at the enormous piles of papers spread over the dining table and spilling onto the floor.

'My husband's research,' replied Miranda as she poured boiling water into the teapot and swilled it around to heat it before making the tea. 'Alberto was Professor of Music at the Conservatorio and a very keen historian. He discovered numerous unpublished scores in the archives of San Petronio dating from as far back as the twelfth century and began to work on a compendium of Bolognese composers. It's unthinkable that all his years of effort and research should go to waste.'

She looked at the photograph of Alberto receiving his professorship – her clever, talented Alberto. She liked to show him off as a proud parent might show off a gifted child.

'Alberto was passionate about music and wrote several books on the subject. He was so dedicated to his teaching, his studies and research ...' Miranda's words tailed off. She paused, keeping her eyes fixed on the photograph of Alberto and sighed, 'I don't know how you found time for it all, my love.'

'Pardon?' said Rinaldo.

'I mean I don't know how my husband found time for it all,' corrected Miranda.

She had never spoken to Alberto's photograph when someone else was present. She feared that Rinaldo must think her quite mad. To be on the safe side she changed the subject.

'So Rinaldo, I hope you'll be very happy living downstairs. If there's anything you need, please don't hesitate to ask. And do you prefer lemon in your tea, or milk, like the English?'

*

There was something else about Rinaldo, apart from the camel overcoat, which had been niggling at Miranda. She couldn't shake off the feeling that they had met before, but despite racking her brains, she couldn't think when, or under what circumstances, their paths might have crossed. She'd definitely heard the name Scamorza somewhere before.

'Scamorza,' she repeated to the photograph of Alberto sitting in the red leather armchair. 'It's an unusual name, isn't it? It's definitely not a Bolognese name. The cheese by the same name is from the South, so it's probably a southern name. Does it ring any bells?'

Obviously Alberto had heard of the cheese and had enjoyed it on many occasions, but otherwise it didn't ring any bells. Miranda thought hard. She was absolutely certain she'd come across the name Scamorza.

'It'll come to me,' she said. 'Perhaps a member of his family was someone I met through the gallery, or someone to do with the church? Or one of your choirs ... or maybe one of your colleagues?'

She took her wool basket to the terrace and settled herself with her crochet work – *shell stitch, cluster stitch, shell stitch* – but found her concentration wandering. What *was* it about Rinaldo that seemed so familiar?

Miranda continued absent-mindedly with a row of double stitches, keeping one eye on her work and looking over the balustrades to the palace garden with the other. The bagolaro tree and the sweet chestnut had come into leaf and the cherry trees would be in flower soon. The garden always took on such a fairy-tale prettiness in the spring when the blossom burst forth. Still the question of Rinaldo bothered her.

'Scamorza. Rinaldo Scamorza. Where have I heard that name before?' she continued to muse.

When the bell at San Paolo Maggiore rang to announce the hour, it came to her.

'Oh, Good Lord! Of course!' she exclaimed, casting aside her crochet work and leaping to her feet. If her recollection was right, Rinaldo's details would be in the file.

She knew that the file wasn't in her wardrobe, but it might have ended up in Alberto's. Miranda flung open the doors and breathed in the smell of mothballs, under which a vague trace of Alberto's cologne was still discernible. She began to rifle through neatly-stacked piles of sweaters and shoe-boxes, but the file wasn't there, so she turned her attention to one of the cupboards under the eaves, which was where items that should have been thrown out or given away were stored. Miranda got on to her hands and knees and began pulling things out. Most of the items in there were Alberto's – more clothing, more books, old teaching notes, piles of music scores, unwanted gifts. Finally, wedged in at the back, she found the file marked *Adoption*.

Miranda spread the contents of the file out over the floor. There were information pamphlets, forms which had never been filled in and pages containing the details of several children. She searched methodically, page by page, until at last she found what she had been looking for. There he was – *Rinaldo Scamorza. Mother – Giuseppina Scamorza. Father- unknown. Born – 21 March 1929.* She had written a note beside his name – *darling boy* – along with a little cartoon sketch of an earring. She had also underlined his date of birth.

'Oh Rinaldo, now I remember you!' she breathed.

Miranda thought back to the day she'd been to see the children at the orphanage of San Girolamo. She would have taken them all home if it had been possible. She remembered little Rinaldo because he had asked whether she knew his mother, Giuseppina. She'd felt her heart break as she'd seen the look of hope in his eyes change to one of disappointment when she'd said she did not.

Alberto hadn't accompanied her because he was opposed to the idea of adoption. He said that it was too risky. One couldn't be sure what sort of a child one might end up with – perhaps the issue of a street prostitute, or a drunk, or some feeble-minded low-life. They should keep trying for a child of their own.

Miranda had maintained that a child's background was inconsequential. All any child needed to grow up well-adjusted was the chance to be loved. Alberto had argued that Miranda could only ever see the good in children, which was both a virtue and a failing. Eventually Miranda had stopped trying to talk him round.

She returned to the living room in a subdued mood, feeling that old heaviness in her heart, and she said to the photograph of Alberto sitting in the red leather armchair, 'Rinaldo is an orphan. He was one of the boys I went to see at San Girolamo that day. I remember him clearly. He was a sweet child. He sat on my knee and played with my earrings. '

Alberto remained silent. He knew what was coming. If there was a subject which was guaranteed to upset Miranda, it was children. It was the one thing which had cast its shadow darkly over their marriage.

There had been nine devastating disappointments. Miranda had been unable to carry a pregnancy beyond four or five months. One had lasted nearly seven and the loss of that baby had been the worst. The doctors had said it was a boy, but they hadn't let Miranda see him because they said it would upset her too much.

Through this accumulation of failures Miranda had felt Alberto grow distant. He had withdrawn from her, both physically and emotionally, and had taken to kissing her only on the forehead – often so fleetingly that his lips barely made contact with her skin. It was after one such cold, dismissive kiss that Miranda had crumbled. She knew that Alberto no longer loved her and she knew it was because she had failed to bear him children. She understood why he hated her, and eventually told him so.

'My darling,' he had said, folding her into his arms. 'How could you ever think that I would hate you, and that I would hate you for such a reason? I'm afraid, that is why I keep my distance. I'm afraid to touch you and I'm afraid to make love to you because I cannot see your heart break one more time. Enough, Miranda. Enough of this longing for children we cannot have. Can we not just be content as husband and wife?' His words were like sighs of relief, as though he had been wanting to express them for a long time, but hadn't been able to.

Eventually Miranda had acknowledged that he was right. Every miscarriage had wrenched the couple further apart. Their moments of intimacy had become mechanical, fraught experiences. There was always the hope that they would conceive, and each time they did there was the fear that they would lose the baby. As time passed, that fear became a certainty. This endless cycle of hope and loss had eaten away at their marriage. It was like water dripping constantly onto a rock. Over time that water had caused the rock to crack – and that crack threatened to break the entire rock apart. They had agreed to stop trying for a child, but it had done nothing to quell Miranda's desperation to be a mother.

They hadn't spoken of it much after that, as though silence was the best way of dealing with all the things that needed saying; by ignoring it, perhaps the pain would go away. It wasn't until a few days before his death, when Alberto was confined to his bed and hooked up to the oxygen machine, waiting for the inevitable conclusion to his illness, that the subject had come up again.

Despite the doctors' advice, Miranda had nursed Alberto at home. He had found the hospital intolerable, calling the smell of disinfectant the smell of impending death. Everybody spoke to him as though he was an idiot, or a child. He loathed the mollifying words of comfort, and swore that if one more person asked him how he was feeling, when clearly he was feeling wretched, he would drag himself out of bed and jump from the nearest window.

But worst of all for Alberto were the sounds of the hospital: the scraping of metal furniture, the clattering of trolleys and bedpans, the constant click-clack of footsteps on the tiled floor, the cries and groans of the sick and the dying – all these discordant insults to his ears which echoed around him, made worse by the music on the radio, played constantly to cheer up the patients and take their minds off the inevitable. They were all silly, commercial songs about pretty girls and pretty boys. The man in the bed opposite sang along, loudly and badly. Alberto said he would lose his mind long before he lost his life. It felt as though he was already in hell.

Those final months at home had been a difficult, but precious time. At first Alberto had resisted, refusing to allow himself to be treated like an invalid, but his resistance had softened as rapidly as his decline and eventually he had let himself be looked after without fuss. The couple had found a new kind of intimacy, fed by the knowledge that they were sharing moments which could never be shared again. Time felt different. It was not governed by work schedules, or appointments, or deadlines. It was simply governed by the knowledge that it was running out.

Perhaps it was the morphine talking, but just a few days before the end Alberto had looked at Miranda with an expression she hadn't seen before and said, 'I've been very blessed in life. I've worked hard, but I've never struggled, or had to get my hands dirty. Although perhaps there were times when I could have been more charitable and more understanding of the plight of those less fortunate than myself ... But I've spent the happiest years of my life with you, my darling. I married a little late, but you were absolutely worth waiting for.' He paused for a moment, wheezing. Then, dragging the air into his lungs with a rasping sound, he sighed, 'My only regret is that we didn't have children, because now I'm leaving you completely alone.'

Miranda had also felt her breath catch in her throat.

'That wasn't your fault,' she said.

'I don't mean the miscarriages. They were nobody's fault. I mean that you wanted to adopt and I didn't listen to you. I was fixated with us having a child of our own, but I know now that if we'd adopted, that child *would* have been our own. I just couldn't see it at the time.'

Miranda hadn't known how to reply. That realisation had been a long time coming. She had leaned against Alberto, listening to the rhythmic rattling of the air and fluids in his chest and smelling the blood on his breath.

Alberto broke the silence in a thin, strained voice. 'I never told you about the little boy who came to choir practice.'

'What little boy?'

'You remember just before the war you talked me into conducting a choir of orphan boys? I used to call them my "rabble of delinquents".'

'Of course. The boys from San Girolamo.'

Alberto paused, letting the oxygen machine fill his lungs, then with great effort found the strength to continue speaking.

'Well, one day during practice I found a little lad hiding in the choir loft. A scruffy, skinny little ragamuffin of a kid. He'd been attending practice for weeks, just learning the chants and singing along, but nobody had noticed him and he'd been too shy to come and join in. I only realised he was there because he sneezed. But I was in a bad mood that day. I thought I'd embarrass him by making him sing in front of the other boys. They were all a fair bit bigger than him and they weren't the most charitable bunch. But the little lad turned out to have the courage of a lion! He just took a big breath and sang his heart out. And he could really sing, Miranda. Obviously he'd never been taught and he was rough around the edges and he didn't know any techniques, and his Latin was pidgin at best, but he sang so well and with so much spirit.'

'What was his name?'

'I don't know. I can't think why I never asked. But I never forgot about him. For some reason he's been more and more on my mind recently. He stayed behind after the other boys had gone and we left San Petronio together. And as we were walking across Piazza Maggiore he just reached up and took my hand. Funny how I remember that little clammy hand pressed into mine. I can still feel it if I think about it. I was telling him all sorts of things about buildings and music and history. The kinds of things which would bore any child. But he listened and he asked questions and I thought what a special little boy he was. I took him to Majani's and bought him some chocolate. I don't think he'd ever been bought chocolate before. I'm not sure he'd ever been bought anything before. I'm sorry I never told you about him at the time.'

'Why didn't you?'

'Because you were unwell and we knew another miscarriage was looming. Telling you about a little boy would have been cruel. But it wasn't just that. I was so judgmental about children like him. I couldn't see past where they might have come from. I nearly asked him to come home with me so you could meet him, then I thought it wasn't really the proper thing to do.'

'What happened to him?'

'I don't know. I never saw him again. The war started.'

Miranda shut her eyes. It had taken a long time, but finally the moment for her confession had come – and it was a confession she knew she had to make before it was too late. She had rehearsed her words ten thousand times, but finally faced with the opportunity to express them out loud to Alberto, she couldn't think quite where to start.

She bowed her head to gather her thoughts and eventually began with, 'The miscarriages, they *were* my fault,' but when she looked up, Alberto had succumbed to the effort of their conversation and with his breath straining in his chest, had fallen asleep.

*

It was early afternoon. The church of San Paolo Maggiore was empty apart from two old ladies engrossed in reciting their rosaries. Miranda slipped in quietly, walking on her tiptoes so as not to disturb their prayers. She dipped her fingers in the stoup, crossed herself and genuflected.

The new parish priest, Don Pagnotta, was standing at the far end of the nave staring up at a damp patch. He would have disappeared into the sacristy if he'd noticed Miranda come in, but by the time he saw her it was too late. He knew he'd been spotted.

'Could I trouble you to take my confession, Don Pagnotta?'

The priest nodded in a slightly resigned way. He wasn't in the mood, but he couldn't say that he was too busy as quite obviously, he wasn't. He'd already heard the confessions of the two rosary-reciting ladies. Their sins had been so tame that he couldn't even remember them.

Don Pagnotta wasn't an unpleasant fellow, but he was an unexceptional priest. Miranda found his endless, oily-voiced Bible quoting rather specious, and all his sermons sounded as though they'd been copied word for word out of textbooks. She couldn't help but feel that he treated his position not as a vocation, as she considered that anyone taking Holy Orders should, but as an ordinary job. He might just as well have been a librarian, or a filing clerk. He talked a lot, but said very little of any substance.

Despite this, Miranda still went to Mass every Sunday, and sometimes once or twice on week-day evenings too. She preferred the evening services as they were quiet, mainly attended by older, widowed ladies and spinsters who sought not just spiritual comfort, but a way to fill their lonely evenings. The Sunday services could be rather rowdy affairs and any hope of quiet reflection was lost amongst the fidgeting and the chatter. Miranda had been thinking for some time that most people only went to Sunday Mass so they could show off their clothes. In the winter, there was such a proliferation of fur coats that the church smelled like a zoo.

Miranda thought that somebody else would probably be better placed to advise her than Don Pagnotta, but what was one's parish priest for, if not to air one's troubles to in confidence? She knelt at the confessional grille and began, as usual, with, 'Bless me Father, for I have sinned.'

'When was your last confession?'

'Two weeks ago.'

'What do you wish to confess?'

'It concerns a young man.'

'Ah!' exclaimed the priest, sitting up. Perhaps this confession was going to be worth listening to.

'This young man is my tenant. We're on friendly terms, but a few days ago I discovered that there is a connection between us.'

'*Let marriage be held in honour, for God will judge the adulterous* – Hebrews, chapter thirteen, verse four.'

'Pardon?'

'*Walk by the spirit and gratify not the desires of the flesh* – Galatians, chapter five, verse sixteen.'

Miranda paused for a moment, somewhat insulted by the conclusion the priest had been so quick to jump to, and said in a rather offended tone: 'Firstly, Don Pagnotta, I am widowed and therefore in no position to commit adultery. And secondly, this has absolutely nothing to do with desires of the flesh.'

'Oh,' said the priest, failing to disguise his disappointment. 'What is it about then?'

'Today I realised that we have met in the past, only briefly, and I doubt very much whether he would remember.' Miranda then recounted her visit to the orphanage of San Girolamo, her desire to adopt, and how she had never forgotten the darling little boy who had asked after his mother and played with her earrings.

'Do you feel guilty for not having adopted the child?'

'I feel guilty for not having given a loving home to any of those children who were in such dire need of love and care. I should have been more forthright with my husband about it.'

'So is it this guilt of which you need to unburden yourself today?'

'No. That guilt was the mainstay of my confessions for years. I spoke about it often to your predecessor. He must have grown weary of hearing about it. What I need from you today is advice more than absolution. Should I mention to this young man that we have met before?'

Miranda's eyes had adjusted to the darkness. She could just make out Don Pagnotta's profile through the grille. His Adam's apple protruded over the rim of his dog-collar. He tilted his head to one side and scratched his chin.

'Would it be of any benefit to the young man if he knew that you had had the opportunity to adopt him, but did not?'

'That's the very question I'm seeking an answer for.'

'By telling him would you simply be trying to assuage your own guilt?'

'Perhaps.'

'Was the young man adopted by another family?'

'I don't know. He's never mentioned any family and I haven't felt it appropriate to ask personal questions, having known him such a short time. I wouldn't want him to think me one of those meddlesome landladies.'

'And now, is the young man in question living a life which is honest and decent?'

'Oh yes, very much so.'

'Then perhaps the matter is best left in the past. We are reminded in Philippians, chapter two, verse three, that we should not act out of selfish ambition or vain deceit.'

Don Pagnotta sat back in his seat. He was rather pleased with his answer and the appropriateness of his biblical quotation, although he knew he shouldn't be because pride was in itself a sin.

'Hmm ...' mused Miranda, speaking more to herself than to the priest. 'I can't help but think there's something more to this.

Imagine, if we had adopted Rinaldo, he would have lived in the very place where he finds himself living now. Perhaps it's some sort of sign.'

'A sign? What do you mean by a *sign*?'

'What I mean is ... never mind.'

'Is there anything else?' the priest asked without enthusiasm.

There was – but Miranda wasn't ready to say, and certainly not to Don Pagnotta.

CHAPTER 13

It was a particularly hot day in the middle of a particularly hot August. The cold taps had been running with warm water all month. The atmosphere was heavy and still, and the sky was blindingly white, making the sun invisible through the haze. This combination of suffocating heat and oppressive humidity was known as the *afa*. Even the word sounded like a gasp for air.

Miranda wandered listlessly from room to room, fanning herself with her hands. Earlier she had spent an hour or so transcribing some of Alberto's research, but had given up as the heat had made typing even more unbearable than usual.

She thought she might try a little crocheting instead and took out the shawl on which she had been working for the past few weeks. Crochet wasn't her favourite activity and she didn't consider herself skilled at it, but the shawl wasn't for her. She had offered to make it as a favour. It was quite an unusual bluish shade of green, somewhere between sage and teal. Miranda laid it out on her knees to inspect it and saw that she had dropped a cluster stitch several rows back. Letting out a groan of dismay, she set about unpicking her work, wishing she hadn't volunteered to undertake the task in the first place. She would have bought a ready-made shawl from a shop, or from the market, if she'd been able to find one in the right shade of green. But her hands were so sweaty that she couldn't even hold the hook without it slipping through her fingers, so she put the unfinished shawl aside. She would try again in the evening when it was cooler.

Eventually Miranda made her way out to the terrace, where

she watered her basil, snapped the dead flowers off the geraniums and wiped down the leaves of the aspidistra, then stood for a while contemplating the palace garden. It was looking parched, but there would be some rain soon. There was always a storm on or around the *Ferragosto* public holiday on the 15th of August. It might erupt at any moment. Miranda could feel the electricity in the air.

'There's going to be a big storm, my love. Hopefully it will cool things down,' she said.

Alberto wasn't in a talkative mood and hadn't been all day, but that wasn't surprising. The thermometer read over 40 degrees and he'd never dealt well with the *afa*.

Every August there was an exodus of people from the city as they escaped to the mountains, or to the seaside, in search of reprieve. These days, the only occupants who remained at number 3, Vicolo Chiuso were herself and the officious lady on the ground floor. Miranda could have gone away somewhere, but she rather liked the place when it was quiet and empty, and anyway, she preferred being at home, close to Alberto.

Rinaldo had left for Milano Marittima the previous week. Miranda was pleased that he was taking a little time off as he worked such long hours. Still, she thought, it was a pity that he had gone alone. It surprised her that such a charming and eligible young man was unmarried and didn't seem to have a lady-friend, or any friends for that matter. As far as she knew, he had not received a single visitor during the time he had been living downstairs.

Miranda wondered whether his rather solitary existence was a result of his orphanage upbringing. Perhaps he found it difficult to make meaningful personal connections. Miranda couldn't deny that she was still curious to know whether another family had adopted him, but every time she steered their conversations towards family matters, Rinaldo would find a way to side-step the subject. She hadn't persisted. After all, she was only his landlady and it wasn't her business. Nevertheless, she thought it rather sad that he should be alone. She felt something in her heart whenever they spoke, either when their paths crossed on the stairs, or when Rinaldo came to drink tea with her on rent day. What she sensed in him was not exactly loneliness, more of a disciplined, self-imposed solitude – as though there was a void inside him which he couldn't, or didn't know how to fill.

Perhaps he would meet a lovely lady in Milano Marittima, mused Miranda, thinking back to the summer of 1928 when she had first encountered Alberto whilst on holiday on the island of Capri.

She had gone back to Capri the year after Alberto's death, but the place had changed beyond recognition. Everything had become commercial. The beach, which had formerly been almost deserted, was impassable with tourists. Miranda had spent more time fending off the hawkers who were trying to sell over-priced straw hats and slices of tepid watermelon than reliving the memories of falling in love with Alberto.

With this in mind, it occurred to her that she hadn't looked through her photograph collection for a while. She always enjoyed the nostalgia and the feeling of comforting melancholy that looking through old, happy memories gave her, so she went to fetch the holiday albums from the bookcase and settled herself amongst the plants on the terrace.

There were no photographs of their first summer in Capri, only Miranda's sketchbook and a series of little watercolours she had painted *en plein air*. Several pages in, after various studies of Mediterranean plants, sail boats and fishermen's shacks, was Miranda's first portrait of Alberto. He had been twenty-nine years old at the time, filled with youthful vigour and gifted with a magnetism which Miranda had found irresistible.

She had captured his likeness in ink and watercolour, sitting in the guest-house garden, reading under the shade of an awning and surrounded by great amphoral pots of oleanders in full flower, which encircled him like an enormous garland. It was a very pleasing composition. The way the awning cast its shadow and fragmented the light into little triangles; the playfulness of the pinks and the greens of the oleanders; the pure blue backdrop of the sky ... and handsome Alberto, leaning back in his deckchair with his bare feet resting on the rim of one of the pots.

His dark curls fell loosely over his forehead, reminding Miranda of an early self-portrait by Caravaggio, or a character from *The Three Musketeers*. He was dressed in his usual flamboyant way – in a peach-coloured shirt, unbuttoned almost to his waist, and blue and white striped loose linen trousers, which he had rolled up like the fishermen on the beach. He had a feather and a little sprig of broom tucked into the band of his hat.

Miranda cast her eyes over her artwork, thinking that it was really rather accomplished, considering she had only been eighteen years old when she had painted it, and at that time had received no formal artistic instruction. She hadn't enrolled at the Accademia Belle Arti until the age of twenty-one, and that had been thanks to Alberto's encouragement.

The sketches which followed would have seemed random to anyone who did not know the meaning behind them, but each one was a little memory, like a sort of pictorial diary entry, a record of her subsequent meetings with Alberto – meetings which had been carried out in secret, away from the disapproving eyes of her step-mother.

The thought of the woman's vicious rages still made Miranda shudder. She ran her finger over her nose, feeling the little bump on the bridge where her step-mother had broken it during one of her frenzies. Glancing up at the sky, Miranda said, 'I wonder whether that wicked woman is still alive? I hope she's not up there with you, my love. If anyone was deserving of the fires of hell, it was her.'

Miranda paused for a moment as she wondered whether her father too was still alive. During the years since Alberto's death she had considered trying to re-establish contact with him, but had always talked herself out of it. As far as she knew, he had never made any attempt to trace her either. The feelings she had towards him were still ambivalent. Her father had never been cruel, or violent, but neither had he protected her from his second wife, which according to Alberto had made him equally culpable.

Miranda shook her head, as though to shake the thoughts of her step-mother out of her mind, and continued turning the pages of her sketch book, until finally she came to her drawings of the Ancient Roman ruins of Villa Jovis, where she and Alberto had spent their last day together on Capri. The light that day had been so clear that they could see the Sorrentine Peninsula and Punta Campanella on the mainland. Miranda had sketched the lighthouse in the distance. If she closed her eyes, she could still conjure the feeling of sitting side-by-side with Alberto under the shade of the pine trees, the air rich with the smell of the sea and the sound of the cicadas.

The very last image, which was a rubbing as opposed to a drawing, was of a Roman denarius.

'Our special coin, my love,' Miranda murmured as she traced her finger around its outline. 'I often wonder what became of it.'

It was Miranda herself who had found the coin. She recalled how she had felt something digging into her leg as they lay together near the ancient ruins. She had scratched away at the dry ground and unearthed the coin. It was very worn and difficult to decipher, so she had taken a rubbing.

Alberto, whose knowledge of history was encyclopaedic, had known immediately that the inscription *TI* on its rim referred to the second Roman Emperor, Tiberius Caesar.

'Tiberius was a great general,' Alberto had explained, 'but history remembers him most prominently as the man in charge when Jesus was crucified. They say he lost his mind after his own son died and that's why he came here, to Villa Jovis, where he lived out the rest of his days engaging in wild debauchery.'

The mention of wild debauchery had made Miranda blush and what had followed had not been wild, or debauched, but they had made love – after which, and completely out of the blue, Alberto had asked whether she would marry him. Miranda said 'yes' before he had even finished his question.

'Come away with me,' Alberto had pleaded. 'Come back to Bologna. We can live together until we're married. And you can continue your studies, or do whatever you would like to do. But please, leave with me. I can't bear the thought of you going back to your father and step-mother.'

'When?'

'As soon as you want. Today, tomorrow, in a week, in a month. Whenever you like. But please, come away with me, Miranda. Don't go back to that unhappy place.'

'We'll have to leave in secret. If my step-mother suspects anything, she'll stop us.'

They had made a plan to leave at dawn the next day.

'Let this be our special coin. A symbol of our promise,' Alberto had said, holding the Roman denarius in the palm of his hand. Miranda had placed her hand over Alberto's so that they could both feel the coin pressing into their palms.

Miranda always liked to think that their first baby had been conceived that afternoon, under the pines of Villa Jovis. She had no way of knowing for sure. He could have been conceived in Alberto's room, or in one of the little grottos which opened onto the cliff path, or even beside the fishing boat which they had found abandoned on the beach one night. But from that moment the coin had become not only a symbol of their promise, but also a symbol of their union.

Until it was stolen, along with the camel overcoat, the Roman denarius had been an integral part of their life together, like a sort of guardian angel. Alberto had carried it with him everywhere.

'I hope that the new keeper of the coin, whoever they may be, finds some meaning in it too,' sighed Miranda, closing the sketch book and turning her attention to one of the photograph albums.

She and Alberto had been fortunate to enjoy many happy holidays subsequently – tours around Tuscany and Umbria; walking holidays in the Apennines; seaside escapes to Rimini, Portofino and the Amalfi coast – not to mention the countless cultural trips to visit the galleries of Florence and to enjoy musical performances at La Scala in Milan and at the Arena di Verona. They had only left the country once, for a trip to Lake Geneva. It was a pity that the black and white photographs didn't do justice to the colours of the place.

In the back of the album was a single loose photograph – a souvenir of the dreadful week spent in Cortina d'Ampezzo in 1953 as guests of the awful Saverio Salvi. The picture showed Alberto and Salvi sitting together with an enormous stuffed bear between them. That holiday would have been best forgotten, but Miranda could recall every ghastly moment. It was a pity, she thought, that their very last holiday had been the worst one.

Alberto and Saverio Salvi were only loosely acquainted and Miranda had been introduced to the latter briefly at a charity fundraising dinner, so she and Alberto were both surprised to receive an invitation to spend a week at Signor Salvi's house near Cortina d'Ampezzo in the Dolomite Mountains.

Alberto had been very keen to take up Salvi's offer. Salvi worked for the Government Treasury and had links to the Ministry of Culture, so he was a useful man to know. Funding for the arts was difficult to secure and Alberto hoped that Salvi might be able to put in a good word for his Cappella Musicale di San Petronio project. It was outrageous that for so many long years there had been no professional choir at an institution as historically important as San Petronio.

Cortina d'Ampezzo was beautiful. The Dolomites were awe-inspiring, with their sharp white peaks contrasting against the clear blue sky. The couple had gone up in late spring after the snows on the lower slopes had melted, exposing lush, verdant elevations and jagged, rocky outcrops. How lucky they had felt to have been invited to such a spectacular place!

Salvi's house was a magnificent chalet set high up with commanding views over the valley. Miranda had presumed that their host's wife would be there and had been looking forward to meeting her, but a young woman was there instead and Saverio Salvi made no secret of the fact that she was his mistress. Miranda had felt sorry for the wife, even though she'd never met her, but not as sorry as she'd felt for the mistress.

Initially Miranda had found Salvi to be a pompous bore, but the more she got to know him, the more she struggled to find anything likable, or even tolerable, about him. He boasted of personal qualities which he seemed to think would impress her, but in reality this did nothing but make her detest him further. Salvi spoke about his work at the Treasury as though he was the President of the Republic and was so inflated by his own importance that there was room for little else. When he wasn't name-dropping, or talking about how influential he was, he talked about hunting. He had travelled to many exotic places in pursuit of big game.

The chalet was crammed with oddities, foreign things and peculiar hunting trophies. A massive tiger's head was fixed to the wall above the dining-room door. An umbrella stand was made from an elephant's foot, while a lion's tail served as a bell-pull. Clearly Salvi had expected Miranda to admire these frightful things, but she'd been so forthright in her disgust for his 'sport' that even Alberto was taken aback by her reaction.

Miranda could have put up with Salvi's narcissism, his grandstanding and even possibly his descriptions of gratuitous animal slaughter, had it not been for his attitude towards the mistress, which deepened her repugnance for him to such an extent that she felt it physically.

It was clear to Miranda that Salvi was a man of perverse sexual inclinations who treated the young woman no better than the ill-fated prey which adorned his house. The poor creature spent the greater part of her days closed up in a bedroom on Salvi's orders. In the evenings she would be allowed to join them for dinner, but she never spoke. She would sit with her head bowed, picking at the food on her plate and taking tiny morsels off the tip of her spoon. She looked desperately undernourished, so bone-thin that the slightest breeze could blow her away. The yellowing remains of a bruise on her cheekbone, poorly-disguised by a dusting of face powder, did not go unnoticed by Miranda; nor did the fresh-looking scar which ran from the corner of her mouth to her chin. The unfortunate girl's name was Evelina Brunelli.

One evening, after a few too many glasses of wine, Salvi had bragged about the advantages of having an obedient woman.

'Stand up!' he had ordered, and Evelina had immediately done as she was told.

Salvi had rubbed his hands together, spat on his palm and landed such a hard slap on Evelina's backside that he had almost launched her across the table. There was no cry from Evelina, just a muffled, involuntary sound made by the breath being smacked from her body. Her expression barely changed. She seemed so consumed by suffering that she was numb to it.

Miranda had been outraged, but Salvi had responded with a drunken, self-satisfied smirk and said, 'I bought her. She's mine. I can do what I like.' He had then glanced over at Alberto and added, 'Every man should have one.'

Alberto had just looked embarrassed and muttered, 'Now, now, there's no need for that,' the weakness of which had incensed Miranda, so she had left the table in protest. Despite her pleading, Evelina had refused to go with her. Alberto had come after her instead, but rather than supporting her, he had begged her not to make a scene because Salvi was just a bit drunk and showing off. They were guests in his house and their host's private life was his own business – but for Miranda there was no excuse for Salvi's behaviour.

'Are you condoning hitting Evelina like that? Would it be acceptable to hit me if you'd had too much to drink?'

'Of course not, Miranda. You know I'd never dream of hitting you. But that was nothing malicious. It was just a bit of over-spirited high jinx.'

He had implored Miranda to consider the funding for the Cappella Musicale di San Petronio project, which Salvi had assured him would be made available very soon. The fact that Alberto was making excuses for Salvi and was ascribing such importance to money had further enraged Miranda. She couldn't believe that he was behaving like such a rapacious, grovelling sycophant – and that was exactly what she had called him. It was the only time they had ever had a row on holiday.

Alberto had argued that Miranda couldn't save everybody. Orphans were one thing, but Evelina was a grown woman with a mind of her own. If she wanted help, she would ask. Miranda had said that it wasn't necessarily as straightforward as that and had threatened to involve the police, even though she knew it was a flimsy threat. Salvi was far too well-connected to be afraid of a police investigation.

On the final day of their stay in Cortina d'Ampezzo Salvi had invited Alberto to accompany him on a day's hunting expedition. Initially Alberto had declined, partly because he knew that Miranda wouldn't like it and partly because he was afraid that gunfire would damage his hearing. He was stunned when Miranda insisted that he should go.

With the men out of the house Miranda had tried to speak to Evelina. She had bribed the housekeeper to stay out of the way and spent several hours outside the locked bedroom door trying to coax a conversation out of her. Miranda could hear Evelina on the other side of the door lighting cigarette after cigarette, but it was a long time before she would utter a word.

Eventually, when Miranda had mentioned Bologna, Evelina responded. In a voice that could hardly be heard, she said, 'Do you know where Via del Pratello is? It's the last place where I know my brother, Aldino, was living. Can you tell him I'm here? Can you tell him to come and get me?'

'Why don't you leave with us tomorrow? Once we're safely back in Bologna I can help you to find your brother.'

Evelina had refused. Miranda could hear the terror in her voice. Even though Salvi was out of the house and probably halfway up the mountain, she didn't dare to raise her voice above a whisper.

'I can't go with you – he'll come for me. You don't know what he's really like. He'll make you pay, and I can't give you trouble like that. Please, find Aldino. He'll know what to do.'

Miranda had promised that she would do all she could.

Shortly afterwards, Alberto and Salvi had returned from their excursion with a couple of bedraggled, blood-soaked birds. Miranda didn't mention her conversation with Evelina to Alberto because he had come back in a bad mood. His ears were ringing and he could think of nothing but the damage which the gunfire might have done to them. Miranda herself reasoned that a whole day spent listening to Salvi's bragging had probably been more injurious than the gunfire. By the time they returned to Bologna Alberto's hearing was back to normal, but Miranda still hadn't confided in him. She didn't want him to try to talk her out of finding Evelina's brother, Aldino.

Miranda had never ventured down Via del Pratello as it had a reputation of being an insalubrious street which was best avoided, but she found that although it was a little run down, it wasn't too squalid. Some of the people going about their business were somewhat unusual, but she hadn't felt threatened.

The address Evelina had given her had led her to one of the better-kept buildings. It appeared to be an ordinary residence, with the exception of a notice which read *No loitering outside the premises*, followed by a list of opening times. She knocked loudly.

Almost immediately the door was opened by a man of such monstrous appearance that Miranda gasped out loud. He was purple-faced and pox-marked, with a nose misshapen by repeated breakages.

Once she had collected herself she explained the reason for her visit. The doorman crossed his arms across his bullish chest, shook his head and grunted, 'You can't come in, Signora,' but Miranda could be very persuasive. Eventually he conceded, 'Back door. Through the yard. Wait in the kitchen,' and shut the front door.

The gateway into the yard was capped with a faded sign which read *Tognazzi Scrap Merchants*, but clearly the premises was no longer a scrapyard and hadn't been for a very long time. Apart from a row of dustbins and a Lancia motor car, the yard was empty. The back door to the building, however, was ajar.

A woman was sitting at the kitchen table peeling an enormous quantity of potatoes very slowly. Miranda introduced herself, but the woman said nothing. She just stared back vacantly, made a peculiar guttural sound and nodded in the direction of another door. Miranda thanked her and went through.

She found herself in a dimly-lit sitting room filled with a fug of cigarette smoke and the murmuring of *sotto voce* conversations. A dozen half-naked women were draped languidly over the couches. They looked like garishly-painted dolls, with exaggerated kohl-circled eyes and their mouths crudely enlarged by great quantities of scarlet lipstick.

There were men too, although they were fully clothed. Miranda recognised two from church. They recognised her too and reacted with a combination of astonishment and embarrassment.

It took Miranda only the briefest of moments to realise she had entered a brothel, but it wasn't as seedy as she had imagined such a place might be. Instead it was clean, surprisingly well-appointed, and furnished with some taste.

Seated on a high podium behind an elegant wooden counter was a portly older woman with a mouthful of gold teeth, who Miranda presumed must be the proprietress. She looked Miranda up and down then snapped, 'What are you doing in here? Who let you in?'

The room had fallen into total silence and everyone stared at Miranda, while the proprietress, using some very coarse language, flatly denied knowing anyone called Evelina Brunelli or anyone called Aldino Brunelli who might be her brother.

Miranda had been ushered out rather forcefully by the frightful doorman, but not before one of the women had caught her eye. She'd held Miranda's gaze just long enough for her to wonder whether perhaps she knew something, or was trying to tell her that the proprietress was lying. But Miranda knew better than to stop and ask. She had no wish to get the woman into any trouble.

Now, back in the present, and contemplating the image of Alberto and Salvi, Miranda said aloud, 'Madama Gioconda's – that was the name of the place. I never went back, but I couldn't get poor Evelina out of my mind. I had to do something to help her.'

Miranda paused, wondering whether it was time to divulge the rest of the story. There were only two significant secrets she had kept from Alberto, and Evelina was one of them.

After a long moment of consideration she said, 'So I went to get her.'

Miranda could sense Alberto's astonishment.

'I didn't go by myself. I telephoned my dear friend, Madre Benedetta, the Abbess up at the convent of Santa Caterina dei Colli, and explained the situation. I asked whether she had room to take Evelina in. She said that she did – eventually.'

Miranda sat back. It still amazed her that she had managed to keep her rescue mission a secret from Alberto.

'We went that week when you were at the lecturers' conference in Siena. A lovely young priest by the name of Don Giacinto drove Madre Benedetta and me up in his car.'

Miranda related how they had left Bologna before daybreak with no set plan as to how they would get Evelina out of the house and away from Salvi. They couldn't even be certain that Evelina would agree to leave with them, and they couldn't force her. That would make them almost as bad as Salvi himself.

When it came to confronting Saverio Salvi, Miranda had been prepared to resort to blackmail if necessary. It was pointless threatening to involve the police, but she could threaten to go to the papers. Men like Salvi were all about reputation, and exposing a scandal would, at the very least, dent his precious political career. It wouldn't be pleasant for Salvi's wife, but Miranda reasoned that was a small sacrifice in the scheme of things. Ultimately she was probably doing the wife a favour.

The little car had struggled up the steep mountain roads, but they had reached Cortina d'Ampezzo in the late afternoon without any major incidents. They had taken the housekeeper by surprise, but she had informed them that Salvi was away on business. She had been willing to help, on condition that her involvement in Evelina's rescue was never mentioned and that she received a little compensation for her trouble. Miranda had paid her handsomely enough to ensure her silence, although she had done so through gritted teeth because the housekeeper had been complicit in keeping Evelina locked up. Miranda mentioned the matter of 'unlawful detention' as the housekeeper counted the money.

'So what am I supposed to tell Signor Salvi?' the woman had whined. 'If he thinks I've been careless with the keys he'll fire me. Am I supposed to say that the girl just vanished into thin air?'

Miranda had instructed Don Giacinto to force the lock on the bedroom door and break a window in the scullery to make it appear that Evelina had escaped, but the housekeeper had protested at that too, arguing that Salvi would dock her wages for the damage. Miranda had stuffed another wad of banknotes into her apron pocket and told her to be quiet.

She had found Evelina lying on her bed, curled into a ball and facing the wall. The room was in semi-darkness, with just a few shafts of daylight pushing through the drawn curtains.

When Miranda first entered the room, there was no reaction. She had called Evelina's name quietly, so as not to cause the poor girl alarm. Eventually Evelina had turned slowly to face her, but her face, which stood out ghostly-grey in the half-light, remained impassive, with its violet half-moons under her eyes and her cheeks so gaunt that they seemed to have collapsed.

'Evelina, dear. It's Miranda.'

In an eerie, almost somnambulistic state, Evelina had raised her head and a glimmer of emotion had broken through her expression – but it was not fear, or relief, as Miranda might have expected. Her expression seemed more one of irritation, as though Miranda's arrival was an inconvenience.

With an enormous effort, Evelina drew herself into a seated position, slowly stretched out her fleshless legs and stared vacantly, seeming to see Miranda, but with an absence of understanding of what was happening.

'Mamma?'

'No, dear. It's Miranda. Remember me? I came here before.'

Again, Evelina repeated, 'Mamma?'

Miranda approached very slowly and crouched down beside her.

'It's Miranda Fiorelli, dear. Don't be afraid. I've come to help you.'

But still Evelina didn't seem to understand. She opened her mouth to speak, but at first all that came out was a series of stuttering breaths.

'Mamma, why did you take so long to come for me?' she wailed.

'Evelina, dear. It's not Mamma, it's Miranda.'

It was only then that Evelina seemed to gain some sense of the situation and understand that Miranda was not some ghostly apparition of her mother, but an actual physical presence in the room. She snapped out of her stupor, recoiled and asked, 'What do you want?'

'I want to help you.'

'Where's Aldino?'

'I couldn't find him, dear. But I'll keep looking until I do. You must come with me now where you'll be safe. Let me help you.'

Evelina had eyed her with an intense mistrust, muttered an obscenity under her breath and spoken in a tone which was both bitter and sarcastic.

'*You?* Why would you want to help me? I'm nothing to you.'

'You're a young woman in need of help, and that is not *nothing* to me.'

'But what about *him*?' Evelina said, referring to Salvi.

'You don't ever have to worry about *him* again,' Miranda replied, praying that it was true.

'Where are you taking me?'

'To the convent of Santa Caterina dei Colli. It's up in the hills near the Sanctuary of San Luca, just outside Bologna. It's a lovely place, very out of the way. My friend, Madre Benedetta, and the other sisters will look after you. Usually they only take in elderly ladies in need of care, but they're more than happy for you to spend some time there too. You can stay there as long as you need to.'

Evelina's look of mistrust had turned to one of utter incredulity and she had laughed, suddenly and piercingly, her voice crackling like a parrot's squawk.

'You're taking me to a *convent*? Do they know what I am?'

Miranda had taken Evelina's hands in hers. They were so cold. Her fingers were like brittle icicles which might snap under the slightest pressure. She had felt Evelina tense at her touch, but she hadn't let go.

'Yes, they know what you are,' she said gently. 'You're a young woman who has been the victim of unimaginable suffering. A young woman who has been treated with outrageous disrespect and cruelty. And also a young woman who will never have to suffer mistreatment or live in fear from this moment on.' Again, Miranda prayed that it was true.

'I've got nothing to give you in return.'

'What makes you think that I would want something in return?'

'Everybody wants something in return. Nobody ever gives something for nothing.'

'All I want is for you to have a new start.'

'I've had lots of those. Nothing's ever changed, apart from everything getting worse. Nobody
keeps their promises.'

For a moment Miranda hadn't known what to say. She had no concrete plan for Evelina, apart from getting her away from Salvi's house and to the safety of the convent. Her motives were solid, but faced with the grave reality of the situation, the execution of her rescue seemed very insubstantial.

'I don't really know what I'm promising you, Evelina, apart from a place where you can be safe. I can't tell you how your life will be tomorrow, or next week, or next month, or next year. All I can promise is that it won't be any worse than this.'

Evelina did not reply, but simply rose to her feet and stripped her nightdress off over her head in a single movement. She was naked underneath and nothing more than a skeleton wrapped in skin as thin as tissue paper. Her white, bony body was marked with many scars – the red and purple spots of cigarette burns, countless thin, straight scars which criss-crossed haphazardly, like a grisly game of pick-up-sticks – and an ugly, jagged track which stretched across her belly. Evelina looked at Miranda very directly, as if to say: 'You can see the state of me, are you sure you want to take me?'

Miranda had shaken herself out of her jacket and wrapped it around Evelina, murmuring,

'There, there, now. Don't get cold, dear. We'll get you some new clothes. I can definitely
promise you that.'

They had sped away from Salvi's chalet like outlaws fleeing the scene of a crime. Had the situation not been so serious it might have appeared comical, even farcical, with Miranda, Evelina, Madre Benedetta and Don Giacinto all squeezed into a tiny Fiat Topolino and hightailing it down the mountain road.

It had been an anxious journey, fraught with fear that the housekeeper might get cold feet and report back to Salvi. Their hearts had leaped into their mouths when they had encountered a police checkpoint, but the policeman had peered into the car, seen a priest and a nun in the front seats and waved them straight through. He hadn't even asked to see their documents, which was just as well as Evelina didn't have any.

They had stopped twice for fuel and once when Evelina had announced that she was hungry. She wouldn't get out of the car, mainly because she was too afraid, but also as she was dressed only in Miranda's jacket and Madre Benedetta's underskirt. So Don Giacinto had pulled over and gone to have sandwiches made in a roadside truck-stop. Evelina ate without restraint, devouring an enormous sandwich stuffed with *mortadella*. When Miranda couldn't eat her sandwich because the salami was far too greasy, Evelina had polished that off too. She had even picked every crumb out of the paper wrappers.

By the time they reached the sanctuary of the convent of Santa Caterina dei Colli it was past three in the morning. Poor Don Giacinto was exhausted from almost twenty hours of driving. Even the Fiat Topolino seemed relieved that the ordeal was over.

'There you have it,' said Miranda, now turning back to the photograph of Alberto. She could sense that although he was appalled that she had put herself in such a perilous situation, he was also rather impressed by her audacity.

'I did intend to come clean with you at the time, my love. I almost did when you returned from Siena as the lecturers' conference had gone so well and you were in such an excellent mood. But something always got in the way.'

It was the week following the rescue mission that Alberto had come home in a rage, fuming that the funding for the re-establishment of the choir at San Petronio had been withdrawn. No reason had been given and Saverio Salvi wouldn't return any of his telephone calls. Alberto couldn't understand what had happened.

Miranda had let him vent. She understood the situation perfectly well and decided to hold her tongue on the matter, at least until Alberto had secured some money through an alternative means. Unfortunately it had never happened and thus Evelina's rescue had remained a secret.

'The thing is,' she sighed, tracing her finger around the outline of Alberto's face, 'sometimes you could be difficult to talk to. When I knew something would make you angry, or upset you, sometimes it was easier not to say anything and just deal with it myself, or let it pass.' Before Alberto could respond, Miranda added, 'Although perhaps if you hadn't fallen ill so soon after our visit to Salvi's, I'd have found the right moment to tell you. But I want you to know that I am truly sorry about the choir funding. Reinstating the Cappella Musicale di San Petronio would have been quite a legacy for you to leave.' She paused. 'I have to admit, my love, that much of the reason I offered to take over the transcription of your research was to try to make up for it. It's my Act of Contrition.'

Miranda could feel that Alberto wasn't angry with her, but rather that he was hurt by the fact that she had kept such a secret. She felt some relief at having confessed, but the guilt for having kept Evelina's story from her husband still weighed heavily on her conscience. That one big secret had led to many other smaller secrets and so many 'white' lies. Whenever Miranda had gone off to the convent for the day, she had told Alberto that it was to help with the old ladies. The sums of money she had taken from the rent of the downstairs apartment hadn't been for repairs to the gallery, but payments made to the convent for Evelina's upkeep. And all those costly medical bills from the gynaecologist – those hadn't been for her fibroids, but for Evelina, whose sterilisation had been nothing short of an act of butchery. But that wasn't all; there had been a thousand other little falsehoods and omissions of the truth, all related to Evelina's rescue. That was the trouble with secrets. They needed lies to keep them alive.

A contemplative period of quiet ensued, partly because Miranda was lost in her thoughts and partly because she felt that Alberto might need some time to absorb the new information. He always liked to mull things over.

Miranda sat back with the album open on her lap and the photograph of Alberto and Salvi still in her hand. Confessing to Alberto hadn't been quite as difficult as she had imagined. There was still the other thing she hadn't told him, but it wasn't the right moment for something as serious as that. One step at a time.

She slipped the photograph of Alberto and Saverio Salvi back into its place in the back of the holiday album, then paused for a moment and took it out again. A man as twisted and odious as Salvi had no place amongst all her photographs of happy memories. Quite frankly, he had no place anywhere at all in her home. Miranda took the picture into the kitchen and cut it in half with her big scissors, leaving only the image of Alberto and the stuffed bear intact.

She took one last look at Salvi's face before starting to snip away at it bit by bit. Little pieces of Salvi fluttered into her kitchen dustbin like confetti and settled amongst the vegetable peelings and old tea leaves.

Suddenly a tremendous rumble of thunder shook the windowpanes and made the crockery tremble. The sky had turned from white to black in an instant.

Miranda slammed closed her kitchen dustbin and dashed back out to the terrace to rescue her precious albums as the first fat drops of rain from the *Ferragosto* storm began to fall.

CHAPTER 14

The bus that pulled up outside Majani's chocolate shop was almost empty. Ten o'clock in the morning was always a good time to head out of town and up to Santa Caterina dei Colli.

Miranda would never have imagined at the time of Evelina's rescue that she would still be making weekly, and sometimes twice-weekly, visits to see her at the convent, all these years later. She had presumed that within a few months, once Evelina had improved physically and gained some emotional stability, that the young woman would want to go and make a new life for herself in the outside world, perhaps with her brother, Aldino – but that had never happened. Evelina had indeed made a new life for herself, but strictly within the convent walls. During her seven years of residency she had never once left the confines of Santa Caterina dei Colli.

Miranda had to admit that she had underestimated the depth of Evelina's trauma. Initially, some nights Evelina had slept hidden under her bed, terrified that Saverio Salvi would come for her. Certain fears were so deeply entrenched that they were hard to dispel. It was one thing to *be* safe, yet quite another to *feel* safe.

But despite knowing that Salvi was no longer a threat, Evelina wouldn't speak about what path had led her into his clutches. She refused to give any details of her former life. At first both Miranda and the nuns had encouraged Evelina to speak about her past, thinking that releasing her pain would be helpful in her healing process, but all that had done was to distress her further. Whenever anything was asked she would shut down and then she would refuse to speak at all. Eventually, in order not to cause her further pain, they had stopped asking. She had never mentioned her brother Aldino again, not even once.

The question of Aldino had bothered Miranda. She had made numerous offers to try to contact him, but each time Evelina had declined. Miranda hadn't insisted, reasoning that perhaps reconnecting with her brother might open old wounds.

Still, although Miranda knew that she must be respectful of Evelina's request not to locate him, the matter had bothered her. Surely Aldino would want to know that his sister was safe? She had made a discreet inquiry at the Public Records Office, but had been unable to find any Aldino or Aldo Brunelli. She had even tried searching for other variations on the name, but there wasn't anyone called Geraldo, or Osvaldo, or Arnaldo Brunelli who might be a match. Eventually she had let the matter go. If one day Evelina decided that she was ready, then Miranda would do everything she could to help, but that decision was entirely Evelina's to make.

The bus made its way out of town, passing through the old city gateway of Porta Saragozza. Miranda rode as far as the ornate two-storey arch known as the Arco del Meloncello, where the road widened and continued flat towards Casalecchio, and the road up the hill known as the Colle della Guardia, which led to the Sanctuary of San Luca, forked off and rose sharply to the left. She crossed over to wait at the little bus stop at the foot of the hill.

The road up to the sanctuary was too steep and full of hairpin bends for a big bus, so a minibus would turn up every hour or so. There was no set timetable. The little bus took a circular route – up the precipitous Via di San Luca, then down the longer but less steep Via di Casaglia, and back to the Arco del Meloncello, where it would start its circuit again.

As there was no set timetable, it was down to chance as to whether one could wait a minute or an hour for a ride. Today luck was on Miranda's side. The minibus pulled up almost immediately – and thankfully the driver was Pietro, who didn't take the bends too fast – unlike some of the other drivers, who treated the road like a sort of racetrack.

'*Buongiorno, Signora,*' he greeted her cheerfully, 'I'm glad to see the back of that heat, aren't you?'

Miranda replied that yes, indeed it was far more pleasant now that the summer temperatures had abated, and she took her usual seat on the right-hand side so that she could enjoy the views along the route. As well as her handbag, she had with her a package for Evelina and a broom. The package contained the crocheted green shawl which Miranda had completed at last. It had taken her months. She hoped that it would meet with Evelina's approval as she had been so particular about the shade of green.

Miranda placed the package on her lap and tucked the broom beside her seat. She was concerned in case the minibus filled up, since it would make things awkward with the broom, but only four more passengers boarded – two ladies with baskets, who were clearly locals returning from a shopping trip in town, and a French couple who made their way to the back and began wrestling with a map.

The minibus began its two-kilometre climb, winding up the steep hill alongside the Portico di San Luca, which zigzagged its way up the Colle della Guardia like an enormous terracotta-coloured snake. It was the longest covered walkway in the whole of Italy – some said the longest in the world. In former times, devout pilgrims had crawled the entire way on their hands and knees, stopping at each of the fifteen chapels en route to the sanctuary in order to recite their Ave Marias. Modern-day pilgrims preferred to tackle the climb in comfortable shoes and stop at the chapels for a chat, but pilgrims had become a minority, replaced by tourists and day-trippers, both foreign and

Italian. The minibus regularly made extra stops to collect weary travellers along the way, as many underestimated the stamina required for a climb all the way to the top.

Miranda rested her head against the glass and looked out of the window at the expanding panorama of the city below with its bursts of green amongst the red roofs. She had been born and raised in Ravenna and was only a *Bolognese* by marriage, but she could name every one of the buildings of historical significance, from the various ancestral seats of noble families, to the football stadium which had been built to resemble a Roman arena, to the sprawling cemetery of La Certosa, which was almost a city in itself, and every single one of the numerous churches and monuments. It was thanks to Alberto that she was so knowledgeable, for he knew Bologna brick by brick.

Miranda came back to the present as the minibus rounded a hairpin bend and shuddered to a walking pace. It had caught up with a group of amateur cyclists on racing bicycles. They were riding standing up, their sinewy, muscled legs pumping away at the pedals. There had been more and more cyclists tackling the route since the Giro d'Italia bicycle race had undertaken a hill-climb stage up that very road. Pietro made a noise of irritation, leaned on his horn and began to gesticulate to express his displeasure.

'*Du maron!* Damned cyclists!' he muttered. He sounded his horn repeatedly, but the cyclists, who were riding four abreast, took no notice. Pietro added another far more colourful oath under his breath, but as the cyclists continued to ignore him and as there was nothing he could do about it without running them over, he just made a noise of exasperation and changed into a lower gear. Miranda didn't mind the slow pace of the climb at all and turned to look out of the window again.

It was only as they neared the summit that the cyclists moved across into single file and Pietro overtook, still complaining, and passing closer to them than was necessary. He was making a point.

A few minutes later the minibus came to a stop in the piazza in front of the Sanctuary of San Luca and Miranda alighted, wishing Pietro a good day. The French couple followed close behind her. The two ladies with shopping baskets remained in their seats.

It was late in the season, but there were still quite a number of tourists, some resting their legs after the long climb and taking refreshments while others were browsing the little stalls which sold novelty hats, postcards, key rings and facsimiles of the Madonna di San Luca, as well as more generic Italian memorabilia. It had always amused Miranda that one could return from a trip to San Luca with a miniature scale plaster model of Michelangelo's *David*, whose original statue resided in Florence, or of the Leaning Tower of Pisa.

Not all the visitors had reached the summit via the portico, or the road. Some had ridden on the cable-car, which approached from the opposite side of the hill. Amongst these was a class of excited schoolchildren. They were being herded by a flustered-looking teacher who was trying to explain that a church had stood on that very spot for over a thousand years.

Miranda crossed the piazza, picking her way through the clusters of visitors, then proceeded down the narrow lane which led to the convent with the broom in her hand and the package tucked under her arm.

It was no more than a five-minute walk from the bus stop to the convent. As Miranda approached, she tutted at the graffiti which had been scrawled on its perimeter wall. More and more graffiti had been appearing in and around Bologna, and it was making the city look awful. Some of it was obscene; much of it was political – Communist graffiti in the form of crudely-painted sickles and hammers, or the initials of opposing political parties. Ugly though it was, that kind of graffiti was trying to make a point – but what had been daubed over the convent's outer wall was an indecipherable scribble, nothing but a gratuitous act of vandalism. She wondered who on earth would take the trouble of bringing paint and brushes all the way up to San Luca in order to deface a wall.

The entrance to the convent was a tall, solid wooden gate with a small door set within it. Miranda tugged hard on the bell chain and heard the jingle in the distance. A few minutes later the little spy hatch in the middle of the door opened and Madre Benedetta's eye appeared behind the grille.

'Ah, it's you, Miranda,' she said, and the long process of unbolting the door began.

Although Madre Benedetta was the Abbess and the rules stated that she should be greeted and addressed formally, the two women had been friends for so long that they had dispensed with official titles and etiquette.

The Abbess hugged her warmly. Miranda would have returned the hug, but the package and the broom got in the way, so she craned her neck to kiss Madre Benedetta's cheek, missing slightly and landing the kiss on her wimple instead. Just as well, she thought, that she wasn't wearing any lipstick.

'How are you, Benedetta?' Miranda asked, to which Madre Benedetta replied in her usual dry way.

'Rushed off my feet, Miranda dear. I'd pray for there to be twelve more hours in the day if I had time. But as they say, *quinon proficit deficit* – he who does not advance, goes backwards.'

The convent garden was laid out on several sloped terraces. The fruit orchards were on the lowest terraces, bordered by a row of beehives, an enclosure for chickens and a heavily-fortified goat-pen. The goats were tricky escapologists whose regular quests for freedom would send the sisters running to catch them before they wreaked havoc by eating the crops, or anything else, whether edible or not.

Above the enclosure was the vegetable garden, where several of the novice sisters were hard at work with their sleeves rolled up and their sky-blue habits tucked into their aprons. Their underskirts and their knee-length drawers were showing, but as it was outside official visiting hours, a blind eye was turned to their less-than-proper state of dress.

The upper terraces, which were flat, boasted a beautiful ornamental garden, coloured yellow, pink and white by rose beds and hydrangea bushes. A number of the convent's elderly residents were seated in wicker chairs on a paved terrazza, enjoying the end-of-summer sunshine. As she had no family, Miranda knew there was a very real possibility that she might become one of those residents one day, but she could certainly think of worse places to spend the winter of her life.

Madre Benedetta linked her arm through Miranda's and they began their customary catch-up about this and that. As they made their way along the path which led to the cloister, the old gardener, Signor Rinaldo Rossi, appeared with an enormous bunch of hydrangeas for Miranda. He couldn't smile, or speak, but he offered up the flowers, nodding his head vigorously and patting his chest, which was always his form of greeting.

'Thank you. They're very beautiful,' said Miranda, taking the bouquet with some difficulty as she was already laden and Madre Benedetta was still holding her arm. Signor Rinaldo Rossi pointed to himself with his thumb and nodded again.

'Yes,' agreed Miranda, understanding the gesture, 'your hydrangeas really are magnificent this year. You have a magic touch, Signor Rossi.'

The old gardener indicated the sky, shook his head and mimed raindrops falling with his fingers.

'That *Ferragosto* storm was not kind to the roses,' explained

Madre Benedetta. 'Signor Rossi was beside himself when they were battered.'

Rinaldo Rossi shrugged and held his hands up to say that there was nothing he could do about the weather.

'I have something for you too, Signor Rossi,' said Miranda, holding up the broom.

The old man's eyes lit up. He nodded his head vigorously in gratitude, then took the broom and inspected it carefully, assessing its weight and the length of the handle. He scrutinised the brush end meticulously, running the flat of his palm along the bristles, then checked the connection to the handle. Finally he mimed a sweeping action before gliding a few strokes across the ground. He repeated the whole process twice.

'If there's anything else you need, Signor Rossi, just let me know,' Miranda told him. 'As long as I can carry it on the bus, I'm happy to get it for you.'

Rinaldo Rossi pointed to his feet.

'Socks?' said Miranda. 'Of course. That goes without saying. I'll bring some more next week.'

Signor Rinaldo Rossi made the gesture of thanks several more times, then tipped his straw hat with his index finger, turned and left, sweeping the path with his new broom as he made his way back to the rose garden.

Madre Benedetta smiled indulgently as she watched him walk away and said, 'He must be nearing seventy by now, but he has the energy of a man half his age. I wouldn't be surprised if he outlives us all.'

'There's a lot to be said for fresh air and good food.'

'You and I both know that he'd have died on the street if it wasn't for you, Miranda,' replied the Abbess.

Although Miranda couldn't recall exactly when she'd first encountered him, Rinaldo Rossi had been a familiar figure in and around Via Val d'Aposa for a long time. He scratched out his living by means of sweeping in exchange for food. When he was not sweeping he could be found wandering about with his blankets rolled under one arm and his brooms strapped across his back. He spent his nights in doorways.

Over the years Miranda had offered to help him find permanent lodgings, but Rinaldo Rossi had always declined, so instead she had provided him with blankets and warm clothing. He had always been particularly grateful for socks. When she had asked how he found himself to be living on the streets, he had given a jumbled, disjointed account about how he had had lodgings once, and a job in a brush factory. But Miranda had trouble understanding Bolognese dialect at the best of times and Rinaldo Rossi's explanation had rambled into something involving a cheese and a policeman, which she was unable to make any sense of. Ironically, he had become easier to understand since he had lost the ability to speak.

It was early one morning , just before Christmas 1948, as she was on her way to work at the gallery that Miranda had found Rinaldo Rossi collapsed in the doorway to Vicolo Chiuso; he was in a state of semi-consciousness and she could see he had suffered a stroke. She sent for an ambulance immediately and went to visit him in hospital every day for a fortnight, during which time she was his only visitor. When the doctors insisted on discharging him, Miranda was incensed, as a man in Signor Rossi's condition was clearly in no fit state to be sent back out to live on the streets. She would have offered him a bed in her own apartment, had he been able to climb the stairs.

When she had asked Madre Benedetta to take him in to see out the last few weeks of his life in dignity, warmth and comfort, the Abbess had agreed without hesitation. The doctors had given Signor Rossi no more than a couple of months to live.

That had been almost twelve years ago. Thanks to the care and solicitude of the sisters of Santa Caterina dei Colli, Signor

Rossi had made a remarkable – some might even say miraculous – recovery. Although he had never regained his speech, or much movement in his face, the rest of him had bounced back to robust health.

Despite this, Madre Benedetta wouldn't hear of him being sent back to live on the streets. Unfortunately, the convent was only permitted to house elderly ladies, so Miranda had stepped in and sought a special dispensation from the Bishop, thinking to herself that Alberto's church contacts could be very useful. Permission was given for Rinaldo Rossi to remain. In return for his board and lodging, Signor Rossi had become the semi-official convent gardener, assigned principally to sweeping the paths and tending the flower beds.

'How's Evelina been this week?' asked Miranda, as the two women stepped out of the sunshine and into the shade of the cloister.

'Nothing untoward to report. In fact, I'd say she's been in very good spirits. And she's had an excellent appetite, which is always a good sign,' replied Madre Benedetta. 'We've been having terrible trouble with one of our more challenging residents. Yesterday Signora Visconti was convinced that there was an infestation of cats in the chapel, which of course there wasn't, but Evelina went to free the imagined cats and then wheeled the confused old dear all the way down to the chapel to show her that they'd gone. And today for some reason she's convinced we're still at war, but Evelina's been wonderful with her. She must have told Signora Visconti at least twenty times just this morning that the war's over, and never once with the slightest irritation. That young woman is blessed with *patientia sancti*, the patience of a saint.'

'Evelina's at her best when she's caring for somebody else.'

'Indeed. Her care work gives her a focus beyond her own tribulations. Who'd have thought when she first came here that she would become such an indispensable member of our little convent family?'

They had entered the main hall, which was scented with the fragrance of beeswax from the convent hives and something delicious wafting from the kitchen. Miranda stopped before the icon of Santa Caterina. Madre Benedetta stood back, clasped her hands and bowed her head respectfully so that Miranda could recite the customary prayer.

'Preserve me, O beautiful love, from every evil thought; warm me, inflame me with Thy dear love, and every pain will seem light to me.'

They crossed themselves in unison and Madre Benedetta's tone became businesslike.

'Shall I take your flowers and put them in some water, Miranda? I have a dozen things to attend to, so I'll see you at lunch. We've got rabbit stew today. Signor Rossi caught three big fat ones in his trap.'

With that she took her leave, cradling the hydrangeas and disappearing hurriedly into her office in a rustle of skirts and veils.

*

Evelina laid her exercise books out neatly on the table. She knew that Miranda must have arrived because she'd heard the gate bell ring. Miranda was one of the few people Madre Benedetta would let in outside official visiting hours.

She knew all the people who came to the convent, and was happy to speak to them. None of them made her afraid now, not even the men. There weren't many male visitors anyway, just a few of the residents' friends and distant relatives, most of whom were pretty ancient, and the odd priest. Don Giacinto would come to visit her whenever he could, even though his parish was in Livorno now, which was quite a long drive away; she knew where it was because Miranda had shown it to her on a map when they'd learned about the geography of Italy.

Evelina had been waiting longer than usual, but Miranda and Madre Benedetta were probably having one of their chats and she guessed that it was about her. She'd hated it at the beginning, knowing that she was the subject of their conversations, but now she didn't mind so much because she understood that they meant well. They had been so very kind to her, even when she'd blasphemed, even when she'd raved like a lunatic, even when she'd pushed them away and told them to mind their own business. Not once had they been angry with her.

At first they had asked her so many questions that she had screamed at them to stop. She wasn't proud of that. There were things that they were better off not knowing and that she was better off not thinking about. How would she explain, anyway? She had seen the worst of men who did the worst of things. How could she tell a nun and a nice, respectable lady like Miranda about that? They'd said that speaking about her past would help her, but all it did was to fill her head with images and memories she wanted to forget.

She pulled up her sleeve and looked at the scars on her arm. Every cut and every cigarette burn had left its mark. Those marks would never go away, but there was no reason to pick at them and turn them back into wounds. It was better just to let them fade; to leave them out of sight and out of mind.

Evelina rolled her sleeve back down and opened up her exercise book to check through her arithmetic homework again, then read through a poem she had copied out. She was still a little slow at forming her letters neatly and she didn't always join them up in quite the right way, but Miranda said that didn't matter.

Recently she'd even had the confidence to read out loud during the Bible study classes she took with the novice sisters, even though they could all read better than she could. They were always patient with her and didn't mind if she stumbled on an unfamiliar word; but whenever she came across such a word, she would break it into syllables, just as Miranda had taught her.

She didn't just read the Bible. Miranda brought her all sorts of books from the public library. Illustrated storybooks were her favourites. Sometimes Miranda brought magazines – usually the kind aimed at housewives, which were full of recipes and articles about domestic things. Often Miranda used them as the basis for their lessons and would set mathematical problems which had practical applications such as budgeting, calculating the costs of everyday items, and working out how much change was owed. Now Evelina knew how much bread cost and how much milk could be bought for 50 lire.

Evelina understood that Miranda set these practical lessons in case she ever decided to venture into the outside world, but the chances of that happening were zero. She felt safe at the convent and enjoyed the routines of care and prayer. She loved all the sisters too. Nobody said mean things to her, or judged her. More than anything, she loved caring for the old ladies – and everybody said how good she was at it. There was no reason for her to leave, and Madre Benedetta had promised that she could stay as long as she wanted, even if that was forever.

The prospect of life beyond the convent walls was unimaginable, but she did enjoy hearing about it. It was like learning about a faraway foreign country whose customs and culture fascinated her, even though she knew she was unlikely ever to visit.

She wondered whether Rinaldo was all right. Recently he had been on her mind even more than usual. He would be thirty years old now – a fully-grown man. He was the only part of her past life that she allowed herself to think about, because it brought her joy. She revisited their childhood pranks and all their earnest plans, wondering what life he had made for himself. But the guilt of having lost his money – and the certainty that she had lost him his mother's precious earring because of it – still cast a guilty shadow over her mind. Miranda had offered to try to find him for her many times, but Evelina just couldn't bring herself to say yes.

Evelina's musings were interrupted by Miranda's arrival. She rose to her feet as she would if one of the senior sisters, or Madre Benedetta herself, had entered the room, even though Miranda had said that the formality was unnecessary. There was no greeting kiss or hug. Miranda respected the fact that Evelina wasn't comfortable with close physical contact.

Miranda set the package on the table. Evelina felt the contents through the brown paper and beamed, saying, 'Is it the shawl, Miranda?'

'Yes. At long last. I'm sorry it's taken me so long to finish it.'

Evelina eased open the paper and clapped her hands in delight.

'Is it all right? Is that how you wanted it? Do you like it?' Miranda asked with some trepidation.

Evelina didn't look up straight away, but the broad smile remained fixed on her face.

'It's perfect,' she said. 'Absolutely perfect. It's just the right green, just like my Mamma's shawl, except Mamma's shawl was rough and this is really soft.'

'Your Mamma had a shawl like that? Is that why you were so particular about the shade of green?'

'Yes,' replied Evelina.

Miranda hesitated before responding as this was new territory. Evelina never spoke about her mother. The only thing Miranda knew about her was that she had died when Evelina was very young. She had volunteered no other information.

Evelina took the shawl from its packaging, but rather than trying it on herself, she turned to Miranda and wrapped the shawl around her shoulders instead, arranging it carefully and in a very precise way.

'There,' she said. 'I've always wanted to see you in a green shawl like Mamma's.'

'You have?'

'Yes. I've seen you before, but only in my mind. Whenever I think of my mother I see her, but with your face. I think of you as my mother. I know you're not old enough to be her, but I don't mean it that way. I mean that you care. You do kind things for me, like a mother would. You're my Mamma now, my Mamma Miranda.'

With that, she planted an enormous and very noisy kiss on Miranda's cheek, then clasped her tightly and whispered hard in her ear, 'Thank you. Thank you for everything, Mamma Miranda.'

This openness and affection was so unexpected that Miranda felt a wave of emotion which made her heart beat so hard she could feel it like a rattling in her chest. The kiss had been so loud that she could still hear its echo in her ear.

Being called 'Mamma Miranda' was a wonderful term of endearment. It meant more to Miranda than Evelina could ever know.

CHAPTER 15

The blazing hot summer had switched to winter with barely a pause for autumn. It was only mid-October and the temperature had dropped below zero overnight. Miranda had had to bring her geraniums in early. Most years she was able to leave them out until at least the end of November.

'I'm going to spend the day with Evelina at the convent, my love,' she said. There was some relief in telling Alberto the truth about where she was going and why. 'Do you think I should wear my sheepskin-lined boots? It's always a few degrees chillier up in the hills.'

She considered the boots for a moment, then decided against them and put on her thicker stockings instead. She also took her yellow beret from the wardrobe.

There was a fresh photograph of Alberto on the bedside table. Perhaps it was the sudden seasonal change which had made Miranda choose it. It was a cheerful snap she had taken across the table of a café a few doors down from the Galleria Fiorelli on a bright December day. Alberto had come by to have a look at a new intake of paintings and Miranda had closed the gallery for an hour so that they could go for coffee. It was chilly, but they had sat outside as the weather was so fine.

He looked so dapper dressed in his camel overcoat, his black fedora hat and the lovely blue and red tartan scarf with the matching tie which she'd bought for his birthday. He was wearing his coat open, as he always did, but Miranda had given up years before on badgering him about doing it up.

As she was making her way down the first flight of stairs she heard the main door open and close and the sound of Rinaldo's footsteps. She always knew when it was Rinaldo climbing the stairs because he ascended quickly, two steps at a time, and was usually humming to himself.

Once or twice before, Miranda had stopped and listened to his footsteps, keeping out of sight with her back pressed to the wall and pretending that it was Alberto coming home. He used to climb the stairs in the same way, two steps at a time, and he would always be singing. He maintained that singing during physical exertion was the best breathing practice, and the acoustics in the stairwell were particularly good.

When Rinaldo looked up and spotted Miranda he called out, '*Buongiorno!*' Miranda nearly fell over the banisters. She had seen her tenant countless times in his camel overcoat, but that morning he had a blue and red tartan scarf tucked into the fur collar and was wearing a black fedora hat. Miranda almost called out Alberto's name, but when she opened her mouth all that came out was a gasp and the word, 'Oh!' As she said it, she missed the last steps and toppled, landing in a heap just outside Rinaldo's door. He leaped up the stairs three at a time and was by Miranda's side in an instant.

'Miranda! Are you hurt?'

'It's n-nothing,' she stuttered. 'I just slipped. It's these shoes – I've just had them re-soled. You know how it is, leather soles can be so slippery until they're worn in. Really, it's nothing – it's just the new soles. I'm fine. I should have worn my boots.'

Rinaldo crouched down beside her and put his arm around her shoulder. Miranda stared at him, so overcome by the sight of him in the camel overcoat, fedora hat and tartan scarf that she wanted to grasp his face, call him 'Alberto' and kiss him, but even in her distressed state she was aware of the madness of doing such a thing. Rinaldo would think her insane, and rightly so.

Instead she sank her face into Rinaldo's shoulder and smothered her sobs in the rabbit fur collar – but it was not the pain of her fall which was making her cry. Close up she could see that the tartan scarf was not just similar, it was identical to the one she had bought for her husband. For a few strange and wonderful moments, as she huddled against Rinaldo, she let herself believe that he *was* Alberto. Even the sound of his voice was Alberto's as he said, 'Come, Miranda. Let's get you back upstairs.'

Rinaldo helped her to her feet, but she cried out when she tried to put any weight on her ankle. They attempted various ways of getting up the stairs, but even with Rinaldo's support, Miranda couldn't manage it. Eventually she looped her arms around his neck and Rinaldo carried her.

Once inside her apartment, he set her down on her armchair, knelt in front of her, took her foot in his hand and unbuckled her shoe. Had the fall happened under any other circumstances, Miranda would have found it an uncomfortably intimate gesture, but in that moment all propriety was forgotten. All she wanted to do was keep hold of the vision of Alberto.

As she looked down at Rinaldo kneeling at her feet she could still imagine her husband. The expression in his eyes as they met hers; the way his brow knitted as he examined her ankle; the forms his mouth took as he spoke. It was all Alberto. Again, she wanted to reach out and touch his face, but she knew that she mustn't.

'Can you move your foot?'

'Yes,' sniffled Miranda, wincing. 'It's just a sprain. You must think me so daft, Rinaldo, crying like this over a silly sprained ankle.'

'It's all right. You're in shock, Miranda.'

'Yes. You're right. I am in shock,' she said. She still couldn't tear her gaze away from him.

Rinaldo took off his overcoat and hat, draped the coat over Alberto's red leather armchair and placed the fedora hat on top.

He was wearing a boldly-pinstriped suit in a rather brazen shade of blue with a yellow waistcoat and multi-coloured handkerchief tucked into the breast pocket of his jacket. Miranda thought that he looked very smart. It was certainly an outfit that Alberto would have approved of.

Rinaldo pulled the footstool across and carefully rested Miranda's foot on the cushion. There was a lump showing through her stocking.

'It looks really swollen. Shall I call a doctor?'

'No, no. It's not serious enough for that. I'm just a clumsy fool for tripping over my own feet. Thank you for picking me up.'

'Well, I couldn't just leave you on the floor, could I? You were making the landing look very untidy and we have rules about keeping the communal areas clear. The lady on the ground floor would have complained.'

Miranda wanted to laugh, but the effect of Rinaldo's good-humoured quip was to set her off sobbing again. It was just the kind of funny thing Alberto would have said to make her feel better.

'Miranda, are you sure you don't want me to call a doctor, or take you to the hospital? Or I could go down to the bar on the corner and get some ice,' offered Rinaldo, sounding rather worried. 'And if you want me to stay with you, I can. I'll just call the office and tell them I won't be coming in.'

'Thank you, Rinaldo. You're so kind, but I'll be fine. I'll just keep the weight off it and take a couple of aspirins. I know how busy you are. I can't keep you from your work. I must have delayed you already.'

Rinaldo was reluctant to leave Miranda in such a distressed state. He sat holding her hand until she had stopped crying.

'If you need anything, or want me to pick anything up, just give me a call and I'll come back,' he promised, 'or I'll send one of my delivery boys round with whatever you need.'

Miranda squeezed his hand, holding it for longer than was necessary, and thanked him again. Rinaldo took his overcoat and hat from the back of the red leather armchair and left, saying that he would call in again after work.

Miranda's ankle was looking rather swollen and it was very painful, but that was insignificant in comparison with what she had experienced on the stairs. She turned to one of the photographs of Alberto and said, 'Am I going mad?' but the image in the photograph remained impassive.

Whenever she spoke to Alberto's photographs and imagined him responding, Miranda was aware that it was a construct in her head. She knew that when he replied to her distracted chatter it wasn't really her dead husband replying. She was just telling herself what she supposed Alberto might have said, or rather, what she wanted to hear. Her imagination might be a little over-fertile, but she wasn't delusional.

She understood that speaking to Alberto's photographs was her way of grieving. It might not be the usual way, but grief was bespoke. It didn't respect schedules, or circumstances, or any set rules. Imagining Alberto's presence and including him in her day-to-day life was her way of postponing the loss. The countless hours of tedious typing and translation she undertook were not just a penance, but a way of keeping him with her. All these loving gestures made her feel less alone, and because she *was* alone there was nobody to tell her she should stop, or pull herself together and move on.

She had never intended it to continue as long as it had. Miranda had thought that eventually she would feel a distancing and the yearning would subside. It had for a while and she had settled into a new normality, but then everything had been set off again when Rinaldo had come to view the apartment wearing that camel overcoat.

From the moment she had set eyes on him, she had had the

feeling that the overcoat was some sort of sign from Alberto. She kept telling herself that it was ridiculous to set such store by an item of clothing – but the feeling had been stronger than her. Then there was the emblem of Tiberius Caesar on each of Rinaldo's delivery bicycles. Surely that too was some sort of sign?

But what she had just experienced with Rinaldo, the overcoat, the hat and the scarf was more than just a bit of wishful thinking. It had felt like a real, physical connection to Alberto and she wasn't sure whether she should feel elated or troubled by it. In fact, she felt both.

Miranda took two aspirins and telephoned Madre Benedetta, offering her apologies and saying not to expect her. She then sat for a while with her eyes closed and her foot on the footstool, breathing in slowly through her nose and out through her mouth, concentrating on a tranquil rhythm so as to calm herself, and waiting for the aspirins to take effect – but she couldn't settle. She felt profoundly disturbed, yet deeply joyful. The sensation that something important was happening permeated through her; the feeling that she should be preparing herself for something momentous – although exactly what, she didn't know.

But when Miranda glanced across at Alberto's red leather armchair, she jumped out of her skin, shock pushing the air out of her body with a strangled sound. She gripped the arms of her chair, gasped for breath and closed her eyes so tightly that she could see stars.

It couldn't be. It was impossible. It must be an hallucination, a mirage, a trick of the light.

When she finally dared to open her eyes again she knew that they were not deceiving her. For right in the middle of the seat of Alberto's armchair was a Roman denarius!

Miranda struggled to her feet and limped to the armchair, then stood over it, staring down at the coin. She knew by the wear and the chips around the edge that it wasn't just *any* Roman denarius. She would recognise it anywhere. It was, without a doubt, their special coin.

At first she was too afraid to touch it. She looked around the room, almost expecting Alberto to appear in some spectre-like form. A prickling sensation spread through her and grew in intensity until it was like a swarm of bees raging through her veins.

'You're here, my love!' she cried.

Suddenly Miranda was not afraid. A feeling of rapture overcame her. This was not a delusion, or a figment of her imagination, nor was it reality warped by grief. Alberto really was still with her!

She picked up the coin and touched the seat of the chair, hoping to sense some other sign, such as a change in temperature, but there was nothing else.

'What is it, my love? Is there anything you want to say? Is there something I need to do?'

There was no response, but there was definitely something in the room – some sort of presence, like a shadow which she couldn't quite see, or the echo of sounds which she couldn't quite hear. Alberto was everywhere, surrounding her, yet at the same time he wasn't there. It was a most extraordinary sensation. Miranda sat and stared at the red leather chair for a long time, clutching the denarius in her hand.

How were such manifestations possible? How could physical laws be twisted for something to appear from nothing – or even for something to appear from another realm? How did the intangible become tangible? And what did it mean to send the coin, and to send it in that moment? But none of these questions really mattered, because whatever the manner of its sending, the result was a miracle.

Miranda had a collection of mementos she had kept from their summer in Capri. There was a pressed oleander flower from the guest-house garden, a pine cone from Villa Jovis, a shell from the beach, a pebble from the cliff path.

She laid out her little collection of keepsakes, including the Roman denarius, in a circle on the footstool, bowed her head and prayed – not specifically to God but to some unknown entity, and partly to Alberto himself. She prayed for clarity and for further signs. If Alberto needed her to do something she prayed that she would understand what it was. Periodically she would look around the room, urging Alberto to come to her. She couldn't see him but she could definitely feel him.

It was in this mystical state of mind that she understood that whatever else Alberto might need from her, sending the Roman denarius was a declaration that his love for her endured. Of all the signs he could have sent, the coin was the most symbolic of them all.

*

At around four o'clock there was a knock at her door. Miranda presumed it would be Rinaldo, although it was earlier than she would have expected him. She was rather surprised to find Don Pagnotta holding a bag of grapes.

'Signora Fiorelli, I understand you've suffered an injury,' he said with an air of great concern.

Although Miranda had thought it unnecessary to inform anyone except Madre Benedetta about her accident, the news had spread. The lady who lived on the ground floor had heard the commotion on the stairs and had quizzed Rinaldo about it. She had told her friend who lived at number 4, who had spoken to the butcher. The butcher's wife had informed the shoe-shop owner and anyone else who would listen. This game of Bolognese whispers had continued until eventually the news had filtered down to Don Pagnotta.

Miranda wasn't in the mood for small-talk, but she didn't want to appear rude and it was kind of Don Pagnotta to take the time to check on her.

'It's nothing serious, just a silly accident on the stairs,' she said, then added cordially, 'Won't you take a seat, Don Pagnotta? But not on the red leather armchair, please.'

Don Pagnotta pulled a dining chair across and offered up the grapes, but Miranda was far too unsettled to eat. They chatted for a while about matters of little consequence until finally Miranda said, 'What is your view on ghosts, Don Pagnotta?'

'Ghosts?' spluttered the priest, coughing a grape out of his mouth. 'What exactly do you mean by *ghosts*?'

'The spirits of the dead who manifest on earth.'

Don Pagnotta put down the bag of grapes slowly and scratched his chin, as though he was planning his answer very carefully.

'Well,' he began, 'one must be cautious in one's belief of such things. I would venture to say that in most cases there is a rational explanation for experiences which are perceived as supernatural events. If something appears to be unbelievable, it usually is.'

'But as Catholics are we not obliged to believe in the unbelievable? If we are expected to believe in transubstantiation and resurrection and to accept the existence of angels and demons, should we not also be open to the existence of human spirits?'

Don Pagnotta hesitated. He sensed that Miranda Fiorelli was more knowledgeable than most on matters of faith and was not afraid to pose uncomfortable questions. He had also realised that his extensive, word-for-word knowledge of the Bible, rather than impressing her, caused her irritation. Miranda Fiorelli was not easy to palm off with a few scraps of scripture.

He nodded slowly. 'There is the belief that God can, and sometimes does, allow a departed soul to appear on earth. The spirit of Samuel appeared to Saul, and a significant number of saints have made themselves visible to people in some form. For example ...'

Miranda stepped in before Don Pagnotta's explanation became too theologically detailed, or unleashed an endless stream of biblical quotations.

'That's all very well, but under what circumstances might God allow these spirits to appear?'

'Far be it for me to second-guess the Holy Father's intentions!' exclaimed Don Pagnotta, raising his eyes heavenwards and making a brief sign of the cross. 'But one can assume that it could be for various reasons. Perhaps to comfort, or to teach, or possibly even to ask for help.'

Miranda had already considered all three reasons. Each was a possibility.

'And what is your opinion on trying to communicate with these souls?'

'Ah, now that is a stickier matter, Signora Fiorelli. There is a line between the spiritual and what may be considered as occult. But the Bible is clear in its position. Speaking to the dead is prohibited, whether it be directly, or through divination. We must not seek comfort or guidance from spirits. Our comfort and guidance must be sought from God. Indeed, there are also clear rules for spirits both in Deuteronomy and Leviticus, which state that spirits should not attempt to draw in the living.'

'Are we therefore to work on the assumption that all spirits have read and studied the rules cited in Deuteronomy and Leviticus and are willing to follow them?'

Don Pagnotta scratched his chin again. He felt on the losing side with Miranda Fiorelli.

'Well, if one were to say, purely for the sake of argument, that a departed soul *was* attempting to communicate in some way, then it would be logical to consider this soul as being in a state of purgatory. In which case, rather than attempting to communicate with it, one should be praying for the soul to be delivered.'

'Purgatory? Not everybody believes in purgatory. I myself have serious reservations.'

The priest was taken aback. 'But the Catholic Church's doctrine on purgatory is extremely well-documented!' he objected. 'It goes back to the second Council of Lyon in 1247 and it has remained largely unchanged since the Councils of Florence and Trent in the fifteenth and sixteenth centuries.'

'Other Christian faiths don't believe in purgatory.'

'Hmm ...' mused Don Pagnotta. 'Indeed, there are those who question it. Protestants, for instance, deny its existence. But many Protestants also deny the premise of the Immaculate Conception.' He tutted to himself at the ridiculousness of the Protestant position, then turned his attention back to Miranda, asking, 'May I know what has driven you to ask me all this, Signora Fiorelli?'

'My husband's spirit is trying to communicate with me.'

'Ah,' said Don Pagnotta, sucking the air in through his teeth. Miranda Fiorelli wasn't the first grieving widow to have been overcome by this type of delusion. In his experience it could generally be put down to loneliness, or in more extreme cases, hysteria. 'May I suggest that perhaps you are in a state of confusion as a result of your accident?'

'I've twisted my ankle, Don Pagnotta. I haven't banged my head.'

The priest sighed. There was little point in arguing. He knew that not everybody could be convinced by reasoning, and recalled a quote from Proverbs which stated that it was easier to live in a dry desert than to deal with a difficult woman.

'I don't disbelieve you, Signora Fiorelli. You may well have had some sort of experience. The question is the exact nature of this experience. The mind is a powerful thing, and as with anything which we don't quite understand, there is room for misinterpretation. I would venture to say that feeling the presence of a departed loved one, particularly a spouse, is amongst the most frequent experiences of this kind. When two people have been unified under God and one party finds themselves alone, the period of adjustment can be very difficult. Many widows and widowers feel as though they have lost half of themselves. This feeling you have experienced ...'

'It's been more than a feeling, Don Pagnotta. I have received a tangible, physical sign.'

The priest swallowed hard and loosened his dog collar with his finger. 'How so, Signora Fiorelli?'

Miranda showed Don Pagnotta the Roman denarius, although she would not let him touch it, and explained the story behind it, being mindful to edit out the more intimate details. She also recounted the incident on the stairs which had resulted in her fall.

'Could there not be a rational explanation, Signora Fiorelli?'

'If there is, I can't think what it might be. I can explain away what happened on the stairs this morning. Rinaldo simply owns an overcoat which is just like the one my husband used to wear and the hats were the same, but lots of men wear camel coats and fedora hats. I can also explain the fact that Rinaldo was wearing an identical scarf. The one I bought for Alberto came from Carluccio's in Via Indipendenza. It's not a one-off item. All that can be put down to coincidence. But this coin? This coin is a different matter entirely.'

'Could it not be that the coin was here all along, Signora Fiorelli? That it was not stolen as you presumed it was, but simply mislaid. In the Parable of The Lost Coin in the Gospel of Luke the coin is just that – lost.'

'If I had found it dropped behind some books, or kicked under a piece of furniture, that would make sense. But how could it turn up out of nowhere right in the middle of the seat of Alberto's chair?'

The priest opened his mouth, but could think of nothing to say. He couldn't even think of a fitting Bible quote.

'I'm afraid I have no alternative answer for that, Signora Fiorelli.'

'Exactly!' said Miranda. 'Alberto is trying to communicate with me and I need to know why in case there's something important he wants me to do.'

The priest's expression darkened and became very serious.

'I would urge you not to stray into the occult, Signora Fiorelli. In matters such as this, prayer must come before all else. I will pray for your husband's soul and I will pray for you to be released from this distressing ...' Don Pagnotta paused as he chose his next word '... haunting.'

'No, you will not!' Miranda told him very firmly. 'If anyone is going to pray for my release from Alberto it will be me – if and when I am ready. I would thank you not to meddle in that, Don Pagnotta.'

At that point, Don Pagnotta had to return to San Paolo Maggiore to prepare for the early evening service, but Miranda was glad to get rid of him. His cursory answers had done little more than irritate her, and what's more had taken up time which could have been spent speaking with Alberto.

Notwithstanding what Catholic teaching might have to say about spirits and ghosts and the apparition of the dead, there was no denying that Alberto was there and that he was trying to communicate something to her. Miranda felt more connected to Alberto's spirit than she had ever felt connected to God, and there had to be something in that.

Then suddenly, light dawned – and she knew why Alberto had come back. He must suspect that there was something she hadn't told him, and he wanted to know what it was. Miranda clutched the Roman denarius so tightly in her hand that it dug into her bones. She knew that she must tell him, and she would, but only when the moment was right.

Rinaldo came up after work, as promised, bringing with him fresh bread and a platter of cold meats, eggs and salad from the trattoria in Via Carbonesi so that Miranda wouldn't have to cook. She thanked him so earnestly for his thoughtfulness that for a moment Rinaldo wondered whether she might start crying again. But Miranda did her best to appear as normal as she could and hoped that Rinaldo hadn't found her earlier behaviour too disconcerting. She took a long look at him, but he wasn't wearing his camel overcoat so she couldn't really see him as Alberto any more, which was both a disappointment and a relief.

Making an effort to smile, she said, 'I have a little something for you, Rinaldo, to thank you for your kindness this morning. I couldn't help but notice your lovely tartan scarf. I thought this tie would go well with it. It's not new, of course. It was Alberto's. But I'd like you to have it.'

Rinaldo was touched. He realised how special it was to be given something that had belonged to Alberto.

'I was curious, Rinaldo,' she went on carefully. 'Where did you get your scarf?'

For a moment Rinaldo wondered whether he should tell Miranda about the rude man in the camel overcoat who had almost pushed him into Neptune's fountain, called him a thieving toe-rag and yelled at him to get a job – and how he had followed the man and taken his coat and hat as a punishment for being so insensitive and bad-mannered. Then he thought better of it. Although Miranda might have understood his motives if he had explained how, at the time, the line between crime and survival had been blurred by his homelessness and hunger, he didn't want her to know he'd been a thief. And anyway, it wasn't who he was any more.

Eventually he said, 'The scarf? Oh, it was a Christmas present from an old acquaintance.'

'How lovely,' smiled Miranda. 'I expect it came from Carluccio's, the menswear shop in Via Indipendenza. That's where the tie came from.'

Rinaldo left Miranda, satisfied that she was all right, but he didn't go home because something very troubling had happened that day.

He'd lost his lucky coin.

He knew that the coin had been in the inside pocket of his overcoat that morning when he left Miranda's apartment after her fall because he'd felt for it as he took his coat off the back of the red chair. He'd only noticed it was gone at lunchtime, after he'd come back from doing his rounds to collect payments due from customers. He had spent most of the afternoon re-tracing the morning's steps, walking along the routes he had taken with his eyes firmly fixed on the pavement, but without success. He had called in to every client he'd been to see earlier in the day to ask whether they had found his coin, but nobody had.

The daylight was fading as he made his way back out again, but at least the streets weren't so crowded. He searched for the lucky coin for several hours in a very black mood.

He knew that it wasn't rational to be feeling the way he was, but losing the lucky coin was like losing a trusted friend. He couldn't shake off the feeling that without it, bad luck would return and some calamity would befall him. Every good thing in his life would vanish. He would lose his business, then his apartment. Perhaps he would be afflicted with some terrible disease, or get knocked over by a tram, or succumb to some freak accident. He would find himself once again living in poverty, in misery, in chaos. He would perish from starvation. The list of possible misfortunes was endless.

As he continued to search, winding his way back in the direction of home, Rinaldo passed a small group of street girls. There had been more and more women working the streets at night since the closure of the brothels. The way they stood in the recesses, under the dark arches of the porticos, often only perceptible by the glow of their cigarettes floating amongst the shadows, had earned them the nickname *lucciole*, fireflies. Rinaldo was no stranger to being propositioned, but he had vowed years before never to become one of those men who bought their services, so he always declined. He would stop and talk to the women sometimes though, just to ask whether they knew anything of Evelina. Nobody had heard of her.

The cluster of women he passed that night paid him no attention. They didn't seem to be working. They were just standing in a shop doorway talking, with a cloud of cigarette smoke hovering above them. Rinaldo thought nothing of it and carried on scouring the pavement for his coin until he heard one of the women call his name. When he turned around it took him a moment to recognise her. It was Fifi la Française, minus her thick mask of make-up and phony French accent.

'Good God!' she said. 'Is that really you? You look as though you're doing all right for yourself, Rinaldo Scamorza.'

'Are you working out there?'

'Yes – but not the way you're thinking. I work for a charity now. We help the girls on the street. Got five minutes for a chat?'

'Sure,' replied Rinaldo, wishing that of all the nights to bump into Fifi, it wasn't on a night when he was so preoccupied. He was about to ask whether she knew anything of Evelina, but Fifi beat him to it.

'Have you heard from Evelina?'

'No,' he said sadly. 'Why, have you heard anything?'

'Not directly. She never got in touch with me, or any of the other girls. But she did send someone to try to find you.'

Rinaldo stopped in his tracks. 'She did? When?'

'It was three years after she left, maybe four. I'm not sure exactly. The years kind of blend together when you're living in a place like Madama Gioconda's.'

'Who did she send?'

'A woman. I don't know who she was, but she was a proper lady. Well dressed, well-spoken. Completely out of place at Madama Gioconda's. She just turned up one day asking whether anyone knew where you were because Evelina was looking for you. She said she was looking for Aldino, so it must have been Evelina who sent her. She's the only one who called you that.'

'So what happened? What did Ardilla say?'

'Ardilla denied knowing you, or Evelina. She was furious with Buttafuori for letting her in.'

'How did the woman know Evelina?'

'I'm really sorry, Rinaldo. I just don't know. I wanted to say something – Carlotta and I both did. We wanted to tell her that although we didn't know where you were, Ardilla was lying about not knowing you or Evelina. Maybe we could have got an address off her or something and put the word out. But we couldn't say anything with Ardilla right there, in a filthy temper. She was so rude to that poor woman.'

'Did the woman say whether Evelina was all right?'

'She didn't really say anything at all, apart from the fact that Evelina was looking for you. But to be honest, Ardilla didn't give her much of a chance to speak.'

'Did she mention Milano Marittima?'

'No,' replied Fifi, shaking her head. 'She said something about Cortina d'Ampezzo though.'

'Cortina d'Ampezzo?'

'It's a ritzy place up in the mountains where rich people go skiing.'

'Is that where Evelina was?'

Fifi shrugged. 'I don't know. I wish I could tell you more. I wish I'd gone after the woman and asked, but I was afraid to, with Ardilla there. A pity, since the Tognazzis threw me out not long after, when they found out I'd been writing to Senator Lina Merlin. Anyway, the party's over for people like the Tognazzis. They've retired. Madama Gioconda's is a boarding house for students now.'

It was difficult for Rinaldo to decide what this news about Evelina meant. It was impossible to say whether her sending the unknown lady had been a cry for help, or simply a message to assure him that she was all right.

'I'd love to stay and chat, but things are going to get busy out there tonight,' said Fifi.

Rinaldo took out one of his business cards and said, 'Here. Take this. And if you hear anything about Evelina, anything at all, please call me.'

'Sure,' replied Fifi, reaching into her bag and also taking out a card. 'Here's a telephone number I can be reached on too. I'll ask around. I promise that if I hear anything at all I'll tell you.'

Rinaldo thanked Fifi and looked at the name on the card. 'Who's Silvana?'

'It's me, you fool! You didn't think my real name was Fifi la Française, did you?'

*

Rinaldo returned home far more perturbed than when he had left. Thoughts of Evelina and her unknown fate filled his head. The loss of the coin was trivial in comparison. On the one hand he was relieved that, if nothing else, Evelina had still been alive three or four years after she'd escaped from Madama Gioconda's, but on the other perhaps she had sent the woman because she was in trouble and needed his help. The worst thing was not knowing.

Maybe he should take a trip to Cortina d'Ampezzo – although in all likelihood it would be another wild-goose chase, just like all his trips to Milano Marittima.

He'd skipped lunch and missed dinner, but he was too agitated to be hungry, so he took a bottle of beer from the refrigerator and began to run a bath, his mind racing and all the possibilities of Evelina's fate turning over and over in his head.

It was only whilst he was undressing that he remembered that Alberto Fiorelli's tie was rolled up in his jacket pocket. He took out his red and blue tartan scarf and looked at them side by side.

'Ha!' he declared. 'Look at that – they're a perfect match.'

It was uncanny. Anyone would think they'd been made as a set.

CHAPTER 16

Since the miraculous appearance of the Roman denarius and her unsatisfactory conversation with Don Pagnotta, Miranda had stopped going to church and didn't miss it at all. She hadn't lost her faith, but rather, felt too constrained by the rituals. Being surrounded by fidgeting people, being told when to sit, when to stand, when to kneel and what to say distracted her from what was important. So, rather than attending Mass, she had begun to take long, contemplative walks and found them to be a far better way of putting her thoughts in order than sitting in church mindlessly reciting the rites and trying to stay awake through a long-winded sermon.

Today she set out heading for Via Saragozza, thinking that she would venture as far as the rather voluptuous statue of the Virgin Mary known to locals as the Madonna Grassa, the fat Madonna; but Miranda was barely two minutes into her walk and was just rounding the corner by the Collegio di Spagna when she came face-to-face with Don Pagnotta.

'Good afternoon, Signora Fiorelli,' he said. 'I trust you're well and that your ankle has fully recovered. I haven't seen you at Mass for some time. May I inquire as to why?'

'I've sought more personal communion with God,' Miranda replied curtly.

'Oh? Am I to assume that this is as a result of your recent *experience* with the coin?'

'Yes,' replied Miranda in a prickly tone which warned the priest not to meddle in her private affairs. 'Now if you'll excuse me, Don Pagnotta, I wish you a good afternoon.'

She quickened her pace and carried on walking, trying to

gather her thoughts after the priest's interruption, but as she proceeded down Via Saragozza she heard hurried footsteps behind her and Don Pagnotta's breathless voice calling her name.

'Signora Fiorelli! Signora Fiorelli, please, if I could take just one more moment of your time!'

Miranda pretended not to hear. She had no appetite for a conversation with a blatherskite priest when there was such a serious matter on her mind.

'I have been very concerned about your wellbeing, Signora Fiorelli, not to mention the effect of your experience on your faith,' puffed Don Pagnotta as he caught up with Miranda. 'As your parish priest I am bound to seek you out as a shepherd seeks a lost sheep.'

'This sheep is not lost, Don Pagnotta, but simply grazing in a different pasture.'

The priest opened his mouth to quote a line from the Parable of the Lost Sheep, then thought better of it.

'Be that as it may, Signora Fiorelli, but I am still concerned for your wellbeing. Have you succumbed to any further *experiences*?'

Miranda slowed her pace. Suddenly she felt readier than she had ever felt to talk about the guilt which had been burdening her for so long, and her readiness came as a great surprise to her. She had never imagined herself speaking to Don Pagnotta, but perhaps there was some significance in her chance meeting with the priest. He was the only one who knew she had been to see Rinaldo at the orphanage, and he was the only one who knew about the appearance of the Roman denarius. It couldn't be coincidental. These things had to be signs.

Turning to Don Pagnotta, she said, 'I understand why Alberto is not at peace. We have unfinished business.'

'Unfinished business? What do you mean, Signora Fiorelli?'

'Something we should have spoken about, but never did. Something of fundamental importance.' Miranda bowed her head, then added very quietly, 'I did a truly unforgivable thing, Don Pagnotta.'

'In the eyes of God, nothing is unforgivable,' the priest said earnestly. 'He has infinite mercy.'

'It is not God's forgiveness I seek. It is Alberto's.'

Miranda stopped abruptly, aware that she felt very weak, as though her knees would buckle if she tried to take another step. Startled by her sudden pallor and change in countenance, Don Pagnotta reached out to support her then guided her to sit on the little wall between the portico columns.

'Signora Fiorelli,' he said humbly, 'I might be a poor excuse for a priest, but if you wish to speak from one human being to another, please share with me whatever is causing you such torment.'

Miranda took a very deep breath and held it in, taking time to gather her strength, then let the breath out slowly. She was ready.

'My wish to adopt resulted from my inability to bring a living child into the world. I suffered eight miscarriages and one premature still birth.'

'Oh, Signora Fiorelli! I can hardly begin to imagine the agony of such ordeals.'

'The agony was deserved.'

'What? How can that possibly be the case?'

Miranda turned her head from Don Pagnotta and hid her face in her hands. She couldn't bear for him to see into her eyes as she spoke, and she couldn't disintegrate, because if she did, she might not have the courage to speak at all. She hesitated, knowing that once said, her words could never be un-said.

'I have never told another soul what I am about to divulge to you, Don Pagnotta. It is a matter which has remained sealed inside me for over thirty years.'

The priest reached across and placed his hand on Miranda's shoulder.

'Signora Fiorelli, you have my word as a devoted servant of God that I would under no circumstances violate the confidentiality of any matter you wish to address, however personal, or however painful.'

Miranda gripped Don Pagnotta's hand, then said, almost in a whisper, 'At the age of nineteen I gave birth to a little baby boy, a living child. I was inexperienced in every way and very much ignorant of an infant's needs. I should have given birth in a hospital, but I chose not to. When my son, Leonardo, was born it was evident that he was unwell. He was suffering from jaundice and he wouldn't feed, but I knew nothing of the condition and I knew nothing of how to nurse an infant. I should have sought medical attention immediately, but by the time I decided to ask for help, it was too late. Leonardo died when he was just one day old, and his death was due entirely to my neglect. If I had sought timely medical assistance I am certain that he would have lived.'

Miranda paused, waiting for the priest's judgement, expecting censure and condemnation, but instead he replied in a tone which was tender and compassionate.

'Truly, my soul is in anguish for you, Signora Fiorelli. I struggle to imagine living with such an onerous burden. But may I ask why you didn't seek medical assistance?'

'Because my baby would have been taken from me. I was a young, unmarried girl with no means of support. I would have had no choice in the matter. But my actions were utterly selfish. I put my own needs and my own emotions before the health, and ultimately the life, of my baby. That is unforgivable whichever way you look at it.' And before Don Pagnotta could reply, Miranda added, 'Although some might think that what I did after his death was even worse.'

The priest swallowed hard. '*Worse?*'

'Yes. You see, I should have alerted somebody. I should have owned up to what I had done and faced the consequences. But I did none of that. I panicked and ran away and simply left Leonardo for somebody else to find and to deal with.' Miranda bit down on her knuckles to stifle a howl. 'I left him, Don Pagnotta. I left him all alone. I abandoned my baby.'

The priest's lips were pressed together so tightly that they had almost disappeared. After a long, thoughtful silence, he asked: 'Do you know what happened to the child after you left?'

'N-no,' stammered Miranda. 'Whatever happened, it happened very quickly. The enormity of what I had done hit me a few hours later and I went back to retrieve him, but by that time he had been removed and there was already a new tenant occupying my room. It was as though nothing had happened. And over the days and weeks that followed I scoured the newspapers for news of the abandonment, hoping that I might find out where Leonardo had been laid to rest, but there was nothing.' Miranda's voice faltered again, then broke. 'My greatest fear was that he was simply disposed of, like a piece of rubbish, and that was never, *never* my intention.'

She reached inside her collar and pulled out a long, fine gold chain. Attached to it was a tiny emerald pendant.

'When I left Leonardo, I left with him the only thing I had of any value – one of my dear late mother's emerald earrings – so that there would be something to cover the cost of his burial, so that he could be laid to rest with some modicum of dignity. But I'm certain that it was never used for that. Perhaps it was kept by the landlord, to whom I owed money for rent.'

Miranda held up the emerald pendant for Don Pagnotta to see.

'This is the remaining earring,' she said. 'I had the hook soldered into a loop so that I could wear it around my neck. I wear it all the time, and the reason it is on such a long chain is so that I can keep it out of sight, but close to my heart.'

She kissed the little emerald pendant and kept it pressed to her lips.

'This is the most precious thing that I own, Don Pagnotta, as it connects me to both my mother and to my son. But it is also a painful reminder of my actions that day. A reminder of how deserving I am of punishment. The sin I committed was a mortal one, because I was fully aware at the time of how appalling my actions were and I *prayed* that God would punish me, in return for saving Leonardo's innocent little soul. If there was ever a glimmer of hope in my heart that God did as I beseeched Him, it was my subsequent miscarriages. Those losses were my punishment.'

When Don Pagnotta replied, his voice was hoarse.

'It grieves me that you should have lived in such expectation of God's retribution. Ours is not a vengeful God, Signora Fiorelli, but a just and merciful one. If repentance is shown, God's love is infinite.'

'I was never lacking in repentance,' sighed Miranda. 'But clearly it was not enough.'

'If I may ask, what became of the child's father?'

'The child's father was Alberto – and he became my husband.'

The priest raised his eyebrows, then frowned, saying, 'Forgive me if I appear confused, Signora Fiorelli. You say that I am the only person to whom you have divulged any of this information. So how were you able to keep a pregnancy and the birth of a child from your husband?'

'It's a long story, Don Pagnotta.'

'Then we shall be sitting on this wall for a long time, Signora Fiorelli.' The priest straightened his spine, then leaned in towards Miranda. 'This matter cannot be left unresolved and I cannot leave you in this state of spiritual and emotional distress.'

Miranda recounted the story of how she and Alberto had met

and fallen in love on the island of Capri, and how their relationship had been carried out in secret because her step-mother would never have allowed it.

'Both Alberto and I knew that ours was more than just a holiday romance and that, despite the short time we had known one another, our lives were destined to be spent together,' explained Miranda. 'We planned to elope. But on the eve of our departure we were observed kissing and it was reported to my step-mother. So when I returned to the guest house to gather my belongings, ready to slip away at dawn the following day, she confronted me and caused a terrible scene.'

Miranda raised her hands to her face. The recollection of her step-mother's fury and her ferocious, whip-crack slaps still made her cheeks burn. The woman had grabbed her hair so violently that she had ripped out a handful of it; and her piercing screams still echoed in Miranda's head – even after all these years: *Slut! Slut! Slut! Slut!*

'So I found myself on the next ferry back to the mainland that very evening, escorted by my step-mother,' continued Miranda. 'It all happened so fast that I couldn't even get a message to Alberto to explain what had occurred. All I could do was to hope that on discovering that I had disappeared so suddenly he would understand that I had been removed against my will. On my return to the family home in Ravenna I was desperate to write to him to explain, but couldn't – firstly because my step-mother locked me in my bedroom and I had no means to communicate with anybody, and secondly because I didn't have an exact address for Alberto. He had told me about the place where he lived, about the attic apartment where we would make our home, but I didn't know exactly where it was. All I knew was that it was in Bologna, somewhere in the old Jewish quarter. But Alberto, on the other hand, did know where to write to me, for I had entrusted my sketch book to him, and on the folio of that sketch book was my home address. All I could do was to wait for him to make contact.'

The priest nodded as he took in the information, paused for a moment's reflection, then inquired, 'And I presume that he did contact you?'

'Oh yes. Alberto wrote to me from Capri as soon as he realised that I had left, and he guessed that the discovery of our relationship was the reason for my hasty departure. In his letter he said that unless I had changed my mind about marrying him, and that the decision had been entirely mine, we should try to make peace with my step-mother and try to reason with my father in the hope that they would be accepting of our plans.' Miranda shook her head regretfully. 'But that letter never reached me, Don Pagnotta, because it was intercepted by my step-mother, who took it upon herself to assume my identity and write back to Alberto to say that I had indeed changed my mind and that he was never to contact me again.'

The priest clasped his hands together and looked at Miranda very directly. 'And what was your husband's reaction to this demand?'

'Alberto didn't believe for a moment that it was I who had replied to him, so he wrote back several more times, but received no responses. He was extremely concerned about my wellbeing. But of course, I knew nothing of this correspondence. And then the whole thing became rather more complicated as I discovered that I was pregnant. '

There was a sharp intake of breath from the priest. 'I shudder to think how your step-mother might have reacted to such news.'

'Indeed, you are right to shudder, Don Pagnotta. I cannot tell you what sadistic punishments were unleashed upon me. It was a miracle that I didn't miscarry. And then before I knew it, plans had been made to send me away to an institution for unwed mothers far away from my home, where my child would be removed from me immediately after birth and entrusted temporarily to a wet-nurse, then farmed out for adoption, or consigned to an orphanage if no adoptive parents could be found. I would then be sent back home to Ravenna pretend that I had never had a baby.'

Miranda clenched her fists as she felt her sadness turn to rage. It was a rage which welled from deep inside her. Not just rage towards her malevolent step-mother and her weak father, but towards the injustice of the situation, of society – and of the rules invented by, and enforced by, the Church – and of the stigmatisation forced upon unwed mothers and their innocent children for the crime of pregnancy out of wedlock. It made her blood run cold.

'Can you imagine that, Don Pagnotta, allowing a young mother no contact with her child? Can you imagine the wrench a mother would feel, having grown and carried that baby inside her? And putting aside the mother's feelings for a moment, what effect might such brutal actions have on the child? I believe that any baby removed in such a way would feel the repercussions of that broken bond for the rest of their lives.'

'Indeed,' agreed a deeply shaken Don Pagnotta, his voice still strained. 'But your step-mother was unable to understand this?'

'Oh, she understood perfectly and gained considerable pleasure from it. She signed those adoption documents with a smile on her face. So, faced with the appalling prospect of being sent to a place where I would have no choice but to surrender my baby, I did the only thing I could think to do and ran away to Bologna. I made my escape in the middle of the night by forcing the lock on my bedroom door and climbing out of the scullery window. And once in Bologna I did all I could to try to locate Alberto. I walked the streets looking for him. I made inquiries at various schools and at the university in my attempts to track him down. I even placed personal advertisements in the local newspapers in the hope that he, or somebody who knew him, would see them, but fate had played a cruel trick upon us. Unbeknown to me, on the very day that I left Ravenna, Alberto had left Bologna.'

'He left? Where did he go?'

'To Ravenna,' sighed Miranda, clutching her head in her hands. 'As he had received no responses to his letters and he knew that my step-mother was prone to violent outbursts, he was desperately worried about me. He went straight to my family home and confronted my step-mother, demanding to be allowed to speak to me in person. But of course, I wasn't there. My step-mother spun him a yarn about how I had run off with somebody else, but Alberto didn't believe a word of it, so he elected to stay in Ravenna for a time in the hope that I would return. Of course, I didn't. I remained in Bologna and gave birth to our child without his knowledge. Our paths didn't cross again until he returned from Ravenna. That was several months after Leonardo's death.'

Don Pagnotta listened, open-mouthed. 'My goodness, Signora Fiorelli, that was indeed a cruel trick of fate ... But may I ask why you didn't tell your husband about the tragic event once you were reunited?'

Miranda wrung her hands so tightly that her knuckles turned white. 'I knew that I should because he had the right to know – and I almost did more times than I could count – but then I would talk myself out of it. Why cause him pain? If I took the entire burden, then he didn't need to feel it at all. Why break his heart as well as mine? But I cannot pretend that my reasons were entirely altruistic. The fact that I knew Leonardo was unwell and did nothing about it, and the unforgivable way I left our little baby boy's body to be dealt with by strangers. How could anyone forgive that? I feared that he would hate me for it – and then I would lose not only Leonardo, but Alberto too.'

Miranda lowered her gaze and twisted the wedding ring on her finger.

'Then as the years passed the keeping of the secret became almost as big a source of guilt as the secret itself. I couldn't see how Alberto could forgive me for keeping such a terrible secret for so long and for lying, not directly, but by omission.'

'So now you believe that the coin which appeared in your house is somehow connected to this?'

'Yes. I believe that Alberto is giving me the opportunity to tell him what I could never bring myself to say when he was alive.'

'Then you must tell him.'

'You're advising me to speak to the dead, Don Pagnotta?'

'I see no other way to bring some closure to this painful matter, Signora Fiorelli. I have no doubt that you are most sincerely penitent, but if forgiveness from your husband is what you seek, then you must ask for it. It is impossible for anyone to forgive if they are not aware of what they should be forgiving. Being granted forgiveness does not make a sin any less of a sin, but the process has to start somewhere.'

Miranda nodded and thanked Don Pagnotta. He had surprised her by not judging her actions, or her situation. He might not be the most inspirational priest at the pulpit, but he had shown great humanity when it counted the most, and she was grateful for that.

Don Pagnotta insisted on walking Miranda home. As they stood at the entrance to Vicolo Chiuso, she pointed to the windows above the shoe shop and said, 'Just up there, at number 7b, is the room where Leonardo was born and died.'

'So close to home?'

'Yes. I know it seems like an impossible coincidence that of all the rooms I could have rented in a city the size of Bologna I chose one which was barely thirty paces from where Alberto lived. If he hadn't left for Ravenna there's no doubt that we would have found each other much sooner and things would have turned out very, very differently.'

Miranda settled her gaze on the windows above the shoe shop and sighed.

'Over these past thirty years not a single day has passed where I haven't thought of Leonardo. Some days he is *all* I have thought of. I have imagined how his life would have been, had events not conspired as they did. I've imagined him growing from an infant to a little boy. I've wondered what qualities and what talents he would have possessed. I have no doubt that he would have been blessed with artistic leanings. Perhaps he would have inherited Alberto's talent for music, or mine for art. Perhaps he might have been blessed with both. I think how Alberto and I would have nurtured those talents, watched him flourish. And I've imagined him growing up, starting school. And older, perhaps obtaining his degree and entering a profession of his choice. And finding love, having children of his own.' Miranda's voice became full of despair. 'One could say that I have lost ten children, Don Pagnotta, for each of my miscarriages was a most agonising loss, and deeply etched into my memory. But Leonardo is the only one who has left a gaping hole in my heart and is missing from my life.'

Miranda kept her eyes fixed on number 7b and added, 'I look up into those windows every time I go in or out of this door, and every time I send Leonardo my love.' She paused for a moment. 'It was so strange, Don Pagnotta. Earlier this year, on March the twentieth, the very day which would have been Leonardo's thirtieth birthday, I saw a figure standing there – the figure of a young man – and for an instant I had a sensation that it was Leonardo.' She turned to the priest. 'I know that you think me quite mad for believing in ghosts, Don Pagnotta.'

'No,' replied the priest, 'far from it, Signora Fiorelli. What I think is that you have lived in an intolerable state of anguish for much too long – and that the time has come to heal the wounds of that suffering.'

Don Pagnotta rested his hand gently on Miranda's shoulder and quietly recited the Act of Absolution, ending with, 'May God grant you pardon and peace. I absolve you in the name of the Father, and of the Son and of the Holy Spirit. Amen.'

But to Miranda, the prayer was just pretty, empty words which provided no consolation. A priest's absolution barely rippled the surface of her deep pool of guilt. She thanked him feebly, without conviction, then bade him farewell before turning and entering Vicolo Chiuso. As she made her way up the stairs of number 3 to the top floor, her heart was beating fast, as though she had ascended too quickly – although in reality she had climbed the stairs far more slowly than usual.

She stood outside her apartment for a long time with her key poised by the lock as she gathered her strength to repeat to Alberto everything that she had just confided to Don Pagnotta. But the moment she opened the door, her courage left her. There was a world of difference between speaking to a priest and confessing to Alberto.

Confession was supposed to uplift the soul, to free it, to heal it like a medicine, but all it had done was to deepen her guilt and plague her with yet more shame and remorse. Confession was a medicine with side-effects.

She went straight to the bathroom and washed out her mouth, then stood clutching the rim of the basin, feeling as though she was perched on the edge of a precipice, and that if she dared to let go, or move, the floor would disappear from underneath her feet. Miranda squeezed her eyes shut, trying to quell the sensation of vertigo. When finally she looked up and caught her reflection in the mirror, the face which stared back at her seemed shrunken, blanched, wrung out. She had aged by a century in the space of an hour.

This wasn't the good Miranda, the Miranda who was kind and who had been a loving, devoted wife. This was the wicked Miranda, who had killed her child through selfishness and neglect, who had lied to her husband from the beginning of their marriage to the very end.

She turned away, cutting the connection between herself and the alien Miranda in the mirror and made her way to the bedroom, being mindful to avoid her reflection in the looking-glass on the chest of drawers. Instead, she took a long look at the photograph of Alberto in his camel overcoat and tartan scarf and picked up the Roman denarius which sat beside it, encircled by the mementos from Villa Jovis. She then pulled the long chain from inside her blouse and contemplated her mother's emerald earring. All these little objects were imbued with so much love, yet now, having spoken about Leonardo, she felt undeserving of any of it. Her thirty years of meticulously-managed guilt, which she had so deftly suppressed, was like a thorn embedded so deeply into her flesh that it was impossible to remove.

She gathered up her mementos and shut them in a drawer.

It was in this state of exhaustion and discouragement that Miranda arranged her pillows; one pillow in the usual position at the head of the bed and the other placed lengthways. She sprinkled a few drops of Alberto's cologne onto the lengthways pillow, then lay down with her arms around it and nuzzled into the softness, breathing in the scent of his cologne.

'I'm so tired, my love,' she said and closed her eyes.

Miranda lay embracing the pillow, just as she had always lain with Alberto – tenderly, lovingly, and as though nothing had happened.

CHAPTER 17

It was over a month since Miranda had been to visit Evelina. Such a lapse had only happened once before, when she had been occupied in nursing Alberto at home during his final weeks of life. She had used her ankle injury as an excuse for her absence, even though she had been fully back on her feet barely ten days after her fall. The truth was that she couldn't face Madre Benedetta. Her friend would know that something was wrong and would want to know what it was.

Miranda's conversation with Don Pagnotta, rather than alleviating her guilt, had brought upon her a wretched feeling. Thoughts of little Leonardo's fate filled her every waking moment and fed her nightmares.

As for telling Alberto, what purpose would that serve? Perhaps Don Pagnotta had been right and the Roman denarius had been there all along, possibly wedged down the side of the cushion of the chair. Maybe feeling his presence had been nothing beyond an extreme case of wishful thinking; and the impression that Rinaldo had been a version of Alberto in his camel overcoat had been a momentary delusion. Alberto was dead. Gone. Only alive in her memory. She had no choice but to reason that way, or she would lose her mind. Her mind felt in some part lost already.

The day was damp and foggy, the kind of late-November day when the mist lay low, veiling the city in a grey gloom. Miranda stood waiting for the minibus at the foot of the Colle della Guardia, wondering whether she should just head back home, but eventually Pietro pulled up and she climbed on board.

As she was the only passenger, Pietro was eager to chat.

Hasn't it been miserable weather, Signora? The Water Board is digging up the Via di Casaglia again. It's going to be chaos! Have you heard that they're going to increase the bus fares? There are going to be more strikes. Got any plans for Christmas? He talked enough for both of them as they snaked up towards San Luca. Miranda replied with one word answers – *Yes. No. Yes. No.* She couldn't even distract herself with the views. The city was entirely shrouded in fog.

By the time she alighted in front of the Sanctuary, she felt as worn out by the minibus journey as if she had made the two-kilometre climb on foot. She paused for a moment in the piazza, gathering herself. The season was over and the place was deserted. The cable-car was closed for the winter and there were no little stalls selling tat to tourists, or groups of schoolchildren.

Where she stood, at the top of the Colle della Guardia, high above the city, the sky was clear and cloudless. A pale ray of winter of sunshine illuminated the lane which led to the convent. As she approached, she saw Signor Rinaldo Rossi painting over the graffiti on the wall, but didn't have the energy to stop for a lengthy sign-language conversation; so instead she wished him a good day and complimented his whitewashing skills. She had completely forgotten about his request for more socks.

The door was not opened by Madre Benedetta, but by one of the novice sisters.

'Good day, Signora Miranda. The Abbess asks whether you would please call into her office immediately as she has an important matter to discuss with you.'

Madre Benedetta greeted Miranda briskly and made a cursory inquiry about her ankle, which Miranda sensed was made purely out of politeness. Clearly her old friend had something on her mind.

'What's wrong, Benedetta?'

The Abbess leaned in towards her, and although there was

nobody else to overhear, she spoke quietly, in a tone which indicated that what she was saying should be treated with the utmost discretion.

'The green shawl that you made for Evelina, do you know what particular significance it has for her?'

'She said that her mother had had one just like it. She was very exacting about the shade.'

'Well, it seems to have had some sort of liberating effect upon her.' The Abbess paused. 'Evelina's been talking about her past.'

'Really?' gasped Miranda, instantly forgetting her own worries. 'She's spoken to you?' This was indeed momentous.

'No. Not directly to me, nor to any of the other sisters. She's been talking to Signora Visconti.'

'Signora Visconti told you that?'

'Oh no, Signora Visconti isn't capable of repeating what she was told two minutes ago. And I think that might well be the reason why Evelina felt comfortable confiding in her. But both Sorella Antonia and Sorella Maria overheard Evelina speaking very openly about deeply personal matters. They came to me to report it, although they were both rather uneasy with the fact that they'd been eavesdropping. Of course, it's not something I would usually condone, and under normal circumstances I certainly wouldn't encourage it, but I think in this case an exception can be made. The sin lies in the purpose behind the action, after all.' Madre Benedetta gave a little half-smile and added, 'God instructed Moses to send spies into the land of Canaan and told Gideon to spy on the Midianites, so I'm quite comfortable asking Sorella Antonia and Sorella Maria to listen in if what they learn is helpful for us to understand the best ways we can help Evelina deal with her past pain. I think that in this case, we can say *exitus acta probat* – the end justifies the means.'

'What did Evelina say?'

'It wasn't possible for either Sorella Maria or Sorella Antonia to hear anything in detail, but she seemed to be speaking about her mother and her brother. The important thing is that she's beginning to open up.'

'Was she upset?'

'No. Certainly not visibly. But we'll have to wait and see how things progress. For now I think that we should keep this between ourselves, *in secreto*, don't you, Miranda? We wouldn't want Evelina to think she's being spied on.'

'Of course.'

As Miranda was leaving the office, Madre Benedetta added: 'It seems quite remarkable that something as simple as an item of clothing should hold such significance.'

Miranda nodded, although she couldn't agree. She understood very well how an item of clothing was more than just the form, the colour and the weave of its fabric.

She made her way to the little room where they took their lessons, but Evelina wasn't there. No matter. She waited for a while, ruminating over what her friend the Abbess had just told her. A full quarter of an hour later, Evelina still hadn't appeared, so Miranda went to find her.

The door to Signora Visconti's room was ajar. Miranda was about to knock, but she could hear Evelina's voice on the other side.

'... I used to call him Aldino-Fagiolino. Did you ever see the Burattini puppet shows?'

Signora Visconti echoed Evelina's words, 'Aldino-Fagiolino. Burattini.'

'He was such a sweet boy. A bit of a rascal, but a sweet boy.'

'Rascal. Sweet boy.'

Miranda pressed herself to the doorframe and listened as Evelina recounted the story of a school smock, but much of what she was saying was muffled and frequently interrupted by Signora Visconti.

'I used to make him come to church with me. He didn't like it, but he never complained. Do you know the church of San Paolo Maggiore? There was a Madonna in there, a really beautiful Madonna. I used to pretend she was my Mamma.'

A draught caused a door further down the corridor to slam shut; Signora Visconti's door creaked loudly and half-opened. Evelina looked up with a start and her eyes met Miranda's. She was wearing the green shawl.

'Oh! Hello, Mamma Miranda!' she exclaimed, then looked embarrassed, like someone caught doing something wrong. 'I didn't hear the bell. Am I late for my lesson?'

'Only a little, but don't fret. Finish whatever you need to do.'

Evelina arranged the old lady's pillows and said, 'I'll be back in an hour to get you ready for lunch,' to which Signora Visconti replied: 'In an hour. Aldino-Fagiolino.'

At first, when she joined Miranda, Evelina was reserved. She straightened out her pinafore, wrapped herself tightly in the green shawl and kept her head bowed as they made their way down the corridor. Although she seemed a little nervy, she didn't appear upset. Miranda could always tell when there was something painful on Evelina's mind. Often what she was doing spoke more than what she was saying. Whenever she was distressed she would scratch the scar on her chin, but as they walked side-by-side, she didn't touch her scar at all.

Should she ask a question? wondered Miranda. Should she mention Evelina's mother, or Aldino? But before she could decide, Evelina herself spoke.

'I was four years old when my Mamma died. How old were you when you lost your mother, Miranda?'

'I had just turned six.'

'Do you remember her?'

'A little. But only when she was unwell.'

'Do you remember what she looked like?'

'I do and I don't. What I remember about her isn't necessarily physical. I remember that she loved me and that I loved her and I've learned to be content with that.'

Evelina nodded and Miranda saw her give the shadow of a relieved smile. 'That's how I feel too.'

Perhaps this was the way in, thought Miranda. Perhaps she and Madre Benedetta had been wrong to try to talk about Salvi, or the other ordeals which Evelina had suffered. Miranda knew that she had to tread carefully, but she couldn't help but ask about Aldino.

'Your brother, Aldino, how old was he when you both lost your mother?'

A look of puzzlement crossed Evelina's expression.

'We didn't have the same mother,' she said. 'He was an orphan too, but we met in our foster home. We weren't related by blood, but we were really close when we were kids, just like a brother and a sister. When you've got nobody, you latch onto anybody in any way you can.'

Miranda stopped, stunned that this essential piece of information hadn't been mentioned all those years ago back in Cortina d'Ampezzo. Why hadn't she thought to ask?

'Oh? So Aldino isn't Aldino Brunelli?'

'No. I thought I'd told you his name. I was sure I had. I'm sorry, Miranda. I wasn't thinking straight back then.'

'Well, then I'm sorry to say that when I went looking for him in Via del Pratello I asked after the wrong person.'

'It doesn't matter. Really. You see, I was relieved that you hadn't found him. He probably hates me.'

'Why would he hate you?'

Evelina bowed her head and did not answer. Miranda feared that perhaps she had gone too far, too fast. Nevertheless, she couldn't stop herself asking: 'Do you not think he worried about you, dear?'

'I expect he did,' said Evelina sadly. 'And all these years I've worried about him too. He gave me absolutely everything he had so that I could get away and start a new life, but I lost the lot and got myself into an even worse situation because I was stupid. He must have struggled so much with no money. I hate the thought of him having been hungry, or not having anywhere to live, and all because of me.'

'Is that why you've never wanted me to try to contact him?'

'Yes.'

'Would you like me to do so now?'

'I don't know. There are times when I want to see him so desperately, but then other times I think that I just couldn't face him. And it's not only because of the money, it's because he'll want to know things about me and I'm afraid of upsetting him, or that he'll do something to try to get revenge on some of the people who've—' Evelina cut herself off and raised her hand to her scar. 'I don't know what I should do, Miranda.'

'Well, I could make an inquiry at the Public Records Office. If he's still in Bologna, they'll have his address. Or he might even be in the telephone directory. I could check both and he would never know, unless you decided to contact him.'

'He wouldn't know that you'd looked?'

'No.'

Evelina seemed to be weighing it up. She wrapped herself tightly into her shawl and after a while nodded and said, 'All right. Have a look. And if you find him, then I'll decide what to do.'

'Then I'll need his full name.'

'It's Rinaldo. Rinaldo Scamorza.'

'I beg your pardon.' Miranda froze. 'What did you say?'

'I know it's unusual. Scamorza, same as the cheese.'

*

Rinaldo had come home from work early because he had things to do. Earlier that week he had taken delivery of a record player, and not just any record player – not some cheap table-top thing which made the music sound as though it was being played through a tin can, but a costly American model with four high-quality loudspeakers and an in-built radio, all housed within a shiny wood-effect cabinet.

He was very eager to play the three records he'd bought, but there was no electrical socket within reach where he wanted to put the record player unless he re-positioned the bureau against the opposite wall. The bureau was one of his favourite pieces of furniture in the whole apartment. It was made of a honey-coloured wood with curly patterns engraved on the front where the desk folded out, and it was carved into a quirky bulbous shape with a keyhole like a lion's mouth and feet like lion's paws. Miranda said that it had belonged to Alberto's father. But it was a big, bulky piece of furniture and even heavier than it looked, and being such a rounded shape there wasn't anything to hold onto. Rinaldo didn't want to drag it, or push it, because that could mark the floor. It would be easier to walk it across the room if he took out the drawers.

He didn't keep much in the bureau drawers, but what he kept in there was of great value – his personal documents, his orphanage records and yellow blanket, and of course, the emerald earring.

Rinaldo had looked through the file so many times that he could recite it by heart, but he hadn't read it for a couple of months, so he forgot about moving the bureau for a moment and spread the contents of the file over the coffee table. He then sat down with his yellow blanket laid out beside him and began to read it again, just in case he'd missed something.

As he finished perusing the police report there was a knock at his door. He hoped it wasn't his dinner being delivered. He'd booked it for seven thirty and it was only ten past six. But when he opened the door, Miranda was standing there.

'Can I talk to you, Rinaldo?' she said. Something in the tone of her voice and the expression on her face troubled him. She was smiling, but gravely. His heart sank. What might Miranda need to talk to him about if it wasn't the apartment? He hoped she wasn't coming to say that she needed it back – and that this was to be the beginning of a run of bad luck. He still hadn't found his coin.

'Of course,' he replied with a certain feeling of dread. 'Come in. Excuse the mess. I'm rearranging a few things.'

Rinaldo prided himself on how neat and clean he kept his home and it did bother him that Miranda should see the living room in disorder, with the bureau drawers pulled out, a mess of paperwork on the coffee table and the record player still in its packing case blocking one of the French windows. But it didn't seem to trouble Miranda at all. If he hadn't pointed it out, he thought, she wouldn't even have noticed.

'I have something to tell you, Rinaldo, which might come as a shock. Perhaps you should sit down.'

Rinaldo sat down immediately on his yellow blanket. Miranda sat at the opposite end of the sofa and began with, 'I have a message for you. A message from your sister, Evelina.'

The words hit Rinaldo like a belly punch and he felt his stomach somersault. It was just as well that Miranda had told him to sit down, or he would have fallen down. He repeated the words in his own head, checking that he hadn't misunderstood. All he could answer was, 'What?'

Miranda told him everything she knew, starting from the invitation to Salvi's at Cortina d'Ampezzo; to her visit to Madama Gioconda's, where she had searched for him by the wrong name; to the rescue mission; and ending with Evelina's residency at the convent. Rinaldo sat and listened without saying a word, his eyes growing wider and wider.

Miranda thought it imperative that she should omit nothing and explain everything truthfully and in detail, even though some of it was very unpleasant. Rinaldo had to be prepared for the fact that Evelina might not be the same as he remembered her and it was important that he should know that despite the great improvements, she was still fragile and that reconnecting with him might cause some of her previous traumas to resurface. The situation had to be treated with the utmost delicacy.

'I cannot emphasise enough, Rinaldo, how sensitive we must be with Evelina. I'm certain that reuniting with you will be an enormous advance in her healing. But I stress the word *healing*, because her experiences have injured her both physically and emotionally.'

It was only as Miranda finished her explanation with, 'She wants to see you, Rinaldo. She asks whether you would visit her as soon as you can,' that Rinaldo realised that the tears which had sprung into his eyes were running down his face. He let them run, even though he had never cried in front of anybody since the age of five, when he had cried to Evelina during his first night at Ada Stracci's.

Miranda moved across, put her arm around his shoulder and passed him one of Alberto's handkerchiefs, which she had brought with her in case of such a reaction. She didn't say anything. She just sat close, letting Rinaldo take in the information.

Then it was Rinaldo's turn to speak and Miranda's to weep. He told her about Ada Stracci and Gigio Lingua and the 'lessons' in the attic, about how Evelina had been taken for her virginity to be sold over and over again and how he had found her by chance at Madama Gioconda's. He spoke openly and honestly, expressing the guilt, fears and regrets to Miranda that he had never confided in anyone before.

'If only I'd been able to do something sooner – as soon as Evelina told me what was happening with Ada Stracci and Gigio

Lingua. I knew that something awful was going on and I didn't do anything.'

'You were a small child, Rinaldo. Knowing and understanding are two very different things. And at that age there was nothing you could have done.'

Rinaldo bowed his head, thinking that what he could have done was to set fire to the vile old bitch's bedroom sooner, and chosen a night when Gigio Lingua was in there too, but perhaps that was a bit much to share with Miranda.

'I should have done things differently when I found Evelina at Madama Gioconda's though,' he said. 'What was I thinking, sending her away alone like that? I knew she was afraid. She begged me to leave with her. I didn't even know she couldn't read. It was a stupid thing to do.'

'You did it with the most honourable of intentions and you thought you were doing the right thing. How old were you then?'

'Nineteen.'

Miranda paused, lowered her gaze and said, very quietly, 'We all do things at that age which seem the right thing to do. We're still children at nineteen, even though we inhabit adults' bodies.'

Rinaldo composed himself a little. He felt an overwhelming sense of gratitude towards Miranda and a deep respect for everything she had done to help Evelina. 'You did what I was never able to do, Miranda. You saved Evelina. I will be forever in your debt for that.'

There was a moment's silence as both Rinaldo and Miranda let all the new information settle in their minds. After a while Rinaldo added, 'Well, now you know that I'm an orphan too.'

And as it was time for things to be in the open, Miranda replied, 'I knew already.'

'You did? How?'

When she recounted her visit to the orphanage of San Girolamo and described the time he had sat on her knee, Rinaldo's eyes grew wider still. He took a long look at Miranda and said, 'So you could have been my mother?'

Miranda nodded, stroked Rinaldo's cheek lightly with the back of her hand and replied regretfully, 'Under different circumstances, yes.'

In that moment Rinaldo thought that the situation couldn't get any stranger. He turned his gaze to look around the beautiful sitting room and the view over the palace garden, wondering, as he had many times before, how it would have felt to grow up in such a genteel environment, filled with music and paintings and supported by the affectionate authority of good parents. Who might he have become, he wondered, if he had been raised a Fiorelli? Miranda seemed to read his thoughts.

'To think that if Alberto and I had adopted you, you would have lived in this very apartment. One would struggle to believe such a coincidence would be possible. It's as if you were drawn here by fate.'

'There's more to it than that,' replied Rinaldo, indicating the papers spread across the coffee table. 'Just a couple of weeks before I came to see this apartment I'd been to get my records from San Girolamo. I'd been thinking about doing it for years, hoping that there would be details in the paperwork that might tell me something about my mother. And there were. Not much, nothing that's helped me to find her, but I learned that she'd left me very close to here. And when I knew that, I wanted to live as near as I could to that place. I know it might sound sentimental, but even though I know nothing about her and have no memories of her, I have feelings for her and this wish to be close to her in any way I can.'

'That's both sweet and heart-breaking,' replied Miranda, dabbing her eyes with the cuff of her blouse.

She was still sitting close, so close that their knees and their knuckles were touching in a comfortable intimacy. In that moment they were more than tenant and landlady. Miranda felt a strangely deep connection to Rinaldo. It pained her that he had grown up motherless and fatherless, but she also felt a certain sense of pride that despite his significant disadvantage, he had grown into such a fine young man of whom any parent would be proud.

'So you know nothing about your mother?' she asked. She could see by Rinaldo's expression that although he was resigned to not knowing, the void of knowledge weighed heavily.

Rinaldo reached across to his paperwork, but he did so slowly, because Miranda was sitting really close to him and he didn't want her to move away.

'Nothing much,' he said. 'This is all I have from San Girolamo. Just a police report which says that nobody knew anything about my mother and a few details to say I was found in a crate on the floor wrapped in this yellow blanket.' Rinaldo pulled out the yellow blanket which he'd ended up sitting on and continued with, 'Apparently it was just as well I was found when I was because I wasn't too well. They said I had jaundice and suffered from convulsions which stopped me breathing and used to turn me from yellow to blue, but my mother had left the stove on to keep me warm, so that probably saved my life.'

When Rinaldo looked back up at Miranda, the expression on her face had changed to something he couldn't quite read. She was blinking very fast and frowning, like a person trying to understand something spoken in an incomprehensible foreign language.

'A-and where exactly was it that you were found?' she stammered, staring from Rinaldo to the crocheted yellow blanket.

'In Via Val d'Aposa, at number 7b. On the first floor. It's just above the shoe shop, right opposite the door to Vicolo Chiuso, so when I heard about this apartment—' Rinaldo stopped abruptly because Miranda had made a noise which sounded as though she was about to choke, or be sick.

'What's the matter?' he asked, concerned.

But Miranda couldn't speak. Her breath stuck in her throat. All she could do was stare at Rinaldo as though she was looking not at a living person, but a ghost.

'Miranda, what is it?'

'W-when?' she stuttered at last, her lips trembling. 'When was it? When was it you were found?'

'March the twenty-first, 1929.'

'Was anything left with you?'

'Yes, it was. My mother left an earring. That's why I was so obsessed with your earrings when you came to San Girolamo. I used to check the ears of any woman I met, in case she was my mother. I had this notion in my head that my mother wore the other earring all the time.'

For a moment Miranda was paralysed, and when she could move again, with shaking hands she scrabbled inside the collar of her blouse and pulled out the long gold chain. She held up the pendant for Rinaldo to see.

'Your mother's earring. Was it one like this?' Her question came out in slow motion.

As Rinaldo stared at the gold pendant with its green emerald set into a golden drop he felt his entire body go hot and cold at the same time. His skin flushed and broke into a sweat, but his blood felt as though it was freezing in his veins. His eyes could see that the earrings were identical, but his brain couldn't believe it. He gazed at the reunited earrings, looking from one to the other, trying to spot a difference. But there was none.

'Your mother did wear the other earring all the time,' said Miranda, so quietly that her words were barely audible. 'She was wearing it that day she came to San Girolamo. The very day you sat on her knee and played with her earrings.'

Rinaldo opened his mouth to speak without any idea of what might escape from it – but all that came out was stunned silence. His mind fired off questions in all directions, searching for a plausible refusal – a way to say, No, it can't be. Not like this. I wasn't supposed to find you this way. I've imagined meeting you in a million different ways, but never like this. Anyway, you're Miranda Fiorelli, my landlady – not Giuseppina Scamorza, my mother. It couldn't possibly be you – lovely, kind, sweet Miranda Fiorelli. Surely you of all people would never abandon a child?

His vision flickered as he scrambled to make sense of what was happening. He stared at Miranda, scanning her face for an image of himself in her features – something to confirm or deny this thing which seemed so impossible. All the imagined versions of the mother who was Giuseppina Scamorza crumbled. All his expectations lost their shape and disintegrated.

Then a feeling of dread struck him. She had discarded him once before, so would she do it again? Was he good enough for her? Could she love him as a son? Should he call her 'Mamma'?

Panic exploded, then came excitement, anticipation. All these feelings hit him in rapid succession, giving his brain no chance to process any of them. He didn't know whether to laugh, to cry, or kiss Miranda or shout at her, or even to run out of the room, or to jump from the balcony, or to hide behind the sofa.

Before he could draw some sense out of his whirlwind of emotions, Miranda folded him into her arms and clutched him tightly, pressing her cheek hard against his and supporting his head with her hand. Rinaldo felt a gentle, almost imperceptible rocking motion as though Miranda was holding not a grown man, but an infant.

As he let himself be cradled in her arms, Rinaldo felt the knot of uncertainty loosen inside him. All the answers were so close that he could feel them.

'When you came to San Girolamo that day, were you looking for me?'

'Looking for you? No, Rinaldo. When I left you in that room, I thought you were dead.'

'Dead?'

'Rinaldo, I would never have abandoned a living child! My sweet boy, forgive me. Please forgive me. Please forgive me! You wouldn't wake up. You'd turned blue. I couldn't revive you. I was so afraid. Please, please forgive me!'

Of all the possible reasons behind his abandonment, being presumed dead was one he had never considered. It threw a completely different perspective on everything. Rinaldo breathed in the warmth and the scent of the skin of Miranda's neck, and in a voice which expressed both happiness and bewilderment, he said: 'We've found each other now. Nothing else matters. There's nothing to forgive.'

Suddenly Miranda had the sensation of being sucked upwards, out of her own body, and hurtling towards the ceiling, where she stopped, suspended in mid-air and looking down, like a spectator in the room, observing herself fused into that embrace with Rinaldo. And for the briefest instant, no longer than the blink of an eye, not even enough time to gasp, she glimpsed an image of Alberto standing by the French window with his thumbs hooked into the arm-holes of his waistcoat. He looked up at her and the glimmer of a knowing smile twitched the corners of his mouth. *There's nothing to forgive, Mimi.* Then, as abruptly as the vision had appeared, it vanished.

When Miranda came back down, what remained was wondrous, miraculous – *and real.*

Miranda held her son in her arms. Rinaldo held his mother.

Ingram Content Group UK Ltd.
Milton Keynes UK
UKHW011812230323
419066UK00005B/441